THE ALZHAMMER

Praise for *Subway to California*

"A beautiful, heartfelt, sometimes funny, occasionally harrowing story of a man making his way through the minefield of his own family history. Di Prisco has lived more lives than most of us, and managed to get it all down in this riveting book."
—Jerry Stahl, author of *Permanent Midnight* and *OG Dad*

"Brimming with humor, heartbreak, and at times the feel an old-time Catholic confessional, *Subway to California* is a one-of-a-kind read."
—Kathleen Caldwell, A Great Good Place for Books

"A book replete with all the rich unfolding and poetic reflection of a novel, and all the focused research and unsparing truth-seeking of biography...an account that is at once an intimate meditation on the author's interior life and a gripping family history reaching back to Ellis Island in the 1920s. Threaded throughout is the author's irreverent, ecstatic love of words, of storytelling, an affirmation of the transcendent grace that literature can offer."
—Laura Cogan, Editor-in-Chief, *ZYZZYVA*

"What Joe DiPrisco has written here is likely to become the standard-bearer for all future memoirs...A comedy and tragedy filled with paternal pratfalls, missteps and odd criminal adventures, all of which cast Joe onto the road as a gambler, teacher, writer, political activist, accused criminal in his own right, father and husband. This *Subway* ride is the real deal."
—Steven Gillis, Publisher of Dzanc Books; author of *The Consequence of Skating* and *The Law of Strings*

"Di Prisco delivers thoughtful contemplation of the human condition and plenty of self-examination that reveals how he made it to where he is, and why he survived when others didn't. His sharp wit and hard-won wisdom make *Subway to California* a story that anyone who's risen out of a hardscrabble life with the odds stacked against them will love and learn from."
—Diane Prokop, *ForeWord*

"Di Prisco tells the wacky tale of his criminal-leaning family's escape from Brooklyn to California in the sixties and his own coming-of-age story. His is an interesting one, full of personal brushings with the FBI plus stints as a student activist and as an Italian restaurant manager and ultimately in the role of caretaker for his dementia-suffering dad. An attention-capturing cliffhanger."

—Judith M. Gallman, Editor, *Oakland Magazine*

"Di Prisco traces the reasons for his dance between decency and delinquency to his Brooklyn boyhood. A fearful, precocious child, the 'perfect schoolboy' grew up with three misfit brothers (all now dead) raised by two profane sociopaths in a home where the only set points on the volume control were 'silence and screaming'...The author can break your heart recalling the most romantic memory of his life or make you laugh out loud."

—*Kirkus Reviews*

"Told with enough tenderness and humor to elevate his pain-filled recollections to poetry at times, pure fun at others, Di Prisco...brings us home—grateful our family is less volatile, or feeling less alone if we, too, survived a wild childhood."

—Lou Fancher, *Contra Costa Times*

"A heartwarming and hilarious sharing of his dysfunctional family adventures, Joe said it best when he wrote: 'stories happen...to people who can tell them.'"

—Ginny Prior, Town Crier, *Oakland Tribune*

"A very fine novelist and poet who has now written a moving and actually quite funny memoir about life with two parents who should never have married, and once they did, should never have had children. But then we wouldn't have Joe to tell us their story."

—A. R. Taylor, *Sex, Rain, and Cold Fusion*

"In Di Prisco's hands, memoir is simultaneously a reflective tracking of oneself and the urge to make sense—or not—of what memory can make opaque. Whether chosen or not, transitions will construct a life of transformation. In these pages, way-finding becomes a philosophy of being."

—Laurie Saurborn Young, *H_NGM_N*

"People struggling to find their place in the world often search for answers in a psychiatrist's office, in love affairs, religion, illegal drugs, gambling, social activism, academia, work, and vicariously, through their children. Joseph Di Prisco visited all those places, and then, coming up short, found himself by writing a memoir."

—*Bay Area Mercury News*

"It's rare to encounter a book so heartfelt and compassionate and yet so incisively hilarious at the same time."

—Heather Mackey, author of *Dreamwood*

"Throughout *Subway*, Joe Di Prisco evokes the past with vivid, often hilarious, prose, describing his Italian-Polish upbringing in Brooklyn, the flight to a strange world called California, his doomed and dramatic love affairs, and his colorful parents—the kind of parents you enjoy reading about and are grateful they were not yours."

—Anara Guard, author of *Remedies for Hunger*

Praise for *All for Now*

"Though Di Prisco takes a heartbreaking look at the scars left by pedophilia, and some readers will surely feel anger at the sins, the tale unfolds, bravely [and] with much humor thanks to Brother Stephen's bemused narration."

—*Publishers Weekly*

"What makes Joseph Di Prisco's novel work is its narrative voice—poignant, rueful, and wise-crackingly sardonic...This is a novel about posthumous discoveries, reunions, and revenge. Readers of J.F. Powers' *Morte d'Urban* and Alice McDermott's *Charming Billy* should find their way to *All For Now*."

—P. F. Kluge, author of *A Call From Jersey* and *Gone Tomorrow*

"What will the afterlife be like? If we're lucky, it would be something like the humorous and humane version Joseph Di Prisco imagines in *All for Now*, a smart, sparkling tale about faith, religion, and devotion under less-than-ideal circumstances—that is, the average existence."

—Oscar Villalon, Managing Editor *ZYZZYVA*

"It is sad and poignant and beautiful. If all deaths occurred in the same manner, I think we would all have a little less reason to fear it."

—Antal Polony, *SevenPonds*

"It is especially moving to read a book that looks so broadly at the ubiquitous issue of Roman Catholicism and pedophilia...Joseph Di Prisco has given us a brave, bumbling, soul-searching hero whose wry humor only enhances his honesty."

—Jan Weissmiller, Prairie Lights Books

"Di Prisco opens each chapter with a question and answer from the bible of Catholic childhood, the *Baltimore Catechism*, wickedly laying out the contrast between dogma and behavior. The novel's surreal tone, Brother Stephen's drily acidic worldview, and the enigmatic portrait of a pedophile all combine to deepen this thoughtful look at the heartbreak left in the wake of child sexual abuse."

—Booklist

"Joseph Di Prisco has crafted a completely original thriller…The quick pace and sharp writing make *All for Now* a book you can't bear to put down."

—Kathleen Caldwell, A Great Good Place for Books

"Deploying intelligence and humor, Joseph Di Prisco examines his subject in an engaging and entertaining way, and the end result is anything but morbid…Catholic or not, religious or not, *All for Now* is accessible to everyone because mistakes and forgiveness are universal."

—Seattle Post Intelligencer

Praise for *Confessions of Brother Eli*

"First-time novelist Joseph Di Prisco must be a very funny guy. *Confessions of Brother Eli* fairly sparkles with humor that ranges from sophisticated to slapstick, in what some believe to be the most difficult writing to carry off."

—Tucson Weekly

"With dry, sardonic wit, Brother Eli questions his faith and vocation, while recounting adventures that take place at his school…The writing and narrative voice in this book is some of the best I've come across lately."

—Akron Beacon Journal

Praise for *Poems in Which*

"Somehow the speaker in Joseph Di Prisco's new poems manages to install himself in the kitchenware of contemporary culture without becoming a part of it. With a wit that questions as it embraces, *Poems in Which* provides us with a strong, original voice."

—**Carl Dennis**, winner of the Pulitzer Prize

ALSO BY JOSEPH DI PRISCO

MEMOIR

Subway to California

NOVELS

Confessions of Brother Eli

Sun City

All for Now

POETRY

Wit's End

Poems in Which

Sightlines from the Cheap Seats

NONFICTION

Field Guide to the American Teenager (with Michael Riera)

Right from Wrong (with Michael Riera)

JOSEPH DI PRISCO

THE ALZHAMMER

OR KEEP YOUR FRIENDS CLOSE AND...
I FORGET THE OTHER THING

A Vireo Book—Rare Bird Books
Los Angeles, Calif.

This is a Genuine Vireo Book

A Vireo Book | Rare Bird Books
453 South Spring Street, Suite 302
Los Angeles, CA 90013
rarebirdbooks.com

FIRST TRADE PAPERBACK ORIGINAL EDITION

Set in Minion
Printed in the United States

10 9 8 7 6 5 4 3 2 1

Publisher's Cataloging-in-Publication data

Names: Di Prisco, Joseph, 1950-, author.

Title: The Alzhammer : or keep your friends close and…I forget the other thing
/ by Joseph Di Prisco.

Description: First Trade Paperback Original Edition | A Vireo Book | Los
Angeles [California], New York [New York] : Rare Bird Books, 2016.

Identifiers: ISBN 978-1-942600-43-5.

Subjects: Alzheimer's disease—Fiction. | Organized crime—United States—
Fiction. | Death—Fiction. | Family—Fiction. | Older people—Fiction. | San
Francisco (Calif.)—Fiction. | BISAC FICTION/Literary.

Classification: LCC PS3554.I67 .A49 2016 | DDC 813.54--dc23

To Dean and Laurie

My heart leaps up when I behold

A rainbow in the sky:

So was it when my life began;

So is it now I am a man;

So be it when I shall grow old,

Or let me die.

—William Wordsworth

PART ONE

Chapter One

Red lights were flashing, warning bells, clanging. That's what they do when a train is barreling down the tracks. This told Mikey all he needed to know. He was parked on those tracks. After midnight the roads were otherwise deserted, some nowhere junction outside city limits, and the zebra-striped gates hedged him in.

Ding ding ding ding ding ding ding ding ding ding...

A cemetery loomed nearby, so by now even the dead and buried could have caught a clue about the train.

He had clicked on his seatbelt. Not that driver safety was a prime consideration. He might have regarded a seatbelt as sensible if it was any night other than this, and if a locomotive was not speeding toward him, and if he had something he wished to live for.

"That train," he said to himself, "that train has left the station."

That would have been funny, he reflected, if it was funny, which it wasn't.

Nobody was around to hear him talking to himself, which was one of the best parts of being alone.

A non-suicidal man with an ounce of sense would be moving his car. It was in this respect that he didn't qualify. Not that anybody was in a position to question him, but if somebody were, Mikey would swear he had never thought as clearly as he was thinking now.

Maybe that's not saying a lot.

Even so, he was done, his horse had already shot out of the starting gate.

This was the moment his big plan was set in motion.

It wasn't really much of a big plan. Not like fixing the World Series or breaking into the vault in Monte Carlo, not quite. But it didn't matter. Not anymore, not here, not now. Only chumps and dreamers who bank on seeing the sun come up tomorrow cook up big plans. It wasn't a brilliant plan, either, nor did it score points for originality. But he made it *his* plan, and he could actually *hear* the wheels turning, louder and louder and louder and louder. And louder.

The environmentally hostile twelve-cylinder car engine purred like some Ritalin-jacked Siamese. In the collapsing distance a not-so-faraway train rumbled, relentlessly bearing down on Mikey, who demonstrated no inclination to give up his final parking space.

He had the black Benz washed and waxed yesterday and it gleamed beneath the starry skies. "See?" he said out loud, though nobody was sufficiently insane to volunteer riding shotgun. "What were you thinking? Detailing your car?"

Time to cash out his chips and the check-out window loomed.

Ding ding ding ding ding ding ding ding ding ding…

The phone in his shirt pocket rang. He assumed it rang, that is, because he didn't hear the ring tone, what with all the racket, yet he did feel the feathery fibrillation in the region of his *rat-tat-tat*ting heart. God, how he despised inescapable mobile phones. Any luck, soon as he met this train, and unless the cell phone company grandfathered in an afterlife plan, he would never take a call from anybody ever again.

Chapter Two

Socks. That's how that day had started off—with Mikey's socks. Motherfucking socks.

Before the train tracks and before he hatched his plan, it was socks that ruined his day. When he had a bad day, he had a tendency to spread the mood around.

He was destined to have an extraordinarily bad day.

The whole thing was complicated, but not in an especially complicated way.

In a sense, it had nothing to do with the motherfucking socks. The problem was, he *forgot* the socks. *His* socks: those are the ones he forgot. He neglected to put them on, those socks of his. On his feet. Inside his hand-tooled thirteen triple-wide shoes. Where socks are supposed to go.

He was not the sort of man who dresses and goes: *Guess what? Fuck them socks.* Everybody knows that type, a swaggering dickwad without socks in their Guccis, their Tod's, their Gravatis. The kind who knows how to get around town, where you're supposed to be seen. Chateau Marmont. Palm Beach. Meatpacking District. The W. He frequents places where drinks are served in chilled, stemmed cocktail glasses and are *infused*. That type has no clue what *infused* means. That's because an ass wipe like that has the mental agility of a billy club and meat balls for brains. You can see his canary-crunching countenance on every other glossy ad page of *Vanity Fair* or *Mook Monthly*.

Don't ever confuse that kind of guy with Mikey.

Just so you know, and not that you would.

When he walked out of the house not wearing his socks that morning, how could he know that today would be momentous for his sockless soul? How could somebody standing in his shoes—the shoes without the motherfucking socks—be without a clue? If he'd known that much, those socks would not be missing and their absence would not be posing the distressing predicament they would soon be posing, of which deficiency he continued to be unconscious.

He wouldn't be in the dark for long. Neither would anybody else.

Chapter Three

Early on the morning of the day that was going to turn balls-out brutal, he had gathered his crew at the social club. This was the time and the place when and where he met his crew, always in the past while unfailingly wearing his socks, which, in case there's any doubt, he had never before forgotten to wear. Until today, that is, when the whole world was due to unravel for a sock-minus mobster by the name of Mikey Festagiacamo. He was the only son of the elderly, bedridden boss, Vincent Festagiacamo, for generations a legend who struck terror in the hearts of his enemies as well as his friends, not that he cultivated many of the latter. Though the man was still alive—barely hanging on for now—Mikey was running the show, or trying to.

As for the club, time and the elements had ravaged the ancient painted sign over the entrance. Letters had been bleached out by the erasering sun and the weathered wood had been warped by countless seasons of rain. Now you had to squint in order to decipher the bleary placard:

OCIAL

LUB

Stale memories of spilt wine, soggy espresso grounds, and Cuban cigar butts still bittered the atmosphere, so crime scene analysis might have authenticated that once upon a time this had been indeed a social club, and somebody with an active fantasy life could imagine detecting the faint lingering echo of disco or Motown. Problem was, nobody alive had the faintest recollection of a wedding or a prison-release or a Teamster retirement or a Sweet Sixteen party or anything of a remotely festive nature having taken place within its bleak confines since dinosaurs and John Gotti freely roamed the earth. No upcoming dates were booked either, and there were openings on the calendar as far as the eye could see. About that supposed calendar: nobody could locate such a quaint instrument if they set out armed with a search warrant, a forensic accountant, and a bloodhound. Then again, the desolation inside the place would not have stunned a sharp observer who noticed the other sign affixed to a window of the ocial lub:

CLOSED

Mikey was positioned in the middle of the creaky, wood-warped dance floor, lodged in his leather easy chair big as the cage of a bobcat, and the sock deprivation, while grave, wasn't the only trouble he seemed unaware of in the moment. In the estimation of his loyal—loyal for at least the time being—crew, he appeared equally oblivious to many more serious troubles. Nonetheless, he forged ahead.

"Who's doing come-to-Jesus with Cutie Boy Keily?" He wanted to know. Judge Keily's nostrils were flattening, the man was getting flinchy in his advancing years. Mikey didn't wish to see surface any evidence of an impartial and therefore non-advantageous judicial temperament when he was issuing rulings from the bench that pertained to him or his business.

"Fatso, you on Hizzonor's case today?"

Fatso nodded energetically. Fatso commanded extra reserves of enthusiasm since he lost all that weight, a cosmetic uptick he attributed to his groundbreaking nothing-but-bacon diet, which he invented and which made him reek like a deep-fryer at the summer county fair, and which explained why he was positioned an olfactory-free zone away from the rest of the crew, all of whom liked their bacon all right but didn't need to smell piggy grease round the clock.

Not very long ago, Fatso weighed—he had no idea what he once weighed, only that his groaning scale begged for mercy one day, stopped keeping tabs at the very round number of three hundred, and didn't dispense a prize when the needle topped the last number on the wheel. Since then, Fatso had disposed of the hundred-pound parmesan wheel around his gut, and the corned beef on his ass, and the angel food around his biceps and thighs. How'd he come up with the bacon concept? Simple. Bacon was his go-to nourishment source and the idea came to him one day at lunch, when he decided he would restrict himself exclusively to the food item he preferred. If he was destined to be fat when he keeled over from a stroke or heart attack, he would make the most of what was left of his obese life and relish what he consumed. What could be wrong with a scheme as elegant as that? That was the day he ordered a BLT sandwich at the diner, and he told the waiter to keep the L, the T, the sand, and the wich.

"Not for nothin', Fatso," said his running mate and nemesis by the name of Dolly, who inserted his considerable nose into everybody's business, "you hear of choler esterol?"

"Yeah, matter of fact I have, Dolly. Y'ever hear of shut-the-fuck-upperol?" Fatso hated Dolly. He made it irresistible to hate him, and Fatso was not alone in his lack of fond regard for the man. Given a chance, Dolly could aggravate the Dalai Lama, or Mother Theresa, or any erstwhile candidate for beatification.

Despite shedding all those pounds, the bacon-devotee retained the name Fatso. Monikers are harder to shed.

"Bring Keily some flowers," said Mikey. "Say they're for his new girlfriend, he'll get the idea."

"Gotcha covered, boss," said Fatso.

"Yeah," said Dolly, "but you got a lousy attention spam."

Then something happened. The precise something that happened was *nothing.* Mikey tried to speak. His lips were moving but silence was coming out of his mouth at an alarming rate.

A hush had seized Mikey by the throat like a pit bull. Emptiness yowled throughout the hall or inside his head, hard to tell which, and though the yellowing, retracted window shades fluttered epileptically, on account of the wind whistling through the cracked panes, they made no sound that he himself could hear. He held his breath, like somebody whose head had been shoved down inside a toilet bowl.

TWO YEARS LATER

CAREGIVER LOG

Use this form to monitor changes and to communicate with doctors, hospice nurses and caregivers across shifts.

PATIENT: *MICHAEL FESTAGIACAMO (59)*

CAREGUVER: *Amanaki* ♥

DATE/TIME: *Monday 8 clock AM mourning*

NOTE CHANGES: *no change for mikee same same*

FOOD: *toast jam butter Ensure rice one bite ham burger bannana; good ! appetite*

MEDICATION: *same as befor, new pill at 9 PM at nite; no morfine (hospis nerse says use jujement call oncall nerse)*

ACTIVITIES: *BM midnite (big)*

PAIN LEVEL: *2-3*

ENERGY: *ressless, mummbling to hisself*

SLEEP PATTERN: *talk talk talk all nite*

Sun come up go to sleep; Sun Downing

Chapter Four

The minutes passed, and it was as if he were watching time itself go by, in the form of a twin-engine softly droning high overhead, until it disappeared through the clouds, over and beyond the receding hairline of the horizon.

"Where was I?" Mikey managed to say out loud after a lull that felt as long as a baseball game rain-delay.

The crew didn't score high on the SATs when they were in high school or ever take the exams or finish high school, but even they knew better than to hazard a response. *Where was Mikey?* That was the question on the table? They had no idea where the hell Mikey wandered off to, only wherever it was, his elevator was stuck between floors.

Talk about bad timing. Mikey's father had been the boss forever, but now that the old man's health was failing, he was in the final stages of passing the mantle of power onto his only son. In his conspicuous and lamentable absence, the crew had suffered an agonizing fall from grace, which, considering the kind of rough trade it conducted, was not an expression ever invoked with respect to them. There was a time not so long ago when Vincent Festagiacamo operated the most professional, ruthless, and profitable shop in the whole city. Not that there was in existence a shop, as in a physical location with a postal address, a company with an inventory of widgets, a bookkeeper, a water cooler, a ream of stationery, a checkbook, a suggestion box, Christmas parties, and so on. The closest they came to having a shop was this closed-up, run-down, once-upon-a-time gathering spot with an incoherent sign listing precariously over the nailed-up front door.

These days, Vince's crew—effectively Mikey's crew now—had become in a heartbeat smaller potatoes. Each day the old man was slipping more and more definitively out of the picture, and his son at the helm was not going to be confused with Don Corleone—or a Michael or a Sonny Corleone, either. If anything, more like pathetic Fredo, last seen dressed as a fisherman going out on that fateful boat on Lake Tahoe at dawn. As a result, they struck knee-knocking terror into virtually no one, including the emboldened teenage vandals who periodically smashed Mikey's mailbox into pieces in the middle of the night or deposited dog turds on his *Benvenuto* welcome mat. What the crew was really good at—

Honestly, not much anymore, and consequently it would be hard to explain how and why they made more than a decent living, working the margins of the streets for their hard-earned money. Maybe it was too simple. The local underground economy was booming, there was plenty of money to go around, and the cooperative local law enforcement and judiciary, like Judge Keily, didn't mind turning a blind eye, for a price.

Today the once and future boss and his subordinates were to review their tasks—the pick-ups, the drops, the ultimatums to the late-payers (whose ranks were increasing), the take at the Italian restaurant Mikey's dad owned, which was called Lorenzo's, the take at the other Italian restaurants he didn't technically own, the visit with the trainers at the track, the no-show union job sites, and the dozen other activities that constituted customary business. There was also the last-one-standing old-school bookmaker, named Brownie, who took nickel-and-dime bets over his phone, like the bygone days, before people had computers and presumed they knew better. Brownie was frozen in Philco and Victrola time. He was also behind in his payments. Old man Festagiacamo would have never tolerated such insolence. Despite everything, everybody had a soft spot for Brownie, who could be reliably located any time of day wearing a Giants baseball cap and a wife-beater t-shirt within striking distance of an overflowing ashtray and the rotary-dial phone that rang every few hours, unlike the old days when he employed three hoarse-throated guys taking bets round the clock. Now Brownie the book played solitaire for hours on end. Not on some high tech gadget phone, either. With real, mucked, dented playing cards.

Somehow, the crew cobbled together enough of a business to get by, or slightly better than that. They realized, almost certainly unconsciously, that their best hope for survival lay in 1) acting and looking intimidating when dramatics were called for, 2) counting on nobody bothering to bring out the big guns to blow them all away, and 3) flying under the radar. As everybody knows, under the radar's where certain types of deadly ordnance fly. Less-often noted: so do other sorts of ordnance.

The good news was, in this city, there was more than enough business for the crew if they were judicious and played it smart. The other kind of news was, with Mikey calling the shots, being judicious and playing it smart were nowhere near bankable propositions. Not that anybody used banks. So far they were not threatening enough for the competition to rub out or law enforcement to crack down on. *Small potatoes.* As for the increasingly skeptical crew, tracking the inevitable demise of the whole enterprise, as long as Vincent Festagiacamo was technically alive they would be formally respectful of his living and breathing disappointment of a son, Mikey, and humor him whenever he blustered. Once the old man passed over to his eternal reward, that might be—which nobody needed to talk about—another story.

Mikey cleared his throat. Unfortunately, that felt like an achievement.

ℭ

ONLY LAST WEEK MIKEY'S crew had spent an unexpectedly fruitful hour or two at a new construction equipment rental company in town, where they stopped by unannounced and introduced themselves, which was reminiscent of the glory days under Vincent Festagiacamo. That is to say, they did not pay a social call. They didn't bring the requisite box of cannoli. They did bring their bats. The new proprietor had no inkling as to how little he had to worry about—how could he be aware, being fresh on the scene? Even so, it took some convincing, at which one particular endeavor they were, somewhat mystifyingly, semi-proficient—they called it taking batting practice—and they came to acquire knowledge that this new business was generating healthy profits, which meant a win-win by Mikey's lights. The guy who owned the company had a goatee and a shaved head, not a bad look for a pro baseball player, but not for a guy with a way of whining that got under Mikey's skin, which factors upped the ask, which was not intended as an ask. The man pleaded for mercy, kept saying he was already paying somebody else, and how was he going to stay in business if this kept up and somebody else walked in the door with another baseball bat?

"Don't you guys compare notes?" he made the mistake of asking.

"Whaddaya fucking mean 'you guys?'" asked Dolly, who swung the biggest aluminum bat, upon which he had added by means of a marking pen decorative red splotches meant to induce terror. "We're here to provide you a service, including a funereal marmorial service if the need should by accidental or not so much that way chance have arose."

"Sorry," said the man tentatively, because it was not always a simple matter to decode what Dolly intended, and he had already gotten off on the wrong foot with these guys, whoever they were.

"It's okay, sir, no offense taken," Mikey said. "Excuse my employee's eagerness. I'm sure your other interested party will be happy to look the other way. Tell him Mikey Festagiacamo would be happy to discuss arrangements for him to disappear because he seems to have made a miscalculation."

"Who's Mikey The Other Name I Can't Pronounce?"

Dolly would have lost his patience had he possessed one ounce of it and he answered for the acting boss he had increasing but masked contempt for: "That would be the someone of which you would not wish to have asked him about if you knew any better which you can't but you might if you're not warning alerted."

The owner was now thoroughly confused, yet again a not-rare byproduct of Dolly's mangling mouth.

In reality, Mikey wouldn't be happy and wouldn't discuss his arrangements with anybody else moving in on him. "By the way," said Mikey, "not for nothing, who is the other party in question?"

"Some guy thick as a retaining wall, said his name was Mr. Smith. Scared the piss out of me." Judging from the tears running down the proprietor's smacked-around face, it wouldn't take much to weaken the man's bladder. "At least you don't look like you are going to tear me to pieces, like Mr. Smith. I swear to God he had the teeth of a backhoe." But then he looked apprehensively over toward Dolly, who was taking menacing practice swings in what he designated the on-deck circle, terrified he may have spoken too soon.

"Mr. *Smith*? You kidding, right?" Mikey pretended to chuckle. "Not to worry, I know him very well," he said, lying through his own teeth. "He'll get out of your hair, no disrespect, after you tell him you and me, we already had a deal you were previously unaware of."

So there was a crew in town he didn't know? A new bunch stepping onto his progressively more vulnerable, shrinking turf? True, he was more forgetful these days, but he would have remembered a man with a pretentiously aggressive name like Mr. Smith. He wasn't too worried about this Mr. Smith, as time to time new crews hip-checked onto the scene, all elbows and ass, but soon limped away swinging dicklessly, unlike his crew, which had been a going concern for decades. What was different here was that Mr. Smith was bold to the point of being possibly reckless and could therefore become dangerous. Mikey was annoyed. So annoyed was he, he'd put Dolly on the job. If Dolly was good at one thing, it was making conversation. His was highly irritating conversation, and irritation was what was called for.

If this poor son of a bitch construction rental guy was being squeezed two ways, Mikey thought, well, that's life in the big city, nobody asked him to set up his business here, did they? This was the United Frigging States of America, Land of the Goddamn Free, wasn't it?

☙

MIKEY NEVER PUT A single word or number down on paper or its electronic equivalent, not one notation, an all-around sound business practice adopted wholesale from his father. This morning at the club was no time to initiate changes on that score. He fell silent once more and struggled to recall the next item on his mental agenda. It was as if he were riffling his chips while the cards were being dealt. One by one the cards flipped over, all of them blank.

Chapter Five

"**A**bout this Mr. Smith," Mikey said in a leading tone, struggling to recover. "You know, like they say? Keep your friends close..." he began, and then stopped, having arrived at a dead end. Expectation surged, everybody leaned forward in their chairs. He tried to hotwire his brain: "Keep your friends close, and...I forget the other thing."

Of course Mo apprehended what the boss wanted to say. You could have entire productive conversations using nothing but dialogue from *The Godfather*. An offer you can't. Take the cannoli. Sleeps with the. You can have my answer now. Who's being naïve? Dying of the same heart attack. Yet it was Mo alone who sympathetically wished he could urge Mikey forward and fill in the blanks—*Your enemies closer, keep your enemies closer*—but wouldn't dare utter the words.

His crew flashed subtle, knowing glances at each other fairly devoid of subtlety or knowingness. It was like he could read their minds, the thought-bubbles eloquently floating above their heads:

Oh, man.

What the.

The fuck.

So it's really, like.

I know, right?

"Anyway, this Mr. Smith," Mikey said, disgusted to utter the name, starting over again, clean slate, hoping nobody noticed but fearing they did, "what we know about this so-called tough guy?"

"I been on it," said Dolly. "Guy's flying under the rebar. So far, can't seem to predeterminate eggs-ackly nothing." In reality, Dolly had invested his typically meager, half-hearted efforts, reasonably enough fearing that if he weren't careful he might accidentally stumble upon some actionable intelligence when he looked too hard in the obvious places, and then what was he supposed to do? Give the guy a box of chocolates, kiss his brass knuckles?

"I want this renegade put back on the reservation."

"Assolutely, Mikey. Just don't want to hark up the wrong tree."

Mikey? Dolly said his name, like he was entitled. He didn't appreciate being addressed familiarly, by his first name. True, strictly speaking, his dad was still the boss, and everybody was used to calling his dad *boss*, but Dolly seemed to enjoy taking liberties too much. Dolly's time was coming.

"Get the fuck, go do your jobs already."

They were prepared to do that, but then the unfortunate development occurred.

☙

MIKEY CROSSED HIS LEGS and shook his shoe in the air. That's the moment he looked down and noticed for the first time: where his sock was supposed to be, on his foot, of course, where it usually was, he saw a flash of lily white ankle.

He had dressed this morning as he customarily did: Zegna sport coat, untucked short-sleeve Tommy Bahama silk shirt, Zanella trousers, buttery-soft slip-ons straight from Italy. But this morning, no socks. He had nothing against wearing socks. In theory, he could have chosen from over a hundred pair in the dresser. It didn't cross his mind this morning to select any of them.

The crew caught on to the sartorial slip-up at the same time, and as if on cue they responded identically, theatrically. Each took off his loafers and removed his socks, virtually in unison, the choreography loosely reminiscent of synchronized swimmers—without the pool and bathing caps.

"You guys some kinda comedians?"

"No, Mikey," said Dolly. He was certainly no comedian, though he was the Number Two in Mikey's crew who routinely voiced ludicrous assertions. "Every single day, you always dress accordionly."

"You making jokes?"

"No, boss," said Mo, Mikey's personal driver and enforcer, who knew better than to try his hand at banter. "We all like the look, no socks. You're a trench-setter." He'd hung around Dolly too long not to be infected by his mangling mouth. Truth was, Mo and the rest had been noticing to their rising alarm for some time now the big change in Mikey: his failing memory, his painful struggle at times to find words.

"Yeah," added Dolly, "very *GQ*." He didn't know what that meant, he admitted, but he heard what he called "sediments" expressed along those lines.

"Don't know from that, but whatever gee cue is better be good." There had not been a time in Mikey's life when the slightest sign of disrespect didn't elicit a double-barrel response. And he grasped instantly when he was being played. He knew *before* he was being lied to that he was going to be lied to. Like right here, with their taking off their socks: he might be being played. For once, he wasn't sure what to do. Only a few minutes ago, he actually felt pretty good going over the mental list. He felt assured he hadn't missed anything. He was in command. Then again, how would he know for certain? The socks were a setback he could not ignore.

He glared at his crew. All of them had stuffed their socks into their coat pockets. Here was his question: were they patronizing the boss? Which led to the next question: did they assume he was weak in the head? And then the logical follow-up question: *was* he?

Beware a man who is aging, a man whose mental powers were slipping, who was therefore more dangerous than ever. And then imagine Mikey.

As long as Vincent Festagiacamo was alive, they would appear to obey him.

Mikey was not as clueless as the crew assumed.

They had no idea that he himself was all too aware his command was slipping away.

Mikey couldn't miss that his crew was up against it, outgunned and outmanned by his rivals.

He also appreciated all over again what his crew did not: he had greater problems than that.

Chapter Six

Ultimately it was the end of that bad day when Mikey first went sockless and those red lights were flashing before and behind him. Actually, it was three o'clock the following morning, usually not the best time for making life and death decisions. He did not go to bed that night and he had already made his life and death decision: he was waiting for a train to blast him away from all this.

He was going to take himself out once and for all. He would do it the right way.

Drastic, sure, but called for. He knew he was living on borrowed time, that he was faking it, pretending to be in control, not convincing anybody looking hard. He grasped that his crew's ship was taking on water.

Going without socks may have been fashionable for gigolos, fanooks, and garden-variety losers, but he realized it was a very bad development for a loser like himself, yet another bad sign of worse things in the offing. It was time for action.

This was the situation: he knew he wasn't right in the head. He was right enough in his head, though, to grasp this fact. He did not always keep a firm grasp on this fact, which slithered around like a line-caught fish on the boat deck, but when he did he also grasped the fact that he did not always grasp this fact, which, when he was aware, he realized was the whole problem.

His brain was coming in and out, like phone reception in the mountains driving up to Tahoe for the weekend.

Socks were one thing. Sometimes, he would stand in his closet half-dressed for a long while, unable to move the ball down the field. Or he'd put on a shirt inside out or fumble for a half hour with the buttons. That's not all. He was behaving erratically. Like the time he left the car engine running in the garage all night. Like the time his signature lasagna baked overnight in the oven and came out tasty as a two-by-four. Like the time he apparently forgot he turned on the water in the tub because hours later there was a mini-Niagara cascading down the stairs.

There were probably other things he couldn't remember he forgot. Which went to the point he was trying to make to himself while he suffered this moment of clarity and understood there were probably things he couldn't remember forgetting. It was maddening. He could go days and days and nothing untoward happened. Crystal clear satellite reception. Then he'd discover a roll of cash, his own money, in the vicinity of the garbage can, or he'd be holding the TV remote and wonder how long it had been nestled in his hand.

Then it happened: the stupid, stupid, stupid, stupid, motherfuck-ing socks.

As Dolly would have remarked had he butted in, that was the saw that broke the camel's back.

Yes, time for Mikey to take action.

But no gun. He figured out that part. No gun.

His father was dying with Alzheimer's—a medically diagnosed condition that Mikey termed the Alzhammer. His mother was already dead from complications of the disease. Based on that store of information, he naturally concluded he was doomed. It was inevitable. That was the fate awaiting him. But he wasn't *waiting* anymore.

One day, no socks. Next day, *what?* Drool on his silk shirt and sitting in a shitted-up diaper? That wasn't him, being humiliatingly dependent on others to clean him up and shovel tapioca into his pried-open mouth. That wasn't him, tied up with restraints in his geriatric chair. For the record, he detested tapioca. He had seen for himself what the Alzhammer did to his mom and dad, and he wasn't going to let that happen to him if he could help it.

And he could.

But he better act before he was smashed by the Alzhammer, while he had the capacity.

No gun, however. That was one thing he was adamant about.

You put a pistol barrel up against your own temple, you got yourself one messy crime scene in your future. Better off aiming the barrel under your chin, that's what you're supposed to do. Of course, there's not much of a future when you have turned such a corner. Either way, it's not a pretty picture when you're done with the gun, especially if your body is the one being bagged and tagged by the coroner. If he did use a gun, he would also consider shooting himself in the heart. That would do the trick, not that taking himself out was all that much of a trick, *ta-da*. But in the head? He didn't think so. Because what if he got a case of the jitters or what if he sneezed, and he's off by a millimeter, and he turns into a two-hundred-fifty pound intubated rutabaga for the next twenty Super Bowls? That's a lot of boring halftime shows starring washed-up rock stars to pass before your unblinking eyes.

Something else, too, something hard to admit to the crew or his father and harder for him to admit to himself: a part of him was done, done with the family business, done with being the new boss even before he formally became the new boss. Who needs it? He was destined to become the undisputed boss, but what difference did that make? He wasn't going to live on a pension and Social Security, not that he paid in, and not that he needed extra financial security, so that was merely a figure of speech, but truth was, he had enough of his life.

Some kind of life. Sitting in cars. Smacking around somebody who needed special attention. Keeping the screws tightened on his crew. Flipping somebody else's cash into financial assets usable by him. Eating too much, drinking too much, smoking too many cigars. On the lookout twenty-four-seven for new business opportunities. Keeping an eye out for competition, which was a growing cause for concern he himself could not miss—despite what the crew assumed to be his failing powers of observation. Always a new young gun might show in Dodge, out to make his bones. Young is stupid, young takes chances, young is sure of himself, and being young was one of many, many things he could no longer reliably remember. Once he had been young and stupid and nobody to mess with, but the fire inside had gone out.

He wished he could have talked with his dad about his troubles, because he could benefit from the old man's wisdom, but that was impossible now. His dad had checked out, Mikey was on his own. He wished he possessed his pain-in-the-ass younger sister's laser-like professional focus and her fanatical attention to detail. Rosetta was the ambitious, the tenacious, the committed, the successful child in the family. She was relentless. If she had to reject her own family to achieve her goals, so be it. Sometimes he envied her. Sometimes he hated her—especially when his father made no attempt to finesse his admiration for her.

Mikey didn't have a gun in the car. To tell the truth, guns made him squirm. He was no sharpshooter, for one thing, so his own toes were more at risk than any targeted adversary. His father had tried to teach marksmanship to both of his children when they were teenagers. He thought that duty came with the territory of being the patriarch and the boss. The most galling aspect was his sister had a dead eye: no prowling skunk, no empty wine bottle, no marauding raccoon was safe in her sights. "Your sister," their dad crowed more than once, "she's like what's her name in the cowboy movies, Annie Oakley. A regular Catastrophe Jane. Too bad we can't use her in the crew."

Guns remained indispensable tools of the trade, but they were more appropriate in the hands of the people who worked for him and specialized in such activity, underlings like Dolly and Mo. And he also wouldn't go home and swallow all the sleeping pills in his medicine cabinet, washing them down with a fifth of Jack. That's what a teenage girl might do, pharmaceuticals and booze, and girls are notoriously inept at this sort of enterprise. In any case, pills were a half-assed if not unmanly way for somebody of his reputation to take himself out. True, he wouldn't be around to listen when others pissed all over the name of Mikey Festagiacamo.

What difference did *that* make? Big difference, that's what. Even in death, a reputation matters. You know what? That's when reputation might matter most.

Besides, in the early hours of this morning he had settled on a much more efficient plan: the train tracks. He thought he had come upon a plan of genius. It was like after a huge earthquake and five days later they discover a baby somehow still alive in the rubble—just like that, only completely different.

∝

HE HAD FOUND HIMSELF inside a shrinking window for taking decisive action. Between realizing what he had to do because he had no choice and forgetting what it was he was supposed to do: that was the precise window. And that window was slowly closing by the day, by the hour.

During a stretch in which he enjoyed crystalline clarity, he had looked to all the legal particulars, he had made the necessary financial arrangements. The fiscal house was in order, though his head most surely wasn't. One thing troubled him. Or he thought should have troubled him. He had heard about how people who were terminal and watching the clock wind down weren't watching the clock wind down at all. They were ticking off items on what they called a bucket list. Like going to Gay Paree. Like racing on the Indy Speedway. Like sky diving out of an airplane or bungee-jumping off a bridge. Things they always wanted to do, but had not done so far. When Mikey considered in the abstract coming up with a bucket list, he drew a blank. Maybe because he hated lists. Or because he had done everything and bought everything he desired.

His hypothetical bucket list, then, was already pre-filled. He once owned a piece of a horse that ran in the money in the Kentucky Derby. He had a Bentley and a Ferrari and a Land Rover and drove around for everyday a top-of-the-line Mercedes. Technically, it used to be dad's Bentley, but he wasn't going to be needing it these days. He routinely stayed in five-star hotels in Italy, and flew first-class all around the world. He copped box seats for the World Series. In theory, he could sport a different diamond-studded wrist watch each day of the week. Maitre d's routinely sat him at the best tables and casinos comped him presidential suites with mirrors on the ceiling. Once, underneath one of those ceilings he'd slept with an actual movie star. Unfortunately, this was an event mainly memorable for being unremarkable, assuredly on this side of fizzled fireworks. The star was so full of herself she appeared disappointed she did not receive a standing ovation afterward. Fat chance on his part, because he was similarly full of himself, not to mention that standing up in the moment posed a challenge for his shaky knees. Probably these days she wasn't any longer a star, but sleeping with him was not the reason her box office luster might have dimmed. Although he couldn't summon up her name and didn't recognize it in any movie billboards, he was pretty sure she wasn't what's-her-name who was good with guns and hot cars and who adopted all those multi-cultural babies or the one who used to be married to that short smiley actor with the funny thing about him, who belonged to some stupid cult called something dumb.

In any case, if those were the sorts of experiences and possessions that filled up a dying man's proper bucket list, his summary judgment was: big deal. Besides, it was too late now for any last-minute no-shopping-days-left-before-Christmas fuck-it list.

Chapter Seven

The red train-crossing lights were pulsing and swinging back and forth and the bells were jangling.

Ding ding ding ding ding ding ding ding ding ding...

That's when he answered the telephone.

"Yeth!" Mikey shouted. His throat was parched, and his inflated tongue lolled in his dry mouth like last week's ciabatta.

"Mikey, that you? Randy."

Ding ding ding ding ding ding ding ding ding ding...

"Where you at, Grand Central Station?"

"Grand Thenthral in New York, we're in Cathafornya." He should have brought a bottle of water. More stupid during his final stupid day.

"No shit. Hey, thought you'd want to know. New suit's ready."

Till now he'd forgotten about the suit he'd ordered at the trunk show a few weeks ago. "*Ith* good newth about the thoot." Then thee added thee would thee him thoon, in a thew hours.

The train engineer's horn blasted ear drums for miles and sounded an irrelevant reveille for the residents of the nearby cemetery.

Mikey slammed the car into gear and his wheels fishtailed around the gate as the force of a wind big and boisterous as a cyclone *oonch*ed him forward. The locomotive had missed his back bumper by a dog's hot breath.

One unexpected phone call away from a not-so-clean getaway. Nothing like a new suit to lift the mood of a suicidal guy with early onset Alzhammer, nothing in the world.

Tomorrow would be soon enough. He'd kill himself tomorrow, if he remembered, when he would be in the right wrong frame of mind.

What was Randy doing at the store at three o'clock in the morning and calling him? That Randy. He respected a guy who took his work seriously, and he drove down the dark road home.

TWO YEARS LATER

To: Rosetta Festagiacamo

From: Dinah Forte

Subject: My visit

Rosetta,

Had a chance to spend a few hours with your brother Mikey yesterday, my initial regular biweekly appointment. I look forward to catching up in real time with you, so this is touching base via email—as you requested me to do.

As a professional in the field you once used to be (someday I hope to hear more about your days at the research institute), you understand better than most people where we are in your brother Mikey's process. He seems to be in his own world, sometimes talking semi-cogently, though usually not. Hard to say what he is cognitively processing.

I think often about the question you asked me when we first met: when he sits there, seemingly lost in thought, is he telling himself some kind of story? That's a question, of course, we can't answer, but it's a tantalizing, if excruciating, mystery to ponder. So much left to learn about dementia and about Alzheimer's, isn't there? Which you understand as well as I do.

But you should know that he was quite alert yesterday (dementia is not a linear process, which makes it so exasperating for you as a loved one), and was his former charming self (he perked up and actually asked me if I wanted a glass of wine!).

Evidently, he takes me to be somebody he thinks he knows, but I don't think he knows who I am. He seems to think I am his mother's old friend, and he continually asks about somebody named Pete (?) and sometimes Sammy (?), who may be family friends for all I know. You might know who these people are.

The hospice nurse said his vitals were as expected, and his pulse remains strong. He is having trouble sleeping, despite the morphine, so I think I will check in with his primary and see about upping his dose.

I will be back out to see him on Thursday morning. If you want to coordinate our schedules, maybe we can have a cup of coffee. He seems to prefer his room dark and cool, so I have advised the caregiver (Amanaki sp? is her name, and she appears competent and genuinely caring despite the limitations of her communications skills) to keep the shades drawn and the AC on. The days are hot at his nursing home this time of year.

This is a long journey you and Mikey are on, and I have little doubt you are going through your own trials. As I have said, I am here for you day or night. I admire his courage and I admire your courage, too. So much adversity for you and your family to endure. It almost makes me wish I were a religious person, so I could pray for him, and you.

Dinah Forte

Dinah Penelope Forte, PhD

Forte Elder Care Management Professionals

TWO YEARS LATER

CAREGIVER LOG

Use this form to monitor changes and to communicate with doctors, hospice nurses and caregivers across shifts.

PATIENT: *MICHAEL FESTAGIACAMO (age 59)*

CAREGUVER: *Amanaki* ♥

DATE/TIME: *tuesday 8 clock AM mourning*

NOTE CHANGES:

no change for mikee same same

egcept some new sores on buttox, used cream

and powder incontience urin and feccal

FOOD: *toast jam butter Ensure rice; refused mc en cheeze*

MEDICATION: *same as befor, pluss new pill at 9; one dose morfine pill (hospis nurse says use jugment)*

ACTIVITIES: *two BMs midnite + 7 AM (big)*

PAIN LEVEL: *1-2*

ENERGY: *ressless, talking to hisself*

SLEEP PATTERN: *all nite talk talk talk himself ajjatated*

Sun comes up sleeps; sundowning like always

Chapter Eight

That Randy. That particular Randy who took his work seriously and was respected by Mikey was in the business of selling gorgeous lies. He was a clothes-salesman par excellence and a master tailor, but that wasn't the real business. He made a very good living convincing susceptible customers that, because of him and the men's store he owned, they looked fabulous. When he was done with them—he wanted them to appreciate—they really couldn't help looking that way.

Randy had the face of an affable wolverine and his head was the proud recent recipient of a garden bed of semi-fresh plugs of freakishly black patches of hair. Better than a toupee, he calculated, though observers who did a double-take seeing Doctor Ruggles/The Hair Doc's transplantation efforts did not universally concur.

After the close call on the train tracks, unquenchable Mikey was guzzling down another bottle of water while Randy was doing business as usual, which was lying to him.

"You know how you look, Mikey?" he said on genuflected knee to his client in the fitting room. Randy was wearing a sharkskin vest with matching sharkskin pants and he was checking the pronounced break of two-inch cuffs over Mikey's severely polished shoes. "I said, 'Do you know how you look?'"

Mikey knew this trick question amounted to an intelligence test. This was one notion he accurately summoned into consciousness. He remembered the drill from all the other times Randy had lied to him so he was relieved to recall what he was supposed to say: "I look *fabulous?*"

"Eggs-ackly. *Fabulous*, which is how you look. Damn, I am like some kind of a Michelangelo." That was Randy. He couldn't stop himself. "Don't you agree I'm, like, a artist?"

Mikey was different from other customers. He was never inclined to believe Randy like-some-kind-of-a-Michelangelo's lies. He was constitutionally reluctant to lend credence to anybody or anything. Same time, you didn't need to stick a gun into his ribs for him to concede that Randy was indeed like an artist, not that he had strong views about Michelangelo or any other artists to whom he might be rashly compared, and the one occasion a genuine gun was introduced to Mikey's ribcage was an experience he longed not to have replicated. Doubtless the gunman would feel similarly today if he had survived to share his thought process. File that incident under occupational hazard for a man in Mikey's line of work.

Only this time, funny thing, when Randy swore Mikey looked fabulous, he half-meant what he said. The half he wholeheartedly meant pertained to the suit Mikey was trying on, a custom suit turned around for a valued customer in no time.

Mikey regarded the ruined spectacle of his haggard self in the full-length mirror. He appeared prepped for nothing so much as the taxidermist's magical touch. Under the circumstances, there was no getting around the disquieting chore of taking a long look at himself. It's what you're obliged to do when you try on a new suit in Randy's exclusive men's store, which in a burst of commercial inspiration the proprietor christened *Randy's Exclusive Men's Store*. Evidently, Neiman Marcus and Saks Fifth Avenue and Wilkes Bashford had been snapped up. To Mikey's eye, the new suit appeared fine indeed, but his judgment was not to be trusted. He was distracted. Two hours of fitful sleep will do that. What about those saggy eye lids of his, that puffy face? Wisps of hair on his head, stubble on the chin? In the moment he also became aware that he had neglected to shave before leaving the house. Not good, not good, not good at all.

Maybe it was a rash idea to avoid that train a few hours ago.

Full of trepidation, he lifted up his pants legs. That *was* good. Socks. The socks didn't match, one being navy blue and the other being black, but at least he was wearing two of them.

Being what his family used to call a hypochondriac, Mikey also detected, from his step-up perch beneath the bank of flattering soft illumination, that unsightly mole erupting on the side of his ruddy cheek. Another man similarly taking stock of himself might have seen a doctor. On the subject of medical doctors, Mikey was—for a supposed hypochondriac—a rarity: he did not frequent physicians' offices. He did not believe in doctors. To him, they might as well have been unicorns. His parents had loads of doctors, and where did that get them, where? Case closed.

As far as he could tell, the suit was something, a new black two-button Brioni. Nice suit, no question, but the man wrapped inside the soft folds of its sumptuous fabric was not ageing gracefully.

"*Fabulous*, Mikey, you got that eggs-ackly right," said Randy. The man was in his rhythm, like a jump shooter on fire who knows he can't miss from anywhere inside the gym. "Didn't I tell you the super 120 fabric would drape beautiful on you? Yes, I did."

"You are an artist, Randy." Randy needed to be reaffirmed, and Mikey would oblige. Unfortunately, Mikey couldn't say the same about the man's professional hair restorationist. That's the thing about a guy's hair job.

You can't stop yourself from staring, and not in an admiring way like with a pretty girl lonely at the end of the bar at closing time.

"Yes, I am a artist. It's like somebody poured you into your Brioni."

Which is the effect a customer might have plausibly desired from a hand-tailored garment that cost not much less than some other Italian exports that came equipped with a steering wheel.

Mikey was a large man, size 52 long American, 62 long Italian, which made it challenging for him to shop off the rack, not that he would buy off the rack if he could, which he couldn't. Last time he wore something bought off the rack, he wasn't buying. His mom was, fifty-some years ago. That was when he was a youth, when his mom—rest in peace—would take him shopping in the Husky Boy section of a department store. And that dated back to when his dad wasn't yet the boss, when he was nothing but an up-and-coming member of a crew he was plotting to take over. Then his old man made his bones the normal way, one big move after another, an *Arrivederci, Roma* to one obstructionist rival after another. Eventually he became capo, and nobody in his household shopped in department stores for clothes anymore. They moved to a much grander residence with spacious walk-in closets to hold all their bespoke clothes, a house on a street where the municipality disallowed cars from parking. That's what circular driveways in the neighborhood were constructed for. Ultimately, the family got used to this custom, and in due course they all but forgot when they lived once upon a time on a street where cars dared to be parked.

Vincent Festagiacamo, Mikey's dad, had made what anybody would regard as very serious money from the horses, the card games, the bookmaking, the restaurants, and the numerous other ancillary entrepreneurial interests—and his secreted cash assets were by any standard considerable. He lived in high style to accord with such wealth, as did his son, who stood to gain half of everything in the long run. Next to being indicted for racketeering, notoriety was the last thing Vincent desired, and his name was not on everybody's lips, like some kind of Dapper Don. Gotti favored nice suits, too, but he was too much in the public eye and it's well known how that turned out for him, the short version of which was: not so good.

For everyday wear, when he didn't throw on the kind of sweat suits Tony Soprano wore on that TV show, which were comfortable, Mikey selected one of his sport coats, many of them in bright spring pastels, and before today he didn't own a black suit. Now he felt the need for a black suit, because no way was he going to go, for instance, to a requiem Mass in a canary yellow jacket like from Palm Springs, so why not pop for a Brioni? He could have gone with the Kiton, which cost more than the Brioni, but he had a sentimental, if unfounded, attachment to the Brioni brand—it was his dad's preferred designer.

"Formal occasion, Mikey?"

Mikey's motto, borrowed from his wary father and subsequently adopted by him: never answer a direct question from law enforcement, significant others, or lying clothes-salesmen.

"Hard to say."

Fact is, Mikey did expect there were some funerals to attend in the future, where a black suit would prove de rigueur. His father's, for one.

His own, for another.

Though Mikey had his issues with the medical profession, he went along with his father's attachment to doctors. On that score, the concierge doctor had already ordered home hospice, which meant Vincent Festagiacamo's final Square Up Day was approaching, probably before kickoff of next football season. Despite not having graduated from a medical school, or any other educational institution after elementary school, his son didn't wholeheartedly subscribe to the doc's prognostication. But say he did, who needs strangers hanging around the house, snooping? Not too long ago, Mikey had moved back into his parents' home, where he could keep an eye out, hired all the care his dad needed, twenty-four-seven, and they reported to him, not some white lab coat with a stethoscope serving as his version of bling. The point was taken, which was this: his dad's time on earth was fast winding down. The timing of that inevitability was out of Mikey's control.

The other funeral he was thinking about, the one a little way down the road but getting closer by the second, was Mikey's. And the timing was going to be in his own control. That was one thing he could see to.

"Nice job. Thanks."

"Thank *you*. When my exclusive men's store customers are happy, I am happy." That was the closest Randy came to an outright not-a-lie.

"Never thought I'd pay this much for a suit, but who knows how long a man has left, and they say you can't take it with you, right?" Mikey framed it as a rhetorical question, though his thinking was anything but.

"You got that right." Randy stood up, bowed his head, and allowed his voice to drop a few registers. "I don't mean to be disrespectful or nosy, but we're all thinking about your father, a great man. We hope he is resting comfortably."

Mikey nodded, slowly, full of big feelings that had sneaked up on him. No need for him to use words when words, which these days could be unmanageable as a fire hose in his grasp, might be avoided.

Chapter Nine

Because no, Mikey's dad wasn't resting, comfortably or otherwise, and he wasn't feeling better, and odds were he wouldn't be feeling better ever again. Mikey took Randy's professed concern to be, on the Randy scale, relatively sincere. At the same time, Randy had a vested interest in Mikey's dad's welfare. He was a man who owned a rack of Brionis and he had to be Randy's best customer. He was smaller in stature than his son, as were most people in the world, so those suits were not going to be passed down to Mikey, not now, not in the future, and not even a lying artist of a tailor was going to alter that fact or those suits. And his dad's time was drawing near: Alzhammer, atrial-fibrillation, congestive heart failure. For an eighty-six-year-old man that was some kind of trifecta.

☙

MIKEY STOPPED OUTSIDE OF Randy's store and reflected day-dreamily as the sun beat down on his black beaver, numbered Borsalino hat. His new suit was packed in a plastic garment bag he had slung over his shoulder. Behind him, "EXCLUSIVE" flashed on the storefront window in red neon, alternating with "MEN," which was flashing in green.

He stood there for a while, soaking in the sun's warmth, but if asked he couldn't have said how long.

EXCLUSIVE...MEN...EXCLUSIVE...MEN...

Mikey was recalling the low-budget zombie movie he watched on television in the early morning hours when he could not sleep, which was not unusual these days. He loved his zombies and he established no discernible standards when it came to the genre. As with any number of zombie movies, in this one some virus of unknown origin had contaminated the human species. Some environmental catastrophe had been hinted at, compounded by some vague, nefarious plot hatched by a mad scientist, and furthered by the power-grabbing military brass. Now the undead lurch about, on the perpetual quest for a lunch of human flesh. That part did not make logical sense to him. Why would you want nothing more than to eat people once you were dead? Why would a hankering for uncooked meat—human carpaccio—motivate a zombie? Why didn't they all engage in some other compulsive activity? Shopping, for instance? Or driving, or dancing? Those activities could be equally terrifying to witness.

Mikey observed the lunch hour crowd ambling down the street and it made him think of nothing so much as a post-apocalyptic world, one with zombies on the loose. Fortunately these were not zombies passing him by. The fog rolled in and canceled the sun and the sky grew overcast and the world was about to be overrun by zombies. It could happen, it could happen, why not, why not?

EXCLUSIVE...MEN...EXCLUSIVE...MEN...

Mikey next became conscious of another equally unexpected development. A homeless guy, green khaki jacket, hooded sweatshirt, was mumbling and exhaling a wine-soaked "Thank you, sir," in his direction. There was a twenty-dollar bill fluttering in the exhilarated or inebriated man's hand and a roll of cash in Mikey's grasp. The fancy new suit bag was lying at his feet, on the sidewalk. Mikey passed out dollar bills to panhandlers, sometimes a five, never a twenty. He supposed the twenty was all right, but he could not say for sure. At least the guy wasn't, as far as he could tell, a zombie.

EXCLUSIVE...MEN...EXCLUSIVE...MEN...

Mikey shoved the rest of his cash back in his pocket where it belonged, picked up the suit bag, dusted it off, and walked away. He hoped to get home before something else bad happened, a hope that would prove unfounded.

"God bless you, sir," called out the beneficiary of Mikey's generosity or gummed-up brain circuitry.

"Keep it to yourself," Mikey called back to him over his shoulder.

He turned the corner and sought in vain for the car key within his pocket. But his new black Mercedes sedan wasn't where he believed he had left it. His first thought took this shape: *Hey, they stole my car*—some mother had jacked his wheels. Neighbors stealing the morning newspaper in his driveway, high school kids TPing his trees, out-of-bounds Mr. Smith putting the arm on somebody in Mikey's territory, now this.

His second thought was that was not the case at all, that somebody had driven him to the store—but upon further reflection, that didn't make much sense, because where was his driver? For one thing, Mo, his bodyguard, was visiting his own mom in her nursing home today, and couldn't have taken him if he had wanted to. He usually told Mo where he was going, but since Mo didn't have the intellectual capacity to keep unarticulated any opinions and information and gossip passing through his head, maybe he and the rest of the crew knew where he was—at Randy's, picking up his new suit, and no longer—as he had secretly planned—taking himself out on the train tracks on the edge of the city.

His third thought was more distressing: his car was not stolen by some motherfucker, but he had no fucking memory as to where he had fucking parked.

He reached into his pants pocket once again to seek frantically again for the car key, but the key if located would have somewhat limited utility unless he discovered the car in question. When he again failed to find the key, he had a sinking feeling he might have left it on the console. That would be like him these days.

His car had keyless entry and ignition, and all he had to do was grab the door handle and as long as the key was in his pocket—but that wasn't going to solve the problem, because the key wasn't in his pocket and there was no door handle for him to touch.

Mikey kept walking around in the neighborhood, searching for ten, fifteen minutes. Then, as he was about to resign himself to giving up the quest, he was excited to see that there it was, right there, parked at the end of the block.

Yes, that indeed appeared to be his car, but this was bizarre: two guys were jumping into the front seat of the car, so possibly it was their car. But their demeanor indicated that they didn't possess clear title. They appeared sketchy, and their furtiveness struck him as being suspicious. He considered running toward them, in case it was his car, and preventing them from stealing it, if that's what they were doing. In a moment, he was close enough that he could hear the ignition at the instant it engaged the engine.

He practically felt the heat blast him in the face before he heard the detonation. That was the moment the car exploded, and pieces went flying spectacularly everywhere. In a blink his former Mercedes was now reduced to nothing but a spectacular, smoldering heap of German shrapnel. There was also a naked human leg that had rolled to rest in the middle of the street.

He turned on his heels and walked in the opposite direction before the fire trucks and the cops could show. He wasn't sure where he was, but he knew wherever it was, it wasn't advisable to stay there.

He came to a full stop and touched all over his face. Good, his eyebrows weren't fried, not that that made a difference. And another thing: when did San Francisco turn into Baghdad?

The thieves had made an unfortunate choice of a car to steal, and Mikey almost felt sorry for the two losers. Even more, he appreciated how fortunate he had been. Now, for the other mystery. Who had planted the surprise? But that was no mystery. Not really. Word had leaked out. He was vulnerable. He had a bull's-eye on his back. His dad was dying and it was worth taking a shot, getting rid of the competition, Vincent Festagiacamo's useless son: Mikey.

⊂ℜ

IT WAS ONE THING if he decided to take himself out. It was another when somebody else had a similar idea. *That* he was not prepared for. That was also what he wouldn't let happen, not if he could help it. He'd do what he had to do on his own terms, and nobody else was going to make the call. Obviously he wasn't destined to teach Logic in college any time soon. No, if Logic were a horse in Mikey's race, she was running on the rail and boxed in, a prohibitive fifty to one shot.

He tried to break down the issue into its constituent parts, from train tracks to car bomb. Yes, he had a desire to die and he was willing to put himself in a position where he would die. But he had little desire to kill, and if he were honest with himself, less desire to kill himself. That wouldn't stop him, however. This posed a problem he was confident he could work out once he was away from the site of the car's annihilation.

As he walked off, he reviewed the facts as he knew them. Somebody had made the first move on him. (Fact.) Mikey wouldn't overreact, he would wait. (First step.) He wouldn't get emotional. He learned how to fake that from his father. Remain calm. (Long shot.) Make somebody pay a price. (The plan.) He liked that car and he would miss it. He added the Benz to the list of many things he was missing.

From his socks to his car to his memory, all his losses were connecting.

What he meant was, nothing was connecting.

Wait. Where was his new suit? What did he do with it? Did he lose that, too?

Oh. There it was. He was clutching the black Brioni suit bag to his chest.

He reached up to tug down on the brim of his Borsalino. But he failed, because no hat brim made itself available for him to tug. The Borsalino must have been knocked off by the explosion and it was probably rolling on the filthy sidewalk. Nothing more pathetic to him than the image of a six-hundred-buck hat tumbling down the street, but he didn't go back to search. Time to cut his losses, all of them.

TWO YEARS LATER

CAREGIVER LOG

Use this form to monitor changes and to communicate with doctors, hospice nurses and caregivers across shifts.

PATIENT: *MICHAEL FESTAGIACAMO (age 59)*

CAREGUVER: *Amanaki* ♥

DATE/TIME: *tuesday 8 clock AM mourning*

NOTE CHANGES: *Bad nite very bad nite. I couldnt sleep winkk. Kept tring to get out hospitle bed. Need to talk hospis nurse*

FOOD: *nothing*

MEDICATION: *same as befor, new pill befor bed; three dose morfine pill*

ACTIVITIES: *no BM; put him on toylet, he got mad took punch swing*

PAIN LEVEL: *7-8*

ENERGY: *very ressless, talking to hisself*

SLEEP PATTERN: *all nite moning hey hey hey hey ajjatated*

Sundowning today like ushual

Try to not let him napp during day so he sleep at nite

Chapter Ten

With his new suit in his clutches and the smell of his burning Benz lingering in his nose, Mikey grabbed the first cab out of the city. Maybe that noxious smell had more to do with the taxi operated by a chatty dread-locked young man. Did he catch the scent of singed hair? Was the back seat the site of rooster sacrificial rites? Coming this close to being blown to pieces might make somebody with a certain temperament conclude he was in the middle of his lucky day. Or at least not his most unlucky day. All to say, he wasn't feeling choosy and wasn't going to complain—and besides, he had to get going.

Once he arrived home, glad to be free of the taxi, he headed into his father's room. He couldn't imagine anywhere else to be.

ᘏ

THE DAY HIS FATHER died would be an awful day, awful for everybody but his dad, who had no—what was the expression all these so-called health professionals were using these days?—right, *no quality of life.* That's how they would put it. The man had no quality of life: yet another thing shared by Alzhammered father and son.

Due to his accelerating dementia, Vincent Festagiacamo did not reliably recognize Michael Festagiacamo all the time, and he was continually perturbed, repeatedly trying to climb out of his hospital bed at home, taking each opportunity to strip off his clothes or fling his food like some bonobo monkey or throw a punch at a caregiver who wasn't fast enough on his feet. As much as he hated to admit, Mikey would ask himself a simple and brutal question: how long was this death watch going to go on? Bad as this sounds, he would be relieved when his father would be freed from the indignity of his cursed existence. He had seen his mom wither away and suffer similarly from her dementia, and had witnessed his dad—well before he himself took this decisive turn—weep nightly until he was too tired to shed another tear for his beloved, suffering wife.

This old age business was purely a bitch, no doubt about it. Mikey had read up on dementia—being a supposed hypochondriac, which he didn't think he was—and its possible connection to the family genes, and he was naturally forced to conclude that as surely as catching a cold in winter, he himself would be inevitably knocked out one day by the Alzhammer wielded by his body and brain's fate. He was already staggering in the second round, bloodied and battered by its relentless assault.

But this was one fate Mikey refused to accept for himself. He had his pride. It wasn't much to have, his pride, but it was his. He wasn't going to passively accept sitting in his own fouled diapers and talking to his shoes and the invisible people under the bed, no way. He knew the signs all too well by now after observing his father's and his mother's torments. And it wasn't like his father would miss him once he checked himself out. The man missed everything already.

Mikey reaffirmed his resolution: first opportunity, he would take himself out.

It wasn't like he was going to be leaving his father to fend for himself. Mikey made the necessary arrangements. Yes, his sister would step up, he was confident she would. The two siblings had not always seen eye to eye, but the prospect of a father's imminent death has a way of sharpening the sight lines. She was probably capable of doing a better job of taking care of her father than he could, and it was past time for her to do the right thing on behalf of the family for a change. And she wouldn't have to worry about the finances, either. To judge by the dowdy clothes she favored and the economy car she drove, she wasn't getting rich anytime soon at her fancy-pants job.

Her dad's estate plan and Mikey's detailed instructions were clear. He didn't put every single detail down on paper—his dad taught him well so he knew better—but she was smart enough to read between the lines. In this way, he effectively laid out the information that amounted to her personal map to the buried treasure—along with the contact information for an Italian barrister based in London. That lawyer had the keys not only to the big money in North Beach, the Italian neighborhood of San Francisco, but also to the bigger stashes in Sicily and Naples. Between the off-shore accounts (Mikey's big idea) and some very useful jam-packed mattresses (the dad's old school idea) as well as the significant inheritance from the trust that would come her way, Mikey's sister would have more money than she could possibly need to take care of both her father and herself. Some day she'd wish she could thank Mikey—once he was out of the picture.

ᴄ

Mikey's father grabbed his hand and would not let go. The old man's fingers felt soft and supple, and they wrapped around his son's hand like rubbery vine tendrils. Not like before. In his prime, his vise-like fingers could cut off a man's circulation. And that day he was talking to his son for a change—if this indeed counted as communication. He said the same thing over and over:

"We're losing more than we're winning."

He asked his father what he was talking about.

"We're losing more than we're winning," he repeated.

Maybe it was obvious to his father what it was that they were both losing and not winning, maybe it was obvious to anyone, and maybe Mikey didn't wish to acknowledge as much.

"Mikey, get me outta here, get me outta here, Mikey."

His son assured him that *here* is where he lived, as if that was what the man had intended.

"Hey! Hey! Hey! Get me outta here!"

Mikey tried to assure his dad it was going to be okay, although he knew for a mortal lock it wouldn't be.

"Hey! Help me," he pleaded. "Help me." In that way he articulated a point of view he had not articulated before. He had never needed help from anybody else before. Other people needed *him*: the essence of the longstanding family business proposition. If necessary, he would make painfully clear how and why they needed him.

Mikey said he was doing all he could to help, but his father was only more outraged.

"Mikey, I think you're fulla shit, Mikey."

This was not an original point of view. He'd heard it before. He voiced it to himself. On the plus side of the ledger, he remembered his son's name, if that was to be counted on the plus side. The son looked into the eyes of his demented father, and witnessed his own future unfolding.

"You're fulla shit, Mikey."

"I know, Dad."

Mikey read the pamphlets the worthless doctor presented him, and sure enough, he noticed the classic signs of imminent mortality. His father's breathing was more and more labored. Apnea was the term. The morphine and the Haldol and the Digoxin might help. Of late, the old man was paying as much attention to his food as he would a torn-up pari-mutuel ticket. Most telling, now he was conversing regularly with his deceased wife, and he seemed to revel in her spectral presence. She could have been advising him it was all right for him to let go. If so, that would have been considerate of her. It would also have constituted a first, getting her husband to go along with anything she wanted him to do. No doubt about it, life was winding down fast for Vincent Festagiacamo, and it broke his son's heart to contemplate the reduced, humiliating circumstances of a man once feared and revered.

At the same time, life would go on for the son and the crew—for a while in any case. Complications loomed on the horizon. Exploding cars, just a start. Then who knows what would happen next?

His dad's decline had been precipitous. Plans for succession in the shop and Mikey's ascendance to leadership of the crew were in place. His dad had made his intentions plain, long before his mind slipped its moorings. Of course, whenever there is such a transition in a business enterprise such as this, you have to count on there being those who refuse to sheep-like approve. No, they were more like wolves. It's not like the shop was run by some ordinary board of crooks like an international banking syndicate, though the world at large would have regarded his crew as nothing but a ragtag bunch of reprobates while on the other hand a bank was no such thing—the lies people told themselves were astonishing. There would be rough spots in the changeover, Mikey felt certain, despite all the preparation, rough spots that would need to be smoothed out, and by "rough spots" he meant his enemies and by "smoothed out" he meant eradicated. Other crews would take a shot, try to take over the shop. That's to be expected. He would be astounded if they didn't keep coming at him. From his dad he had learned all about running the family business, all the facets and nuances of the shop, and he was as ready as he could be, which didn't necessarily mean he was ready at all. He was nearly sixty and had spent his whole adult life learning at his dad's knee. Until he succeeded in finally offing himself, he would have to solve the problems that came with running the shop and the crew.

All this was no longer an abstract or theoretical proposition. Somebody had already made the first move. That really was a man's leg in the street. A dumb thief's leg, yes, but a real leg detached from a dumb thief's body which could have been Mikey's own leg. And he had taken a filthy cab home and his car was history and he was sitting in the room where his father was dying of the Alzhammer. And the smell. This is what death smelled like.

ᕤ

A SHAFT OF LIGHT sliced through the heart of the room. If the sun could make a sound it would have been *zing*. Mikey wondered if he was hallucinating.

In that instant something dramatically changed about Vincent, whose face now seemed illuminated, only from within. His eyes gleamed. His rigidified mouth softened. Mikey's father held up his hand, like a benevolent traffic cop at a school crosswalk. He was giving evidence of an intention to conduct, for lack of a better term, a dialogue with his son. He now seemed calm, reflective, what somebody might call rational. What happened to his dementia Mikey had no idea, but he knew enough about the Alzhammer to know that it did not proceed on a straight-line course, and that, especially approaching the end of life, somebody could briefly, temporarily, evanescently become himself again. That end of life stage was called, weirdly to Mikey's ear, "actively dying." A self-canceling term. He himself had been freshly reminded of that concept of actively dying. That's precisely what somebody had had in store for him that morning.

"Mikey?"

"Yeah, Dad."

"Been thinking."

This had happened once or twice before, when his father would appear lucid for a couple of minutes. It was always a shocking development, like old times. If past experience was any indication, the mood would not last long, so the son listened carefully, wanting to take it all in. He lamented his father's absence, yearned for his presence in these travails.

"You feeling okay, Mikey?"

He said he guessed he was.

"It's hard being the boss, I oughta know, people counting on you, people always wanting to take a shot, they get an opening. It's predictable, people are animals."

He seemed to know about today, but how could he?

"Don't worry about me. I'll be okay."

"You might could need a rethink."

"About what?"

"Like rethink it all. This life, is it what you want?"

"I got a choice?"

"You always got a choice. You should step back, take stock, life's short, you know. How's Rosetta? Your sister's a good girl, but she oughta visit her old man."

Mikey told him that the two of them had been talking and she was planning to come by soon. This was not a true statement, but there was nothing to gain from the truth, and candor would merely upset his father.

"Her work's hard, she's got her hands full," Mikey said. And she was a self-centered prima donna, too.

"She got brains and ambition, don't she? And she's kinda cold-blooded, which," he smiled, "is a compliment. I mean, she has made a little name for herself, some kinda doc, ain't she? So I understand. Life belongs to the living, my old man used to say. I coulda been a better father to her, too, I know that, I know that now. Funny thing is, she'd have been good to work alongside you." The man laughed at the preposterous notion. "Only with girls, you can't do that. But if there was any girl could help you run the shop, Jesus, Rosey could."

"Obviously," Mikey said, "obviously." He didn't believe that for a second. The man was going sentimental, and he couldn't fault him, a man in his spot had justification.

"Take care of Rosey, okay?" Deftly leaving out this part: *when I am gone.* And also the other part: *not that she needs being taken care of.*

The mood in the room was growing more nostalgic by the moment. Mikey was fearful the man was going to ask for a priest, make his last confession. That would have been worth overhearing. Yet priests were as useless as doctors in his estimation. Was his father on the verge of implying Mikey should hurry up with his bucket list?

"There are people you can trust and people you can't, remember that. Trust counts for everything in this life. That's the secret to family, which it ain't no secret."

"I trust *you*, Dad."

"That's why I'm saying, maybe the time's right to step back, take a break, rethink the whole thing, the shop, the business, the life. You got plenty money, enjoy it. Take a break, make a trip to Italy, drink wine looking at the boats on the bay in Napoli, you can always come back when you want. The problems don't go away, for long at least."

"Actually, I been feeling kinda off lately, not thinking clearly."

"You're not so young anymore, time's running out on the game clock. You should re-invalidate what you want to do the rest of your life. You might do something else you really want. Maybe being boss ain't you."

"Crosses my mind, it crosses my mind. Today something happened." It was a bad idea, to go where he was going. He went there anyway. Maybe his father could help him somehow. He needed his dad. Mikey told his father what happened with the car. As soon as he did so, he realized that was a mistake.

"Motherfuck," said his father.

Eggs-ackly, Mikey thought.

"Got an idea who?"

He ticked off the obvious suspects and didn't add what had him most concerned: that Mikey Festagiacamo no longer inspired fear.

"That's the life, that's the thing about this life. You worried?"

"Not really."

"Talk to me."

"I can deal."

"Of course you can, of course you *can*, but do you want? What for? To make more money? How much money you need? We made a ton. You could live high on the hog, rest of your life."

"You might could be right."

"Where's your mother? She out shopping?" The man's eyes glazed over. Back to square one. "Get your mother in here when she comes home. Have her make me meatballs tonight."

"She's in heaven."

"What the?"

"Mom's not here. Gone. Up in heaven." *Where you'll be seeing her soon.*

"Fulla shit, Mikey."

"Calm down, Dad."

"You calm down. I think you're fulla shit. You are fulla shit. Get me outta here!" The veins popped along the man's neck as he groped for the water on the counter and summoned up all the strength he had in him to throw it at his son. He didn't have the muscle power, this man who once could practically pull up a light post, and Mikey didn't budge when the water bottle fell to the floor and dribbled near his shoes. So the Alzhammer had slammed the man's brain all over again, and that was Mikey's cue to get up and leave his father's room so as not to further disturb him.

"You rest up. Everything'll be okay." Not that he could and not that it would be.

"The boat is here. We gotta get on board. The boat is here, it's early."

"Okay, Dad, the boat is here, you're right, I can see for myself the boat is here."

Chapter Eleven

Mikey lifted the garage door and popped the trunk of his dad's black Bentley. He had work to do. He went down into his wine cellar and carried up cases of Gaja Barbaresco, choice selections from what he had been advised were the great vintages. That was his favorite brand, and he possessed numerous cases, and this activity took some time. He methodically packed the car with thousands of dollars worth of rare Nebbiolo, till there was just enough room to wedge himself behind the wheel.

Wiping his brow, he was pissed off all over again, pissed off at what he could only manically define as the whole fucking world. A world of bombers and Brionis and Borsalinos and Bentleys and Barbarescos and brain-disease. So no, he was not thinking clearly. A world of bull-shitters and beat-downs and betrayals in Baghdad by the Bay. Bottom-feeders, all of them. No way was he going to leave this wine for those bottom-feeders and bottom-drinkers who came after him, like the guys in the crew who would come around in his wake to celebrate his passing by drinking these tremendous wines while pretending to mourn his passing. And yes, there was a note of self-pity. Because no way was he going to let his kid sister drink these bottles because she would not appreciate them.

 CR

She could have helped run the crew? Rosey? Get the. His dad really said that about his kid sister? She and her brother had drifted apart, and she had systematically ignored her family. Hotshot shrink professor doctor, if that's what she was, and he was continually tempted to write her off.

Once, Rosetta used to be a good girl, when she was young and Mikey looked out for her. But the last time they talked was several months ago outside their dad's ICU bed after his latest scare. She was carrying on about the research they were doing at her institute, tracking the DNA, or whatever it was she said, cutting edge research, all to the end of coming up with some magic potion for arresting the onslaught of Alzheimer's if not curing it.

"Glad you could take time out of your important life to be here for your dad," he said to her that time both of them were standing in the hospital corridor, looking to throw down.

"Don't bust my balls," Rosetta said. "Not the time, and not in the fucking mood."

She did have a wicked tongue, being a Festagiacamo, which was one thing Mikey begrudgingly approved about her. He wondered if she talked like that around her smarmy, pointy-head colleagues, and he half-hoped she did.

"How come you always dress all-black, like there's a funeral?" he said out of the blue, apropos of nothing, but maybe that was not true.

Which took her aback, and which he was surprisingly good at doing: disarming somebody, of their weapons, their attitudes, their assumptions. "Black's academic chic," she said, not sure where this was going but knowing she couldn't flinch.

"And when'd you start wearing glasses? And can your glasses possibly get any smaller?"

She had had enough. "When I need a makeover, I'll let you know, Mister Coco Chanel."

"You want to be a good academic sheik sister for a change," he told her, "get me and dad a goddamn pill for the Alzhammer."

"*Alzheimer's*. You realize every time we talk, you want a pill? You ever gonna stop talking about this? What, you think you're going to catch dementia? It's not contagious like poison oak or the flu or the clap—which is one thing you do know all about."

"Well, I been reading up." If she was so smart, why wasn't she herself worried about getting clobbered by the Alzhammer?

"*Reading up?* You mean, like, *books*? You got a library card now?"

"What, you sarcastic, saying I can't read, perfesser?"

"I'm not a professor and there's no goddamn pill, not yet, and not anytime soon, either." Again she explained, yet again, there were many types of dementia—vascular, frontotemporal, dementia with Lewy bodies, and so on. It wasn't one hundred percent certain their dad *had* the Alzhammer. *Alzheimer's!* In the eyes of others, she may have possessed some intellectual authority on the subject, but her brother never got straight her tenuous academic standing, which in her own mind was lower than krill in the research university ocean food chain, but why should he bother to focus on her, which would restrict time for his self-involvement? He could not appreciate how she had reached the limits of her patience with regard to the nasty politics of her work. She lost count of how many married vice presidents and directors, all of them MDs, had made anything but subtle passes at her.

"*You really know how to fill out a lab coat, baby, in all the right places.*"

"*Legs like yours, what do you look like in high heels?*"

"*Want to go for a ride in my Porsche?*"

The last time, one of them had approached her from behind and attempted to massage her shoulders without the slightest encouragement on her part. She wheeled around and slapped him. But when he reared back to respond with a closed fist, he didn't stand a fighting chance with a Festagiacamo. She kneed the man between his legs and calmly walked back to her desk as he crumpled at the waist and sucked for air. No wonder, professionally speaking, she had had hit the glass ceiling of her failing career. She was not going to be named either director or vice president, because in that sort of hidebound universe no female staff member had ever been elevated. She shouldn't have been shocked that nerds like her bosses turned out to be assholes and cut-throats and creeps, but she hated to admit she often was.

"How come no pill, Rosetta, how come?"

"We have gone over this before. Because there isn't! Listen to me. It doesn't work like that. Yes, there are drugs that may or may not slow down the disease's progress, maybe, but it's not a game-changer. And because we may have isolated the gene for Alzheimer's doesn't mean we can wave a magic wand and cure or even effectively treat the disease. There are these experimental treatments that are trying to block a protein called beta amyloid, which makes plaque deposits on the brain, but it's way early."

"How about one of them tests?"

"It's not like pissing on a stick to see if you're pregnant. I thought you read around, tough guy. There are imaging technologies, PET scans, CT scans, and MRIs, but again, whatever they find, no matter if they determine there is plaque in a certain area of the brain, it's far from conclusive. Though now all of a sudden there is a new and powerful scanning mechanism out there. Yet the problem's the same. So what if they find reason to think somebody has what you insist on ridiculously calling the Alzhammer, what difference does it make? There's no goddamn treatment!"

"Thank you, doctor, I think you have made it all very clear to me."

Yes, she did make it clear, although he couldn't quite register that she was not quite a doctor. He knew what he had to do.

"Look, they can do what they call a simple clock test, which is very accurate, it seems. They ask you to draw a clock, and to position the hands, which is always ten after eleven."

"Great, you gave me the answer. In high school, you didn't give me the test answers, but now you do, thanks for nothing. How can they test me now, when I know the right answer?"

"If you've accurately diagnosed yourself, you'll probably forget it, asshole."

"Just get the goddamn pill, Rosey hotshot. I know they must be testing some new drugs they don't want the public to know about."

"On second thought, chances are you are also paranoid and delusional."

"Told you."

"Good news, Mikey. There *are* pills for that."

~~~

ROSETTA HAD BROKEN MIKEY'S heart, which he would not admit, and she was a complicated egghead know-it-all with all her advanced degrees, none of which he could name or understand. Her father had always adored her with pure abandon, while her mother started pulling away from her daughter and cursing her out every chance when she was in high school—which might have been one symptom of his mom's early onset dementia.

Growing up, Rosey was a lissome and pretty, though frankly not arrest-me-pretty, girl, somebody who never got into any trouble worth getting into. She resembled more her elegant mother, while Mikey looked more like his scuffed-up dad. She received straight As—whereas his grade point average hovered permanently below the Mendoza line. She also ran cross-country, to him an activity that qualified as inane. Baseball, you whack a ball with a bat. Football, you plant somebody's head in the ground. Those games made a kind of sense. But running? Why? It seemed so unnecessary. Why go to all the trouble running? Drive the car. When she ran, she tied her long black hair in a pony tail, but otherwise her hair flowed down like those moon-eyed teenage girls in the movies that his dates wanted to see and that he walked out of after they clawed his hand when he tried to get inside their jeans.

At the same time, she was ferociously competitive and Mikey found it strange how she, for such a geeky girl, bragged, how she trash-talked her rivals.

"You got no chance, bitch," she would say, sometimes with a smile.

"Give up and grab a smoke already, all you gonna see is the bottom of my shoes."

"I got a feather for you to tickle your throat, that'll make it easier for you to throw up on schedule."

"Don't get near me, those acne scars might be contagious."

"Nice sneaks. Where'd you get them, drug store?"

A few times, frustrated, angry girls threw punches at her at the finishing line, blows she returned with interest.

Mikey also never got the part about being on some high school team. The football coach tried in vain to recruit him, because he was so outsized. "The Monarchs need you," the coach once said in a quivering voice, because, like everybody, he was intimidated by the boy. Mikey honestly wanted to know who the Monarchs were and what it was they needed him for. The coach gently informed him that was the name of the school mascot. If Mikey was familiar with any Monarch, it would have made no difference back in the day. He was too busy. He operated a thriving cigarette vending machine business in two hundred locations that required vigilance and maintenance. Some kids had newspaper routes to make spending money. Mikey was entrepreneurial, and he earned more than his teachers, which wasn't saying much, but he had major walking-around money for a teenager.

Whatever his problems with his sister, Mikey, being her big brother, had a sacred, familial, hard-wired obligation to look out for her. He did not allow anybody he didn't approve of to get near his sister. The roster of boys he approved of was highly exclusive. Actually, there was no roster and if there were one there would have been no names on it. No boy was good enough to get next to his kid sister because, being a boy, he knew what boys were all about, which was, to him, come on be serious, self-evident. And as for anybody who stupidly tried to romance her, when Mikey caught wind, he had a little one-way chat to lay down the ground rules, the violation of which would necessitate what he termed a swift response. Mikey was smitten by the term *swift response*, which to him sounded the perfect tone of subtlety. He could not recall where he acquired it.

"What does *swift response* mean?" asked some dumbass she liked who shouldn't have rolled the dice.

Mikey punched him square in the nose. Obviously, that's what it meant.

"What the!" Nobody can recite the Gettysburg Address or say much of anything at all after being punched in the nose and staggering back against a wall.

"Coming attraction."

One day Rosetta made the terrible judgment error of waxing rapturous over the ziti at dinner about her allegedly fantastic, dreamy, young, new English teacher.

First off, English teachers? What kind of self-respecting male goes into the English teaching line of work? Assuming teaching English is work, but how could that be? So he paid a visit after school, and tuned up the fledgling instructor, a little. He was semi-respectful, not doing too much damage. That minor-league beat down explained why Mikey did not don the cap and gown at commencement or attend the ceremony at all, and which accounted for his dad's proudly celebrating instead Mikey's popping his cherry: his first arrest, assault and battery. Judge Keily placed the teenager on probation and fined him a hundred bucks, which the distinguished jurist paid out of his own pocket.

Despite Mikey's religiously performing the due diligence, Rosetta never lacked for admirers in school or afterward. Her one marriage in her thirties had ended practically before it began, for reasons Mikey and the rest of the family were not told. Of course he never cared for the guy in the first place, so he wasn't nostalgic. That suitor, too, had asked what Mikey meant when he pulled him aside one day and told him he had to be good to his little sister because something would happen if he wasn't.

"What precisely would happen?"

He shouldn't have asked that. He was advised there would be, of course, a swift response.

"What kind of swift response?"

His query produced the same tried and true results as before. When Mikey landed on a successful approach, he tended to stick with it.

"You're a maniac, like your sister said!" Or so claimed the observant, nose-bleeding bastard.

Mikey gave him his linen handkerchief. "Let's get you cleaned up and head back to your engagement party. Rosey's waiting, man."

It wasn't long before she was living alone again—like her brother.

◆

"You're no help, Rose. All you doctors, no help, you ask me, what's new?"

"I'm not that kind of doctor, when are you going to get that straight? And because mom had Alzheimer's and dad may have Alzheimer's doesn't necessarily mean you will. It was only the other day, before this new scanner came out, when we used to think only an autopsy can confirm an Alzheimer's diagnosis. The new scanner can also determine if somebody has what they call frontotemporal dementia, which is more insidious than Alzheimer's."

Mikey shook his head violently. "Man, Rosey, man, why you gotta use a word like *that*, why, Rose, word like 'autopsy,' what's the fuck's wrong with you?"

She had a clinical perspective and had done her share with cadavers, but her brother had a point.

"Come on, don't make this harder than it has to be."

"Wait. You saying, *don't mean necessarily I have the disease*? So there's a good chance of getting the Alzhammer?"

"*Alzheimer's! Alzheimer's!* But yes, there's a chance, yes, a chance, but statistically nowhere near a sure thing, nowhere near. And Alzheimer's doesn't run in families, except in very rare cases. And okay, and I shouldn't say this to you, but if somebody has a parent or a sibling with Alzheimer's, they may possibly have a slightly elevated risk—very slightly. Genes play a role, there's nothing you can do about that. But the bottom line is: live to eighty-five, like Pops, it's fifty-fifty for everybody."

"Go on explain to me why I am forgetting so much shit these days?"

"Anybody in his fifties starts to forget things. I'm looking forward to one day forgetting we had talks like this. Forgetting's normal. You might at worst have mild cognitive impairment, MCI."

"I read about that on my computer."

"Stay off your computer till I tell you it's safe to go back in the water. The whole science is so fast moving."

"And this *M see* thing could be a sign of the oncoming Alzhammer?"

She gave up correcting him. He preferred his own terminology. "Not necessarily."

"But it *could* be?"

"Okay, it could be. But you're a long ways from being debilitated. It's a long journey, and you may not be on that journey yet. So keep the faith."

"Where do you want me to keep it, that faith, where? Cause lemme tell you, Rosey. I believe you're holding back."

"In the meantime, instead of worrying, there's some things you can do to keep the threat at bay. If you're worried about forgetting stuff, put up signs around the house, in the car, everywhere you need to, so you remember. Make up lists."

"Now who's the crazy one? I don't make up lists—didn't you hear Dad on that subject?"

"Take long walks, get good exercise every day. Stay active socially."

"Great idea. Me and the crew, we socialize together. I think we're gonna join the choir at church."

"Now you should be actively retraining your brain. You need to learn new things, forge new cognitive synapses. Your brain's not some old dog. You can learn new tricks. Study a foreign language, in your case English. Start doing tai chi or the tango."

Now she had gone off the deep end. "Tango? You say 'tango' to me?" She might as well have advised him to become an English teacher.

"It's true. Don't give up. In fact, I read a fascinating new study—"

"Do tell, perfessor." He smirked and lifted a pinky in front of his face with the force of a middle finger.

"Screw yourself, Mikey." Researchers tracked a large cross-section of subjects as they aged, she said, and they concluded that those who conceived of themselves as having a purpose in life were much less likely to develop Alzheimer's.

"A purpose in life, huh? Wow. That's your big-deal inside information shit?"

She considered refining the point but, considering his negative reaction, thought better of it.

"Look. One thing I don't need is no life purpose, Rosey, all's I need's a fucking pill."

So put that down as yet another unsatisfying sibling exchange. Besides, if there were a pill, she couldn't prescribe one, not being an MD, a distinction lost on her big brother.

"Dancing with the fucking stars," he muttered as he walked back into his dad's hospital room, where the man was tearing at the sheets and attempting to pull the IV out of his arm.

೧

THE CAR WAS PACKED with cases of the noble wine. Contemplating the work he'd accomplished filled him with a strange sense of satisfaction, he couldn't quite say why.

He went back inside, showered, and put on Randy A Artist's new black Brioni. It seemed to be the thing to do. No point *not* swinging into action the suit—at least once in its life. At least once in *his* life. Black bespoke shirt, French cuffs, black Brioni tie, white Brioni pocket square. Upon review, he replaced that white one with a silver pocket square. Details were important in all stages of life, yes, even this one. Oh, and black socks, good, he remembered. He couldn't do much about the facial puffiness and the mole, but he knew how to wear a suit. Not everybody is capable of wearing a suit. Ask Randy, and for a change he probably would not lie. Lots of people bought clothes and threw them on. It was a mystery why some guys who owned beautifully made fabrics and designs ended up looking like mopes, like the clothes belonged on somebody else or a manikin. Men like Mikey and his dad, they got dressed. You had to see it, you could not explain it. Talent like that was in his DNA.

Also in his DNA was his Alzhammer. Nothing he could do about either.

He zoomed out of his driveway. He thought about waving goodbye, but he couldn't figure out goodbye to whom or why.

It probably wasn't a wise move, driving around with somebody coming after him. He would think about that later. Though he probably wouldn't.

His goal was the coastline, and he was on the lookout for a high, accommodating cliff.

TWO YEARS LATER

CAREGIVER LOG

Use this form to monitor changes and to communicate with doctors, hospice nurses and caregivers across shifts.

PATIENT: *MICHAEL FESTAGIACAMO (age 59)*

CAREGUVER: *Amanaki* ♥

DATE/TIME: *thursday 8 clock AM mourning*

NOTE CHANGES: *Another bad nite like before*

Tring craal out of bed tugging on oxgin line

FOOD: *this is good ate a lot incl one hole ham burg*

MEDICATION: *same as befor with new pill befor bed; one dose morfine pill*

ACTIVITIES: *big BM*

PAIN LEVEL: *4-5*

ENERGY: *very resslass, talk to himself, like yousual;*

SLEEP PATTERN: *all nite the yeling hey hey hey*

Sundowning

Amanaki so tired

Chapter Twelve

He was speeding headlong on Highway 1 and hitting hard the endless series of curves, recklessly passing on a bend any lumbering, speed limit law–abiding vehicle that had the misfortune of being in his way. The Bentley was impressive. He enjoyed driving it more than the Benz, the loss of which still pained him, enjoying the Bentley almost as much as his Ferrari.

The wine bottles were jingling in their cases like coins in a jumpy man's pockets, the beautiful bottles of world-class Barbaresco, a lot of them too young to drink, which was theoretically foolish, because why did he buy wines in the first place that wouldn't be drinkable till he was on the other side? Or worse—till he forgot he owned them. He enjoyed those Barbarescos when they were ready, which usually meant vintages at least ten years old, and more like twenty plus. What the wine-snobs who sold him the bottles said was, these wines will last fifty, a hundred years, unlike him, who wasn't going to last till "Auld Lang Syne" broke out next year and champagne corks lamely popped. He was no wine aficionado, obviously, but he had the money to spend, and his dad, who knew his wines far better than his son knew them, preferred a world-class Barbaresco with dinner, so Mikey bought them and opened them for the old man—that was long ago, when he could sit at a table with a glass of wine in front of his plate. A few cases of the Gaja cost about as much as his Brioni, but the point was now moot. That wine was not going to age much more.

He had not personally taken people out before, not even the unquestionably very bad guys who needed to be taken out for the good of everybody else from time to time. That wasn't his thing, and from the start his dad didn't want his son to get his hands dirty that way. True, the very bad guys were taken out by somebody, an out-of-towner specially commissioned, not that he wanted to know the details, no, that was up to his dad, a task the boss assigned Dolly, the crew's principal go-between with the imported, rented muscle. On the other hand, it would be possible for Mikey to arrange his own exit. He wasn't going to sit around someday in his wheel chair with sauce on his chin, no way, pissing himself and forgetting what day it was or who was playing on the television whose remote he forgot how to operate.

What day *was* it today?

Thursday. Forging that connection felt like a sad triumph. Yes, it *was* a Thursday. And this was the Thursday he was going to drive off a cliff.

Geronofuckingmo.

Here, cliff, here. Here, cliffy cliff cliff.

After an hour or so of coast side driving, there it appeared, the perfect precipice, on the approach to the picturesque and dramatic Jenner. There was no traffic. He came to a full stop in the middle of the two-lane highway and contemplated the short-term prospects. He visualized smashing through the inconsequential highway barrier and arcing airborne down several hundred feet to the reliable ocean below: *crash, kaboom, splash, glug, glug, glug.*

Of course, that he remembered it was Thursday and that he was going to drive off a cliff slightly complicated his plans. Not that he was doubting the wisdom of his course of action. No, he wasn't doubting his decision.

What decision?

The decision to drive off a cliff.

That one.

His phone rang. One additional benefit about driving off the cliff, he'd drown the phone. But he answered. What difference did it make?

He knew it was Dolly, he could see the mope's name and number on the screen.

"Hello, Dolly." Cheery as he could manage, because he knew Dolly hated it when people said that to him, *Hello, Dolly*, the name of that Broadway show he claimed to hate though he never once saw it.

"Mikey, that you?"

"Who else'd be answering my phone?"

Dolly scrambled. "Nah, only that…you don't sound like yourself."

You mean, I don't sound dead, Dolly? Mikey would play along for now.

"How's, ah, ah, how's your pops?" Dolly was an idiot.

Dolly was aggravating when he called his boss and Mikey's dad *Pops*. Yet again too familiar. Dolly would not have done that if his dad were on the top of his game. So he was being disrespectful to both Mikey and his father.

"My *father* has bad days and horrible days. Today was somewhere in between."

"Anything I can do?"

Why don't you blow your head off, Dolly, and save us all the trouble?

"Can't think of anything to say, Dolly."

"The crew's getting together for to eat dinner tonight, Lorenzo's by the estuary." As if Mikey didn't know where the place was. "Why don't you come by, for to join us?"

What an insolent rat Dolly was. Mikey was going to be the guy and Mikey was the one to be making arrangements and issuing invitations that were not invitations, not Dolly. Besides, Lorenzo's was controlled by his father, and any day now the restaurant would have been controlled by Mikey if there had been no cliff standing in his way.

"Ten o'clock," said Dolly, "when business slows. Lorenzo reserved the back room for us, you know where that is? Osso buco, some chianti wine, a nice cigar for smoking, like old times. We can have a private talk and conversation and powwow, all the guys and you."

And where and when, if the timing proved right and Mikey's hunch was on the money, Dolly would take his shot.

Over my dead body.

"Good idea, Dolly." Mikey had known Dolly for going on thirty-five years. He despised him for what felt like several lifetimes. When he pressed his dad over his choice of working with the man, he always heard some version of the same point: he knew the extent to which he could trust Dolly, and a man without a conscience like Dolly can be useful when the work called for an absolute minimum of a troublesome conscience. Mikey would have to figure out sooner or later how to manage Dolly. Either that, or have *him* taken out.

Dolly was in a talkative mood and he naturally assumed Mikey was interested in the talk. He mentioned that he had pulled a muscle in his back, but he took a Percoset so he was sure he'd be okay by tonight. He did sound more loopy than usual.

"I'm not an advice nurse. Go see a stupid worthless doctor, why don't you?"

"I was thinking I would go see, like what do you call them, a chiroproctologist?"

"You more than anybody else could probably use one of them type specialists."

"Where you at? What you doing? You sound far away, like we got a very weak connection."

They sure did.

"Nothing, drove out of town to do some bird-watching, calms me down, after a big day."

"F'real? Never did that kinda thing."

"Matter of fact, saw a bird everybody thought was extinct."

"They give you a ribbon or trophy when you see one?"

"Better, I get to see a bird nobody's seen for like forever."

"Like your aptitude, Mikey. Some guys fix hate, only see what's missing, but you and me, man? We're birds of a father. Hey, you taking the Benz out for a spin?" He couldn't resist, could he? His curiosity was killing him.

You and me, man? "No can do. Somebody blew up the Benz."

"What the?"

Mikey shared the barest of details.

"The fuck?"

"Yeah, just the luck, couple of losers who were trying to steal it, they got the big kiss-off."

"You're not joking me, Mikey?"

"Oh, yeah, me, I'm performing all week, tip your waiter."

"Jesus, get back to the house so we can pretect you." He sounded authentically concerned. Was Mikey wrong to be suspicious of Dolly?

"You got any idea who wants me out of the picture?"

Dolly gasped. "Jeez, lotsa people, you shittin me? The Windy Street bunch, Cleo the Douchebag, Antny Decalzo, the Mexicans from the races, Peter the Wolf Russians, the fucking list goes on and on. You know there's a new crew in town, too, don't know much about 'em—what's his name, Mr. Smith. But they all know your Pops is…"

"Okay, stop."

"We got your back, Mikey boy. We'll all be strappered up for tonight. And I'll make sure Mo is handy, too, when he drives you. Now you gotta fly away from the birds, Mikey boy."

Mikey boy? Who was he to call him Mikey boy?

"I'm gonna head back before long. Nobody's gonna wanna meet me in my current frame of mind mood. Mo'll be at the house, so I'm okay. Meantime, I'm gonna look at these birds."

"This ain't really the time for bird-watching."

He couldn't defend being out on his own, but that's where he was. "Yeah, Dolly, with birds, sometimes people think a bird's gonna be extinct that ain't, it's keeping a low profile. I like that kinda thing."

"If you really want, I guess, keep bird-watching them unextincted birds, you're calling the slots. See you tonight, Lorenzo's, ten."

ଔ

MIKEY MADE A U-TURN, and began the journey home. He was wondering what possessed Mo to put all this Gaja in his car.

Phone rang again. How did his dad, or any other capo, get anything done before cell phones?

It was a call from his home, and after he answered it, Mikey wasn't going out for dinner tonight.

"Mikey," said his dad's doc.

"What's wrong?" He sensed his was an absurd inquiry. The doc's tone of voice spoke volumes.

"Sorry."

"Heart attack?"

"Could have been a stroke. Or complications from Alzheimer's. He could have had enough. It happens."

"He know what hit him?"

"He passed during a nap."

For Mikey, despite all his mental preparation for his dad's demise, it was easier to imagine being inside his Mercedes when it blew up.

Who is good at dying? *Nobody,* Mikey thought, *absolutely nobody.* You would think we would all be better at it by now. People have had all the practice they could possibly need. But there his dad had been, in bed, where he had taken bitter refuge for months, oxygen tubes in his nose, mouth slightly puckered like a pale, prehistoric fish. The incessant, rhythmic noise of the oxygen concentrator machinery and the dimmed lights of the room combined to suggest they were all swimming around inside a very large aquarium.

"His boat showed up," Mikey said, mostly to himself. His voice was small and faint, like that of a little boy, which he felt like, and it was as if the sound came from great distance, like the far side of a mountain.

"What'd you say?"

"Nothing."

"Something about a boat?"

"Why would I be talking about a boat, why?"

If you didn't know how useless doctors were, here was your proof. Look, his father was dead.

TWO YEARS LATER

To: Rosetta Festagiacamo
From: Dinah Forte
Subject: hello

Rosetta,

I put in a few calls to you today, but went to voice mail each time. When you get a chance, please give me a ring.

Mikey was in high spirits today, and when I got there he was outside with Amanaki in his wheelchair. I wouldn't have assumed in advance that would be such a hot idea, because he hasn't been in a wheelchair for a long time, which requires some strength on his part to hold his head up. But there he was, sitting in the sun on the patio and seeming in a good mood, which was very heartening to see.

Did you hear about this next part? The hospice people had also arranged for a therapy dog volunteer team, and your brother was happily petting this beautiful and very sweet black Labrador. Did you happen to have dogs when you were kids?

These hospice people, they are amazing.

In any case, I hope you had a good day. Wasn't the weather spectacular? I love these days, summer ending, autumn coming on, leaves falling, like a picture book.

Look forward to catching up at your convenience.

Best wishes,

Dinah

Dinah Penelope Forte, PhD
Forte Care Management Professionals

Chapter Thirteen

Better going in his sleep at home than wickedly lingering in some ICU, Mikey supposed. His dad had signed the do-not-resuscitate order. In one of his last extended stretches of lucidity, he decided that was how he wanted to go, clean and fast. It was neither particularly clean nor fast how he finally went, but some things were out of his control. He admired his dad all over again for the fortitude and foresight. He wished he himself had more of that. But probably like everybody else, his dad whiffed when it came to recognizing the overwhelming force of the Alzhammer. As smart and tough as his father was, he missed that one, as possibly everybody ultimately did, and Mikey was resolved to improve upon the plan.

When he got back to the house from his drive to the coast, his sister's car was already in the driveway alongside Mo's.

Mo came out to the garage from the kitchen, shoulders slumped, shaking his head. "Sorry, boss."

Mikey nodded, saying nothing, because he could think of nothing worth saying, and he headed inside.

"First the car, now your dad. But you shouldn't go out on your own now, boss, after what happened, what Dolly told me. All due." Mo was strapped up, and on the kitchen counter, next to the olive oil and the bread, there were four automatic rifles and two handguns. "Got your piece here, boss."

Mikey still didn't want a gun. "Rosey?"

She was in her father's bedroom, Mo said, talking with the doc.

"You wanna go back there, boss? With your dad?" he added irrelevantly.

Not yet. Besides, he didn't really want to see any doctor, he'd had his fill of them. "Go tell Rosey I'm here." At first he didn't really want to see Rosetta, but she was part of his job now as head of what was left of the family.

After a few moments, she rushed into the kitchen, threw her arms around her brother's neck, and softly sobbed into the shoulder of his new suit, and though her tears fell on the beautiful new fabric he was glad she was here. He sought for the words—wished to hit the right note of *there, there*—but nothing came out. He was a little bit taken aback by her emotion, considering her family history, but he shouldn't have been. He was simultaneously undone by his own emotion.

"Mo," he said over Rosey's shoulder, "there's wine in the car, take it down to the wine cellar."

"You bought wine? Today?" Mo looked flabbergasted.

So did Mikey, not for the same reason. "No, but do it."

He was two steps ahead of his sister in his grief. In his mind, he was already planning the funeral, and at the same time he was steeling himself for the next move somebody was going to make on him.

They released their hold on each other. "Want a drink, Rose?"

"No, I need one. The doctor signed the death certificate, he's going to leave out the back door, nothing left for him to do." She looked at the kitchen counter, strewn with guns: another good reason for the doctor not to come this way. "You going to go back there, one last look? I think you should."

"You think I should?"

"You should."

"I should why?"

"So later you can't say you didn't."

"Makes no sense."

"Things should make sense now?"

❧

THERE WAS HIS FATHER, lying in his bed.

But no. That was his father's body lying in his bed. Which was not his father lying in his bed. Except it was. The doctor must have pushed down shut his eyelids. For the first time, he grasped why they did that.

Mikey wanted to think that the man had at last found peace. He wanted badly to think as much. He wanted very badly to think anything, anything at all. He tried and tried some more to think. Small problem in this regard. Or a big problem. He concluded he wasn't looking at his father at all. His father still somehow existed, though he existed only in Mikey's mind, and though the man's words and his counsel and the experiences of his life would always be alive to him, that had nothing to do with the inert corpse lying before his eyes. But Mikey had it completely wrong, which he also knew was right. He had seen more than his share of dead bodies in his lifetime, but this was different. Vincent Festagiacamo was dead. Not only that, his father was dead.

He had imagined this moment so many times in the past—but somehow that anticipation did not relate to the unvarnished reality. He had visualized his father deceased a hundred times. Each time he did, he felt guilty. But not guilty enough to stop visualizing. Each time, he thought his old man had suffered enough, and he wished him to let go. Death would be relief from the torment visited upon him by the Alzhammer.

Each time, that notion shriveled up, withered like desiccated fruit, fruit turned to stone, long gone in a crystal bowl—sad and worthless. Only each time he thought of his dad as dead, his dad died a little bit more. And considering what he himself was going through, he died a little bit, too. He stayed in the bedroom as long as he could, until he concluded the situation was not going to change.

No, now his father was dead and this time he was going to stay that way.

"Bye, Pops," he said, because he didn't know what else to say, and because he should say something before he left his side. Words and doctors, useless when you need them most.

How many times does a man have to die before he is really dead? That was a question he had for both his father and his father's son, himself.

ʘ

ROSETTA AND MIKEY DRANK the very good Scotch in the parlor and looked to the necessary arrangements. They made the required calls, and well past halfway into the bottle a couple hours later they watched through the bay window when the mortuary showed up in an unmarked, shiny black van. Two men stepped out into the driveway, stood there a moment, took a few last puffs on their cigarettes, and assembled the features on their faces to convey the requisite solemnity of the occasion. Once they came inside the house, they spoke in measured, practiced, compassionate voices and asked at the right moment if the "family" was "ready."

"No," said Rosetta, who was too incapacitated to get up from the couch.

"Shall we wait?"

"What I mean is, I'll never be ready. Want a drink?"

Without using any words, they indicated they understood. It was possible to believe they did. And no, but thanks for the offer, they said, they were on the job.

That came out wrong, and they apologized, but it didn't matter.

The two of them were wearing identical black suits, neither of them Brionis, more like a men's discount, and Mikey believed his dad would not be caught dead in suits like that. He wished he hadn't framed it that way.

They walked solemnly in the direction of the back bedroom, where they could be heard snapping on their latex gloves, and after a while they wheeled out on a gurney the father and one-time boss, Vincent Festagiacamo, in a zipped-up black bag. Eventually, the van slowly drove off, a single vehicle that seemed like a cortege, and when it reached the end of the long driveway, they could hear from inside the house the blasting pop music that seeped miserably out of the vehicle heading off into the night.

"So that's that?" Rosetta said.

"I have no idea, but I doubt it."

Brother and sister resumed drinking till the very good Scotch was a very dead soldier and around midnight both of them fell asleep, exhausted on opposite ends of the couch and at opposite ends of their lives.

ॐ

MONDAY AFTERNOON BROTHER AND sister stood in the rain locked arm in arm while one of the undertaker's assistants held an oversize black umbrella over their heads. They listened to the priest's last words and watched the casket as it was lowered into the earth. The two of them had run out of tears, and they were depleted of energy, and she leaned against her brother to steady herself. A hundred people had made the trek to the cemetery, and they somberly began to make their way off, and to get out of the downpour. She took the umbrella from the assistant and he wandered away.

"Nice suit," she said, trying to say anything.

He cleared his throat.

"New from Randy?" she said.

Mikey had other things on his mind. That's because Brownie, the old school bookie who hadn't paid up for a long time, approached. In a way that was a brave move, and in a way it was a stupid one, which summed up the life story of the guy. The man must have found a madras sport coat in the back of his closet and he was wearing, as usual, his Giants baseball cap. He had the gambler's sunken cheeks with shadows around his eyes and belly hanging over the belt.

"Loved your dad, Mikey, my condolences."

"Sure, Brownie, sure."

And the bookmaker headed off disconsolately in the direction of the cars.

"Wait here," Mikey said to Rosetta.

"Where you going?"

"I'll be right back."

Dolly and the rest of the crew were positioned off to the side, by a spreading dogwood tree, all of them under their umbrellas, and Mikey made his way toward them, his handmade Italian shoes squishing the muddied ground while the rain fell on his Brioni. He didn't care. This time he remembered to wear socks. His dad's death had momentarily sharpened his thinking, or so he had reason to believe.

"Condolences, boss," said Dolly, which was an accomplishment of sorts, not referring to him as Mikey. "Your pops was a great man."

"Let's meet at Lorenzo's in a few nights, I'll let you know when."

"Good idea, Mikey." Dolly's habits died hard. "Your pops'd want us to keep the static quote going."

"I didn't catch what you called my father."

"Sorry, boss, trip of the tongue."

"Another thing, Dolly, Mo. You see Brownie?" He pointed. "Somebody gonna talk to him?"

Mo looked surprised. "All due, boss. Now?"

Mikey didn't bother to answer and he walked back to his sister.

"That was fast," she said.

"Like a snake bite. Let's go," he said to her.

Then the rain halted momentarily and he guided her down the slippery incline where the cars were parked. He tried to open the door of a black Mercedes. But the door didn't cooperate.

"Mikey," said Rosetta in a leading tone of voice, since she knew it wasn't his car. That car was history and they had been chauffered in a limousine.

"Yeah?"

She pointed into the distance. "Our limo's over there."

"I knew that," he tried, unconvincingly. "I knew that."

"It's okay. Grief can scramble anybody's brain."

He bristled. "That a professional medical opinion?" He didn't mean to bristle, but he didn't check himself in time.

"It's your sister's opinion. Come on, let's go home. People will be arriving at the house and the caterers have to feed them."

"You gonna stay at the house for now, or do you gotta get back to work?"

"I was thinking about camping out for a while, if that's okay with you, till we can get things organized at home." Later she would let on she had quit her job, which she had grown to despise, and there was no going back. She was finished with the cutthroats of academe, which she might or might not tell her brother in time. The familiar cutthroats of her brother and his crew were good enough for her.

"That could be arranged, Rose." He couldn't believe he said that. He couldn't believe he meant it.

That was when he heard a small voice calling out his name, and he turned to see someone advancing upon him, a saddened smile on his face, which closely resembled the saddened smile of his own. The voice belonged to a handsome young man, tall and willowy with mocha-colored skin and dressed in a hooded sweatshirt, carrying a pack on his back, and wearing wrap-around sunglasses under his baseball cap.

"Jeremiah! What're you doing here, buddy?" Mikey had to know the answer to his question, but he had to ask anyway, and he was surprised—and also pleased to see him, which wasn't always the case.

"Mom dropped me off."

"She's here?" Mikey looked around expectantly, but Zayana was nowhere in sight. The sky was clearing all of a sudden.

"We were in back of the church for Mass, guess you didn't see us, there were so many people. She wanted me to tell you she was leaving town, not coming back. I was hoping I could stay with you, till I figure out what to do, where to go."

That was a lot of news to absorb, especially under the circumstances, but Mikey instantaneously processed the idea and, though it constituted a big change for himself and his sorry social life, he was okay with that and didn't press for details—not now, not yet. "Of course, buddy." It might be good to have the house full of people. And of course this would be the sort of unannounced move Zayana would make, leaving it up to Mikey to pick up after her. Then again, from her point of view, she had cause, if anybody did.

"Thanks, Mikey," Jeremiah said.

It was the least Mikey could do for his only son, and his now deceased father's only grandchild. True, the boy and his father had a sometimes-rocky nineteen-year history. Those were the bad days. Zayana could be ambivalent about, if not obstinately opposed to, involving Mikey in the boy's upbringing, and truthfully, Mikey wasn't always sure he wanted to play a role—or knew how.

"Boy needs a father," she once told him as they fought about something now long-forgotten. "Know anybody?"

"You get your money every month, Z, long as I feel generous."

"You don't scare me, you know that, right?"

"Why would you be scared've me? But use the money for the boy and don't put it up your pretty little picture-perfect nose."

In the rare, better days with Jeremiah, it was the zoo, the movies, a pizza, shooting baskets at the park. Couple of times, he and the little boy flew to Disneyland. But then months would slip by without any contact between the two. Zayana didn't always make it easy. She had boyfriends. A regular conga line, it seemed like sometimes. Jeremiah did not adjust well to his mom's changing domestic and romantic entanglements, and, frankly, neither did Mikey. Not quite the picture of Family of the Year. As he got older, Jeremiah turned into trouble and his mother could not manage him. Couldn't keep him in school or out of handcuffs in the back seat of a squad car. One petty offense after another, shoplifting and vandalism and graffiti mostly, not to mention the pot-possession and the not-so-petty offenses that included a residential break-in and burglary. That time Mikey bailed him out and paid for the lawyer, who got him off on a technicality—the incriminating evidence having magically disappeared, imagine that, and Judge Keily issued a ruling favorable to the defense: case dismissed. It was prudent to invest long-term in friends you can count on.

"Sorry about Nonno," said Jeremiah and he took a deep breath, as if it had required a great effort to articulate those three words. Mikey was rocked by his using the Italian to refer affectionately to his grandpa, and it took effort for him to sustain his composure. It had been a long time since Mikey had observed the sweet side of the boy, who was not really a boy anymore, something he probably should get used to in a hurry. "He was always good to me."

"I need to give you a hug, Jeremiah," said Mikey's sister, who extended both arms toward him.

"I could use one, Aunt Rosey."

"Here you go, baby boy," she said.

"Let's go home," said Mikey. "Rain's gonna pick up again."

Chapter Fourteen

Jeremiah bounded down the stairs wearing a crisp white dress shirt. It was a shirt of Mikey's, which he had given him to go out tonight, and in which article of bespoke clothing he was fairly swimming. You could practically slip a baseball down the top-buttoned collar. Mikey's made-to-order shirt had French cuffs, which is what he preferred on a white shirt. The sleeves were too long for the boy, but the gold cufflinks compensated and made the fit almost snug enough at the wrists. He used to think it was too bad the cuffs couldn't be monogrammed with the initials of Mikey Festagiacamo. "MF" had unfortunate associations.

"You gonna tuck that shirt in?" said Mikey.

"Think I should?"

He communicated without words that of course he should, what kind of look was that with a nice shirt? At least the boy wasn't wearing his flat-brimmed hip-hop cap today. That wouldn't have gone with Mikey's gold cufflinks.

"You're getting dressed up." Mikey was pleased and the boy was more than willing to look past his father's statement of the obvious. The boy *was* getting dressed up to go out with his aunt in a few hours, and he was sheepish about it.

"Can you help me tie your tie?" he said as he neatly tucked in the shirt.

The gearshift box shifted inside Mikey's head, the one that operated the working of his eyes, and he blinked. Hearing that innocent question, he had come this close to tears.

ʒ

FATHER AND SON WERE in the foyer. That was where only a few minutes earlier he had stood alone contemplating terminal thoughts. Seemed like a million years ago he had been staring up at the blown light bulb in the chandelier and shaking his head. And not because he detested domestic chores like changing a light bulb, though he did.

That was the instant his mood had gone very dark. He couldn't help himself, going dark at some point in every day. He had studied closely the redwood crossbeam, twenty feet above his head. If he got the ladder from the garage, he could sling a rope over the crossbeam, slip a noose around his neck, and jump, bye-bye. A few technical issues presented themselves. One, no rope in the whole house he was aware of. Two, no background as a Boy Scout or sailor or hit man, hence no skill or practice tying reliable, fancy knots. One other disconcerting problem. He heard that when you are hanged, blood rushes to your dick. That would be embarrassing, dying like that with a pathetic hard-on. There must be a less humiliating way to go.

Perhaps the reason he had gone dark and got to thinking about the crossbeam and the rope was on account of his feeling miserably disoriented. Earlier in the day, he couldn't locate his gold money clip, which he was sure he had left on the dresser as he always did, and which held, as usual, five grand in cash, fifty Ben Franklins. He had not lost that sort of money before—except at the track, which was different.

☙

CLOSE, BUT NO TEARS. Mikey was relieved. And maybe Jeremiah was, too.

"You don't know how to tie a tie?" That came out wrong. That sounded like a criticism of his son.

Jeremiah appeared disconsolate. Fact was, he had never owned a tie.

"No big deal," said Mikey, fast reversing field. "I'll show you a simple knot." That was one knot he could make. *Unlike a hangman's,* he reflected.

They stood there before the full-length gilded mirror on the wall, Mikey positioned behind his son, peering down, a head taller, his arms reaching around his shoulders. He was thinking about how his own dad had taught him how to tie a tie when he was a boy. He admiringly held up the Marinella tie, bought in Napoli. In Mikey's opinion, this was the finest tie maker in Italy, and in that opinion he wasn't alone.

"I tell you a secret. Girls, they see a man in a red tie like this, they get weak in the knees." He had seen on TV some psychologist actually proved what Mikey knew was obvious. "Okay, here you go. You flip up your collar and then you wrap the silk tie around your neck—you always want silk. Like that. See? Then you begin with the fat end like this, and then you pull this around, and then you pull this under and over, and then collar down…there it is, *boom.* In no time, magnet for babes. See?"

The boy marveled. "I couldn't do that trick if my life depended on it."

"We'll practice."

"Thanks, Mikey."

"You going out with your aunt tonight, that's nice." Another declaration of the self-evident.

"I'm looking forward."

"One day how 'bout I get you a job at the restaurant? You like that?"

"Really?"

"Bussing tables, helping out waiters, it's an important job. You'll make a few bucks, have some fun, meet girls."

Mikey flipped him the car keys. He enjoyed owning so many cars, and Mo was driving him tonight. But then he worried.

"You got a driver's license?"

He did indeed. That was good to discover, but Mikey was also dejected to realize that a father like himself didn't know such an essential fact about his own kid's life. Becoming aware that he hadn't been there to teach his boy how to tie a tie had been bad enough, now this. He had a lot to make up for, assuming Jeremiah would let him. And assuming he wouldn't throw himself off a bridge before that.

"Tank's full in the Range Rover," Mikey said. "Drive slow."

"I think Aunt Rosey wants to drive her own car, but maybe I can talk her into letting me take yours. I would love to get behind the wheel of a Rover."

"If not tonight, some other time."

"Mom used to work at Lorenzo's." The boy had a faraway look in his eye.

Mikey nodded.

"That's where you guys met."

Where was Jeremiah going with this?

In the grand scheme of things, yes, that's the place where the boy was conceived, not literally, as far as Mikey could determine, though there were a few steamy occasions when their body heat brought up the temperature of the wine cellar after hours. In any case, Lorenzo's was where Jeremiah's mom and dad had indeed commenced their doomed romance, true.

"You got what you need here, buddy? Like in your room, I mean."

"You got a great house—used to be Nonno's house, I still remember from when I was a kid. I think it's kind of cool. You've been great to me."

"Chances are we all come full circle. So you know, your aunt's always late, don't tell her I told you. Women can be like that. Now forget you heard me say that. But a man keeps his appointments, that is a man you can do business with." Another thing he should have told him before. Lots of catching up to do. Better late than never being a dad. He wasn't sure that was always true, but it was all he had to offer under the circumstances.

"I could use cereal. Like Cheerios."

Mikey stepped back and took stock of Jeremiah. He was having a brainstorm, one unrelated to breakfast foods.

"Something wrong with Cheerios, Mikey?"

"You're about the same size as your nonno."

Jeremiah waited apprehensively for the other shoe.

"Your nonno had some nice suits made over the years, Brioni, and these type Italian suits don't go out of style. I think you might fit in them with some adjustments. We'll try them on tomorrow and I know a good tailor. A young man needs a fabulous suit or two in his wardrobe. Girls like guys who can wear a suit. Right clothes, a good-looking young guy like you can go anywhere he wants."

"Really?"

"Sure thing."

"I got the right tie already."

"You do, yes, you do."

"Thanks, *Dad*."

Mikey couldn't remember the last time he heard himself addressed as Dad.

"Shouldn't say this," said Jeremiah, "and I don't know for sure, but my mom might still have a thing for you. She kinda told me, before she took off. I hope she's okay, you think she is?"

"She's a good mom and I guess she got some problems she needs to work on, but she can take of herself." As for the mom's supposed interest in him, Mikey realized even nineteen-year-old children were capable of fantasizing reconciliation. He himself did, too, to be honest. But one thing he could always count on about Zayana: she was continually making a getaway—in her case, inevitably, being who she was, a not-so-clean getaway. She could not be corralled by anyone, least of all a man.

That she was a good mom was something he wasn't always certain of, but he wasn't Father of the Year material, either. At the same time, there was nothing to lose starting out the evening on a high note. He had a good feeling about tonight, and he didn't shoot another glance at the crossbeam overhead.

TWO YEARS LATER

CAREGIVER LOG

Use this form to monitor changes and to communicate with doctors, hospice nurses and caregivers across shifts.

PATIENT: *MICHAEL FESTAGIACAMO (age 59)*

CAREGUVER: *Amanaki*

DATE/TIME:

NOTE CHANGES:

FOOD:

MEDICATION:

ACTIVITIES:

PAIN LEVEL:

ENERGY:

SLEEP PATTERN:

TWO YEARS LATER

To: Rosetta Festagiacamo
From: Dinah Forte
Subject: today's unfortunate development

Rosetta,

It was important to talk, thanks for being available. That was quite a terrible thing that happened with Amanaki—with your brother, I should say. I would not have suspected her capable of doing what she did. To me, here's the only encouraging part. The admin staff of the skilled nursing facility was vigilant, they picked up on Amanaki's pilfering pain meds from the nurse's central station. They actually found her unconscious in the easy chair with stolen Oxy in her lap and Mikey flailing in bed. Thank God he didn't fall out onto the floor, thanks to the rails Medicare paid for. All in all, we got lucky.

I don't think the police are going to press charges, but they put a good scare into her, and she'll get no reference from the home or from me or from the primary or from hospice. So I feel bad for her—but not really.

The important thing now is that Winona is on the job. As you noted, she is very professional and pleasingly eccentric and charming and her references from London are glowing. She is trustworthy, or at least let's hope so. I will monitor the situation like a hawk.

Hang in there, Rosetta. You are doing a great job of caring for your brother, and even if he cannot express his appreciation anymore— well, in the grand scheme, that's not significant, is it?

Onward, somehow onward,
Dinah

CAREGIVER LOG

Use this form to monitor changes and to communicate with doctors, hospice nurses and caregivers across shifts.

PATIENT: *MICHAEL FESTAGIACAMO (age 59)*

CAREGUVER: *Winona Wilder is on the job!*

DATE/TIME: *Friday 11:00 AM.*

NOTE CHANGES: *A new caregiver is bound to pose some initial complications for a patient with Alzheimer's, and I am doing all I can to minimize the difficulties in the transition. Mr. Festagiacamo doesn't seem to remember his former nurse, which is good in a way, so there is no nostalgia.*

FOOD: *I encouraged him to eat, and he ate what he wanted, which consisted mostly of buttered noodles. To tell by all the vowels in his name, he probably thinks that he is eating pasta!*

MEDICATION: *Uneventful administration of meds.*

ACTIVITIES: *Minimal.*

PAIN LEVEL: *Negligible, apparently.*

ENERGY: *Limited. He has a dreamy look when his eyes are open, which isn't all that often. Sometimes, he struggles to speak, but the language patterns are impossible for me to decode—so far, but give me time and I will crack the mystery!*

SLEEP PATTERN: *Fitful. I would estimate he slept 2-3 hours. I will work on this and coax him to sleep more. Sleep is important!*
—WW

Chapter Fifteen

Mikey would run to the grocery store before dinner at Renzo's with his crew, and he headed into the garage with a sense of purpose. If Mo had caught him in the act, he would have accompanied him, or more likely, would have done all he could to dissuade him from leaving the house in the first place. Mo would have argued this was risky, leaving the house after somebody already tried to take him out, completely crazy. "All due, boss," he would have added, because next to "Dolly's a dick," "all due" was his go-to.

Immediately upon closing the door behind him in the garage, he could not summon back that sense of clear purpose. That's because he forgot what he was doing in the garage. He rummaged around in the tool drawers because he couldn't think of anything else to do. *Where did all these tools come from*, he wondered. He picked up a wrench and marveled at it in his hand: he never once saw his dad hold a wrench.

Then something clicked, like the satisfying combination for a safe-cracker. That is when he recalled he had to shop at the store. But then he suffered another setback: shopping for what? That's when he decided: he would start writing out lists for once, not of important business items pertaining to the shop, of course, but the other things. He would buy packs of Post-its and leave notes here and there as reminders. Like, "WEAR MOTHERFUCKING SOCKS."

He was hoping his memory would kick in any second once he got in his Benz, but that was another problem: no Benz for him to hop into. The car would not ever be there again for him, not that he grasped that in the moment. He went back into the house, chasing vindication like some two-dollar horse-player.

He noticed the wide-open refrigerator door, which further discouraged him, because somebody had left it open and, for all he knew, it might have been left open by him—no other candidates were nearby to be blamed. He looked at the empty shelves where the milk was supposed to be, and it suddenly occurred: *milk*, it was important to have *milk* when you have your boy living here in your house. Parents were supposed to be provisioners. Milk was important. And cereal. That's right. *Cereal.* What kind of cereal did his kid like? He had no idea. Yet another paternal failing.

Oh, but that was the good news: the errand was to go out and buy some *milk* and *cereal.*

I am an idiot, he thought, and didn't disagree with himself. Then he placed on the refrigerator shelf the wrench he was for some inscrutable reason carrying.

He tracked down a notepad and wrote in big letters with a felt-tip pen "MILK" and "SEREAL" on a piece of paper he shoved into his coat pocket. He felt ridiculous penning the stupid note, but he exulted when he triumphantly closed the refrigerator door.

The Range Rover was in the garage when he returned, though he had promised that to Rosetta and Jeremiah—and it struck him as funny how some things he could remember, like promising the Range Rover, and how some things he couldn't. It was exhausting, rummaging in his memory bank. In any case, the Bentley was there, and the Ferrari, but once again, no Mercedes. Was the car at the shop? He would try to remember to figure that out later. At this point, he opted for the Ferrari, a car he usually hesitated to drive, on the grounds it was too flashy, and activated too many eyeballs on the street, which made him wonder why he had bought it in the first place. At the same time, it was good to occasionally give that thoroughbred of an engine a little run, for no other reason than to keep the battery from going dead. He wasn't dating a stable of girls these days, and hadn't for a long time, so there was nobody left to impress anymore with his fancy wheels, that was for sure.

ଔ

IT DIDN'T TAKE LONG driving through town till he realized why he had bought this car in the first place: the Ferrari was a lion and he felt like a lion-tamer behind the wheel.

The lion-tamer roared up to a stop light, and the car's pipes made that intoxicating rumble that put another zero on the sticker price. This was a notoriously long stop light at a much-traveled intersection. His car was closest to the crosswalk, first in line to take off when the light changed—in what seemed like an hour or two. There was a lot of traffic, being five o'clock, and the wage-earners were headed home to kids and family, settling down for a night of television and a couple of cold ones. He was not in the least nostalgic for a life he had never known nor ever yearned for.

He had forgotten to strap up. That was very stupid of him, not packing a gun. As much as he hated guns, the situation had radically changed, and a man like him had to do what a man like him had to do.

Out of nowhere an uneasy feeling crept up on him.

He quickly identified what stimulated that intuition—and who it was who was creeping up on him.

Mikey had long ago mastered the art of watching in all directions, like an owl, three-hundred-sixty degrees, and that's why he was never surprised when somebody came up behind him. Like now. In his side-view mirror he noticed somebody had stepped out of the car two back, which was odd, abandoning his vehicle on the street like that. The blurry-faced man was wearing a big black coat and was methodically advancing on foot on the driver's side.

Mikey didn't recognize the man but he had no reason to think he was going to helpfully mention his brake light was out. Mikey was already anticipating the move the guy was getting ready to make: getting closer to the Ferrari and then reaching into his coat pocket and pulling out his semiautomatic piece. That's why Mikey instinctively, unthinkingly floored the Ferrari and zoomed into and through the intersection, somehow incredibly not making contact with the oncoming cars honking, their brakes screeching, the swerving drivers no doubt cursing him out, at which point he hit hard the steering wheel and executed a perfect one-eighty, a trick he acquired in the professional driving school class he once took. He downshifted and waited while cars whizzed by right and left. If Mikey had been thinking more clearly, if the adrenaline hadn't flooded his brain, he would have completed the three-sixty and kept going straight ahead and counted his blessings after speeding away from the threat.

He wasn't interested in counting any blessings. What he was about to do was from about any point of view highly unwise. He might have been serious about taking himself out by driving off a cliff or semi-serious about jumping off a ladder, but it was different when somebody else was trying to take him out. He wasn't sure what the difference meant, only that there was an important, if impossible to quantify or define, difference. Somebody coming after him in broad daylight was one thing he wasn't going to tolerate—and so soon after blowing up his other car.

Right, *that's* what happened to the Mercedes.

So he shifted into gear and slammed down on the gas pedal and roared off in the direction of the would-be hitter. As Mikey accelerated toward him, knifing through the intersection, the guy froze in place. He looked astonished to be standing there with his gun, which amounted to his own dick in his grasp in the very place vacated by Mikey's beautiful red roadster.

Plainly glad to get another opportunity, the man lifted the gun to aim, which confirmed that he was a pro, but like everybody else who never owned a car like this Ferrari he failed to calculate the velocity and power of this vehicle, and he was slower than the wheel-pealing Ferrari. *Nice car, good car,* Mikey was thinking, *and very handy now.* A ninja of a car, and a Jedi mind trick of a car, too, perfectly missing traffic coming in both directions. The gunman was an antelope on the veldt and lions don't usually miss antelopes grazing in the open.

The man may have squeezed off a shot, but if he did, he missed both Mikey and his car. Mikey, on the other hand, did not miss him, and when the car made crunching contact with his would-be killer's body, and slammed on his brakes and avoided by no more than two inches plowing into the next car waiting at the red light and the dazed man behind its steering wheel who couldn't believe the misfortune of his being in the wrong place at the wrong time, the crazy physics sent the gunman head over heels on top of the roof of the Ferrari whereupon he flew up and then rolled fifty feet into the middle of the intersection, where his body came momentarily to rest. But his was only a momentary resting place because—as Mikey could witness in the rear view—a Berkeley Farms Dairy truck rumbled over him. It all happened so fast. The prospective assassin must have been caught under the chassis somehow, possibly snagged by his coat, and dragged away from the scene, because when Mikey looked back there was no body visible anymore in the intersection. The truck driver probably missed this development until he got back to the plant and discovered to his surprise the large piece of stinking dead human garbage lodged underneath.

Mikey drove off carefully down the street and away from the scene, not making eye contact with anybody, as if nothing had happened, and since there was no body, there was a good chance nothing had. Nobody dared follow Mikey and his eye-magnet car. Eyewitnesses are especially unreliable when they cannot believe their own eyes.

Mikey immediately headed back home, drove into the garage, and realized he was shivering. He wondered if that was a good thing or not. It did confirm that nobody had killed him yet today. When he reached into his pocket he pulled out the hand-written list—which he had forgotten to employ: the crucial list that itemized *MILK* and *SEREAL*. He had come home alive, but, he realized, without the groceries. One out of two: a deal he had no choice but to live with, for now.

Funny, he almost laughed, *that was a Berkeley Farms* milk *truck.*

This was getting a little bit serious. That made two attempted hits on him in the span of a few days, four or possibly five if you counted the two or almost three he made on himself. Sooner or later, he had to believe, one of them might do the trick.

Mikey got out of the car as Jeremiah opened the door into the garage, and walked in. His son was holding a wrench.

"Dad, where you put your tools? Found this in the fridge. Funny, huh?"

Chapter Sixteen

Mo was behind the wheel and he looked up to address the windshield, with Mikey in the backseat: "Boss, you sure? Renzo's tonight, boss?"

Mo was determined to practice calling Mikey *boss* at every conceivable opportunity, as well as all the other times, too. He had driven around Mikey's dad for many years, when Vincent Festagiacamo was the unquestioned boss, but it was relatively new driving around him in the Bentley—once upon a time his father's Bentley, and the vehicle from which he had not so long ago bizarrely offloaded all that inexplicable wine.

He had sentimentally assumed whoever was coming after him would observe the proprieties, and not take another shot at him so soon after his father's interment. They'd normally wait a while, as if this made a difference, and as if they had any standards. Today's events put a different spin on matters. So much for mob conventions and supposedly honorable traditions. All that was thrown out the window. As a consequence, Mo arranged for Beppe and Scoop to follow in the car behind and Fatso in the car ahead in case. Nobody liked riding with Fatso—that bacon-soaked eau de cologne was more than anybody could stomach. The attempted hits had put his crew on notice and they appeared jumpy—all except Mikey.

He was glad that his dad had reinforced the car's panels and replaced the windows with bulletproof glass, rendering the car impregnable. Only a military tank would have afforded him more protective fortification.

Mo seemed to take pride in being the boss's chauffeur. At the same time, he was troubled, so Mikey might as well find out why that was.

"Can't believe I'm going to ask, but what's on your mind, Mo?"

"Just axing, boss, 'bout Renzo's, boss."

"I gotta eat dinner, and I do like Lorenzo's chicken under a brick. Not to mention, I think I own the place now, so I can count on pretty decent service."

It was going to take some more getting used to, being in the back seat and being called *boss* every three seconds. But he really was hungry. Tonight, he vaguely recalled, Rosetta and Jeremiah said they were going out to dinner, and he didn't feel like eating alone.

"You make a good point, boss. A man's gotta eat, keep his strength up."

"You worried?"

"No. Yeah. Maybe."

"Covers all the friggin' bases. You drinking again?"

"I don't drink no more, boss."

"You might should start up again."

They reviewed the plans for the Ferrari, which needed to be disappeared as a precautionary measure.

"I don't need to know nothing about the car, do I?"

There weren't many such cars around, and in case somebody on the street today made an observation they wanted to report to the police, it was wise to dispose of it through a reliable subcontractor. Mikey loved the car, but such was the cost of doing business. And cars were flying out of his garage at an alarming rate. First the Mercedes, now the Ferrari.

"Took care of it with Petey at the shop, it's probably on a boat halfway to Chiner already. And if John Law asks us or checks with the insurance, the car went missing last night over by Lorenzo's, which you was at all day and where you stupidly left it by mistaken error."

"You gotta say *stupidly*?"

"Sorry, boss. I'll miss that car of yours, boss. It was a beaut."

Mo's back of the skull barely reached the bottom of the head rest. Mikey sometimes suggested Mo should sit on a telephone book, but these days telephone books were in short supply, much like Mo himself. Nobody was more loyal than Mo. Or shorter. Or tougher. Or more tested. Short guys get tested all the time, of course. Mo passed each test, flying colors, sometimes at great cost to himself—but much more often to others.

Mikey had watched from a distance a few times when somebody got the bright idea of challenging Mo—like, say, at that new dive bar they were once analyzing for business maximization purposes, some place where they were unrecognizable to the local denizens, the kind of bar and grill nobody in recorded history risked ordering the soup of the day. He observed Mo metamorphose on the spot. He visibly swelled up, and his shoulders expanded, and his eyes gleamed. And as for the guy with a Mohawk and a leather bomber who was in his face, you could clock the precise moment he regretted coming up against Mo. It was that crazy look that came into Mo's eyes, like they were set on fire, and those scars on every inch of his face took on prehistoric life. His facial creases resembled the tread of road-tested snow tires, and a man who looks like that is not somebody you want to make the acquaintance of. Every time before the other guy had ultimately backed off, apologizing. The time that guy at the dive bar did not back off, he had to be carried out on his back, with facial contusions for mementos.

"I got a bad feeling, boss, 'specially after what happened to your Benz in the city and then, in the sport car."

"Hanging with Dolly always gives me a bad feeling."

"I got you covered, boss, in case." Mo patted himself under his armpit. He wanted his boss to know he was equipped.

"I think you watched *The Godfather* and *The Sopranos* too much."

"All due, I rest your case, boss."

He asked Mo to put on some music. Change the subject.

"Your dad, he liked listening to what's his name. That Bo Cello guy."

Mo popped in the CD of the great blind tenor singing Italian opera greatest hits. Anything to distract Mo, to keep him from getting more apprehensive. Minutes passed and then Mikey spoke up.

"I have a question."

"Shoot, boss. Sorry, came out wrong."

"Where you driving?"

"Funny, boss."

"Really, Mo, I mean it, where we going?"

Mo was lost for words to respond, not even a "boss."

Mikey had forgotten. This abortive exchange indicated to him that he should wait and see, not seek further illumination.

That instant they pulled into the mostly vacant parking lot of Lorenzo's, bracketed by his crew's backup cars, he remembered what he was doing tonight. Tonight was the night Dolly was going to make some kind of a move, his power play. The nature of the move he figured he would soon learn, and in the meantime he could tolerate the suspense.

The salty breezes were picking up off the estuary as he stepped out of the back seat. Beppe and Scoop and Fatso hustled out of their cars and walked alongside Mikey, heads swiveling on their necks, keeping a lookout.

He noticed the university decal that was on the back window of Rosetta's car, which for some unfathomable reason was parked outside the restaurant.

Chapter Seventeen

Lorenzo's was where Mikey and Zayana met, about twenty years ago. She was a cocktail waitress and the first black employee managed by Lorenzo, who worked for Mikey's dad and was the front for the restaurant. She was a no-doubt-about-it knockout, with magnificent, finely situated, shapely legs that went on all day long and into the night, and provided the perfect excuse for the high heels she unswervingly preferred, and immense sparkling onyx eyes. Her hair flowed down in shiny ringlets. This was a long time ago when she and he made acquaintance, when that hairstyle was fashionable. Looks like hers, though, never go out of fashion.

That first night he saw her, he was sucked into her magnetic field. Before he said a word, he couldn't help yearning to put his hands on her—but not in that kind of way, he'd want you, and her, to believe.

He stepped right up, introduced himself.

"Good to know, Mikey." For a girl who was accustomed to being hit on all night long, she wasn't completely hostile, and the sleepy sweet smile took the edge off.

"My father owns this place, I lend a hand."

"Lorenzo's your dad?"

He didn't confirm that.

Her eyes narrowed. She was not tracking. "You cook, you tend bar, what?"

"Not really."

"'Mikey' you said your name was? Mikey, you're confusing me. Most men, have to say, aren't tough to figure out."

"You're the prettiest girl ever walked into Lorenzo's." Facts were facts.

"You a crazy mad tipper? I like that in a man."

"What else you like in a man?" He wasn't wasting time.

"Need to ask, you don't need to know."

"You looking for a boyfriend?" he said, going for it.

"Why bother? They're always tracking me."

"They can call off the chase." Those were the days when his eyes were brighter, when the hair on his head was full, when his skin was taut, when his teeth glistened, when he stood straight and tall and nobody was actively trying to kill him.

"You're pretty confident..." she started—and coyly paused.

"For a white boy?"

"Okay, but I didn't say it." She instinctively liked him, too, taken by the self-assurance bordering on arrogance. Dominant men were like catnip, especially once she dominated them.

"You going to tell me your name?"

She would.

"Pretty name. Think there's any way you and I can see each other, Zayana?"

"You're seeing me right now. I can tell because you haven't stopped staring since you walked in."

"I mean, outside the restaurant."

"Like a date? You work fast. Since you say your dad owns the place, I don't know how I can avoid you."

"You want to? *Avoid* me?"

"Not sure, but something tells me that won't stop us from seeing each other. I'm off tomorrow night, case it matters."

It did, it really mattered.

Eighteen months later, she gave birth to her only child, whom she christened Jeremiah, who would be having dinner a couple of decades years later with Mikey's sister, the boy's Aunt Rosey, and Zayana had evidently skipped town, leaving Jeremiah for Mikey to take care of him. An unexpected turn, but all in all, not a totally bad deal, he realized. Second chances were rare in the world at large, and rarer in Mikey's.

His vintage memories of Zayana were fairly reliable even now and they helplessly kicked in as he stared at the bar where he first met her and instantaneously fell into a condition that even then he recognized as related to being in like what people sang songs about, maybe called love. He could visualize her standing there, all over again. His remembrances of her were not uniformly happy ones, to tell the truth.

For the record, his father was not to be confused with some civil rights activist. He was more like a pragmatist who recognized that trustworthy restaurant employees were a rare breed, and as a consequence he was open-minded when it came to race. This may have appeared surprising to Vincent's circle, considering the long-lost time ago when he was born, and factoring in the casual racism embraced by Italians in general, but he regularly professed admiration and even affection for Zayana, who reciprocated. And also for the record, his dad never ran girls. That was a distasteful occupation, an unmanly business and uncivilized. Besides, there was plenty of easy money to make elsewhere.

"She got spunk, plus she's a very pretty girl," he said to Mikey, but he warned him: "Don't abuse the help, we got a business to run. And don't take advantage of the girl, the way you did all the others, and break the girl's heart, good waitresses are hard to find, and she's a great one."

As it happened, it was she who ended up breaking Mikey's heart. Dolly himself fruitlessly, ludicrously schemed on Zayana before Mikey planted his flag on the top of a hill that was no flag on nothing like a hill. Once he boldly volunteered his opinion: "Can't believe you don't join that beautiful broad in holy bedlock." But marriage and related social conventions never appealed to Mikey. This was cool with Zayana, who shared the same prejudices. Not that they saw eye to eye on everything. Tough and hardened and street-smart as he once may have been, she stimulated unmanageable, tender feelings within him. Even so, one time as they got into bed he made a naïve mistake he would pay for.

"You asking if I've dated a lot of white guys?" She sat up. "Define a lot. Don't bother defining white guys."

He wished he had never asked. At some point during that first blow-up he also made the ill-advised move of asking how she learned to speak the way she did. He was intoxicated by the music in her voice and by the way she talked, and he intended the question as a compliment. This was not going well. Sometimes, you're in a hole and you keep digging.

"What, I'm supposed to talk blacker?" She had completed community college, he hadn't graduated high school, so they were even.

He tried to defend himself. He said he wasn't dissing her.

"You ain't *dissing* me? When white folks fake talk black, I get depressed, just want to smash them with my handy watermelon."

"You made your point an hour ago, Z." At the same time, he didn't completely understand what she meant by her point. He had a lot to learn. Bizarre as it sounded, he wanted to learn Zayana. More than that, he wanted her to know he loved her—as soon as he knew he did. All he was trying to say was that she was unlike anybody in his life before and he felt differently about her—in a good way. If any aspect of that bore some connection with her race, he might have been the last to know.

She lunged and switched on the bed lamp. "I get it, I get it, light bulb went on," she said. "You never slept with a sister before."

He could not argue. "What do you want, Z?"

"Let me break it down, homie."

"You can stop now. Said I'm sorry."

"Tell me. Me being black—you believe you're colorblind, Mikey, or does me being black turn you on? Which? Is it both?"

She had it completely wrong. He couldn't say why. So he tried to turn the tables, a tested and true tactic with people—white people—in his world. "My being white, not important, or turns you on?"

"Thing is, when *you* ask *me*, it's the wrong question." Besides, she believed he wasn't really white, he was Italian. "You got a long way to go, Mikey."

"Maybe both of us."

"Ain't this when we have make-up sex?"

As a matter of fact, yes. The way he saw it, white pussy was never this complicated, or this good.

☙

MIKEY WENT UP TO his son and sister's table in the mostly deserted dining room, Mo waiting patiently at the host stand, his head barely reaching the countertop.

"What are you guys doing here?"

Rosey answered him: "I told you we were coming here tonight, remember? Want to join us?"

He flinched, but not detectibly, he hoped. "Meeting with the crew. How was dinner?"

Jeremiah spoke up: "I could eat here every night, it's so good."

"Let me talk to Lorenzo, see if I can get you started, Jeremiah." That was a formality, Lorenzo did what he was told. "Catch you guys at home later, don't wait up."

Mikey turned to go.

"Ready, boss?" Mo called out. "Everybody's in the back, boss."

Mikey was ready as he could be. His dad's body was barely cold, but business was, as people who ought to know better always say, business.

Except when it wasn't meant to be, like tonight.

Lorenzo hustled out from the back office. The wiry thatches of gray hair sprouting freakishly from the sides of his otherwise bald head gave him the look of somebody who had been rudely awakened from a nap—either that, or he had been freshly electrocuted. Reading glasses hung precariously on his Roma tomato nose. "Mikey, phone for you, some broad says urgent."

Mikey informed Lorenzo that Jeremiah would work the floor tomorrow night. Then he went back to the office and came out a few minutes later, not looking gleeful as a man who won a big bet.

Mo asked who called.

"Wrong number."

Mo looked unhappy to be blown off like that.

"We gotta go right now."

Mo looked more unhappy.

"What's up, boss?"

"Never mind."

"I should get Beppe and Scoop to drive behind us."

"Not necessary, let's go."

"That's crazy, boss. All due, boss."

"Two things. Lighten up on the *boss*, you making me feel like a Teamster president."

"Okay, that's one thing. Other thing?"

"What other thing you talking about? Let's go."

Chapter Eighteen

Once they reached home, Mikey told Mo to wait in the car.

"You sure, boss?"

"You gotta stop asking me questions like that."

"Really, boss?"

Mikey had his fill of Mo and walked off shaking his head. How did his dad deal for so long with a hen-pecking guy like him? Good and loyal crew member Mo was, but if he wanted to be nagged, he'd have gotten married.

When he reached his front door, he saw on the landing the person he was expecting.

"Long time. Looking gorgeous as usual, Zayana."

"Gorgeous enough to invite me inside?"

Of course, he would. He was nothing if not curious why she had called.

They settled into chairs across from each other at the dining room table.

"How about a drink, Z?"

A glass of water. He could make that happen, too.

"Mind if I smoke?"

"Yes."

"You got an ashtray?"

He went into the kitchen and found a conch shell under the sink. How it got there: no idea. And no point fighting her about smoking in his house. Or about anything else now that so little was at stake between them. When he returned, they studied each other across the mahogany table. The lights were dimmer than they should have been. Well, so was he. She still had that effect on him.

She had an unreliable smile, sometimes a very inviting smile, when it wasn't sending a mixed message. He couldn't help it, he smiled back. Somehow it was uncomfortably comfortable to see her, on account of their history, and their current, so far unexplained, circumstances.

"When'd you start smoking?"

"Day you left me." She exhaled and the smoke ascended, encircling the elaborate chandelier in a zig-zaggy spume. She could be such a drama queen.

"You left me, Z." Once he used to be crazy for that drama queen.

"I would have remembered."

He had come to abhor with increasing vehemence any reference, no matter how unfounded or remote, to his or anybody else's defective memory. The former lovers and on-again off-again parents were off to a rocky start, which may not have been a bad thing. Knowing her, if he could really say that he did, and he couldn't, he figured that state wouldn't last indefinitely.

"How'd you know I'd be at the store?"

"It's the only number I found for you. You're looking fabulous, Mikey." It had been more than a few years, but no point looking too close.

"You talking with Randy?"

"Why would I be talking with that freaky deaky tailor?"

No logical reason he could generate. Silly off-kilter talk. She must have a big problem. Did she have some exotic terminal disease?

"Sorry about your dad. Always liked him a lot. He was a sweetheart, he treated me with respect."

"He thought you were aces. Or as told me a hundred times, you were too good for me."

"How's our Jeremiah?"

Now he was *their* Jeremiah? "He talks about you a lot, misses his mom, which you gotta know. Lorenzo said he could start him at the restaurant tomorrow, I think he'll be a natural. He can make some money, learn a trade."

"It's better this way, being with you, not with me, given what's going on."

He wouldn't argue with her keeping a low profile, but then, why was she at his house, where Jeremiah was due back?

"Been meaning to ask. Given what's going on, eggs-ackly what *is* going on?"

"Nothing much. Could use some money. Think you could help me out, for old time's sake?"

Part of him didn't care to know the details. Most of him, actually. Without hesitation, he pulled out his roll of cash, he didn't think about holding back, and he peeled off the bills.

She counted them out: twenty hundred-dollar bills.

"Guess you forgot, Z. You don't do that, count money in front of somebody, you don't."

"Not gonna cut it," she said, but she did slip the cash under her shirt, between her breasts. Whatever else he may have thought about her, he knew that was one lucky, profitable bra. "I gotta be on the down low for an indefinite period, is why."

No way around the next step. "Want to tell me what's wrong?"

"Not particularly."

"Going into rehab?"

"Don't get it twisted, cause look at me, do I seem like I'm using?"

He guessed not, but one could never be sure. He didn't get why people started using in the first place.

"Take your coat off." He knew that much.

"I'm not going to do that." She had her pride.

"For old time sake."

Need trumped pride. "Fuck it, Don Mikey." She slipped off her coat. She could have been mistaken for being in her thirties. Same beautiful body he had reveled in, like in the past when she was working out two hours a day with that muscle-bound, knucklehead trainer who was too stupid to be scared of Mikey and whom Mikey, for good and obvious reason, never trusted, and who one day didn't show up for work and was not heard from again. Afterward, Zayana never mentioned the guy, which, in Mikey's eyes, may have redounded to her credit. Nobody would call her sentimental.

"Roll up your sleeves."

"Oh, no you don't."

"Is it a thing for black women? The *thing* you just did?"

"You have a lot to learn about women, black *and* white."

"You did that finger wag and your head goes side to..."

She denied that again, and she wasn't lying, though she had to admit to herself that maybe it was unconscious.

"Forget it, roll up your sleeves."

"What the?" But she complied. Her arms appeared trackless, unviolated. "I could be smoking crack, you know, if you're doing the due diligence."

"Are you?" Not that he suspected, rock wasn't her.

"I been a good mom, clean fifteen years."

"So what's the deal, Z?"

"Some people have a serious problem with me is all."

His raised eyebrows and scrunched-up shoulders and outstretched, pleading hands indicated precisely how thoroughly he didn't understand.

"Yeah, you couldn't always follow the bouncing ball."

"You got a bookie wants to break your legs? I told you not to..."

"I don't gamble, Mikey, come on, you know that."

Not on games she didn't gamble. Only the serious shit.

"You borrow from the wrong guy, meaning any guy?"

"Look, some people, they want me to not be around with a national election coming up."

"What'd you do," he shook his head, tempted to laugh at her preposterous attempt to play him, "date some politician who's, what, married, running for office?" He wanted to use a word other than "date," but didn't want to blow up the meet and greet.

She sighed. That always was an easy tell for him to read. She did that when she needed something, or when she was hiding something.

"No fucking way," he said.

Damn, Mikey *was* following the bouncing ball.

ଔ

SHE LIT ANOTHER CIGARETTE. "You see his name in the papers."

"Actually, I don't, on account I don't read the papers, 'cept sports."

"He's one of your senators."

Which would have given a clue to almost anybody besides Mikey, who didn't have any senators he knew of, and who didn't vote in the first place. Only losers voted. "What difference does it make, happened a long time ago?" He was making lots of assumptions, which might have been understandable under the fast-shifting conditions.

She sighed again.

"Really, Zayana, *really*? How'd you get so dumb?"

She told him she didn't need his judgment.

But she did need his money.

"I knew this was a bad idea, waste of my time."

It wasn't her style to be frightened for no reason, so he had to bet the story was real and the man was a heavyweight.

"His wife's the real problem," she said, "because her family fortune is bankrolling his campaign."

He didn't want to ask the next question, but not being a lawyer—a professional who doesn't ask a question he didn't want to know the answer to—he went for it: "You love the guy?"

"I must look like I'm begging for your abuse."

"*Did* you love the asshole?"

She shook her head every which way to indicate *maybe*, which told Mikey everything, none of it good. "I might have had a weak moment," she said. "Or couple."

Who doesn't, he was thinking, as he was having one of those weak moments himself looking at her. All these years later, it was amazing to him how she had this power over him. As for her being in a fix, if he pressed her for details, she might say more. But he didn't need to know any more, not yet, what she had said already was plenty.

"Tell you what. I'll help." His father dying the way he did had somehow rescrambled his brain and his principles.

She dabbed her eyes. She didn't need any tears to fall, not now.

"Hate to see even you jammed up, Z."

"You're the only family Jeremiah and I got left. If they eliminated him and me, nobody'd give a shit. And I burned my bridges and I got a bad history a long time ago, from when I was using, which I'm not using now. Thing is, listen, you'll love this. His people tracked me down, saying they want to help me with my rent and, you know, expenses, but that's bullshit, I know they only want me to go away permanently, I don't trust them."

"That's my girl. Well, you use to be."

"You going soft? That was never a good look on you."

"Where'd you meet? Curious, is all."

"What did you use to tell me? 'Nobody was put in the electric chair for something he didn't say?' You gonna help or not?"

"I'm helping Jeremiah's mom, the boy's been through enough. You really think this guy's people are capable of bringing on the pain?"

"Look who's asking. Who isn't, given the right set of conditions? I'd say winning or losing a big election is in the ballpark of right set of conditions."

She had a point. She could have been making a similar point about herself, he supposed. *But nobody's done stupider things than me,* he added to himself. Like losing her and his kid, for one thing, not that he wished to make that case under these increasingly stressed circumstances.

She put her coat back on and cinched the belt, and looked impatient, like somebody whose plane was late. Sensing her mood shift, he pushed across the table his whole roll of cash. He might have gone into his suit coat pocket to take out more cash, which might have been all she would need for a long time, but that was why he didn't reach into that other pocket. He wasn't thinking altogether clearly, but he had a feeling he didn't want her to completely disappear again. No, he was definitely not thinking coherently.

"We don't have a future, Mikey. You do remember that?"

Again with the remembering, *again.* "I forget a lot of shit these days, but not something like that. And hey, we didn't have much of a past, either, long enough to accidentally make a good kid, little mixed up, and with a dicey track record, but somebody who didn't ask to come into the world and who deserves being taken care of by us."

"By us?"

"Sounds corny, give you that."

"Along with the money?"

"You never know who might get next to Jeremiah, which you don't want. I'll keep an eye out for him. You also never know what law enforcement could be up to, they might go on some fishing expedition. Speaking of which, you're not setting me up, are you?"

"You always were a good guy, don't care what they all say."

"Now you're calling me names."

"Say, isn't this your table from the old house? I served you up some good meals, back in the day."

"You made pretty good veal parmigiana for a…"

"Don't even. Hey, you remember? One time we didn't make it up to the bedroom and right here on this table…"

There was no need to flesh out the recollection, though it was true, and they had enjoyed some sweet, hot times.

"That's enough Memory Lane," he said.

She cooperated. She would be in touch as soon as she settled in somewhere. "I won't say goodbye."

That almost sounded encouraging. "Unlike last time," he couldn't resist adding. There was one other thing eating away at him. Suddenly pieces were falling into place. He asked her if she had tried to blackmail the senator. It was the next natural question for a guy like him to ask of a girl like her in a fix such as this.

"I'm not that stupid."

"You sure?"

"Define blackmail."

That's all he needed to know. "Blackmail's like, I don't know, goddamn, *blackmail*, Z. What'd you ask for?"

"Enough to tide me over, for a long while. He said he'd do it, but it got me to thinking, he said yes too fast, and I got a bad feeling."

"Not good, Zayana, not good. He's coming." He told her that she needed to communicate with the senator, tell him that she didn't want anything, not a dime, that she would be a good girl and keep her mouth shut. "You ready?"

Made a sort of sense, she supposed, not that she was much for being sensible.

"You got his number."

"Stop, come on."

"Call him right now."

"What makes you think I'm going to call him now?"

"Call him, Z."

She took out her phone and in a few moments he listened to her side of the conversation.

"Yeah, it's me... You prick... Don't mess with me... I wanna say, nothing to worry about... Leave me and my boy alone and nobody needs to know anything... No, really, that's all I mean... No, it's not a trick... Tell your bitch-on-wheels wife, nothing's gonna happen... We cool?... Okay, we're cool... I don't know why, your lucky day, I had a change of heart... I want to live my life, I want to start over, no point keeping in the past... No, I don't think you and I will grab a drink anytime soon... What?... You want me to say what?... You're a madman, but okay... Good luck in the campaign... Yeah, sure, I am going to vote for you, why not?... Soon as I register to vote... Gotta go... Bye... Enough... I said, 'bye'... Hang up now..."

Her next words were addressed to Mikey: "He hung up."

There was only one thing to do. "Now you gotta get outta Dodge."

As for Zayana, she *could* be playing him, he knew that perfectly well. He wouldn't put it past her. He wouldn't put it past anybody. But sometimes you have to take care of your own. Including when they weren't quite yours anymore. But truth was, she made him remember feeling things he didn't otherwise feel. Like caring for somebody. So yeah, sure, call him crazy.

Soon enough, they all would.

Chapter Nineteen

Jeremiah and Rosey came in through the back door, Mo trailing. So much for keeping Zayana's boy in the dark for his own good.

"Mom, you're here!" The boy's eyes lit up. It's a good thing, usually, a boy loving his mom.

"Only for a minute, honey. Wanted to give you a kiss and say I'll be back soon, don't you worry."

They hugged. A real, true hug. And Mikey realized there was also a strong chance Zayana had somehow orchestrated this fleeting homecoming scene. She knew she'd get her money and she'd be able to see her boy again, if only for a minute.

"What a nice surprise," said Rosey. "Very heartwarming." She seemed to mean it.

"Amazing, ain't it?" said Mikey. Little too amazing.

"You left Renzo's fast," said Rosey.

He pointed in Zayana's direction so she would know why.

Then he addressed Mo: "I told you to stay in the car."

"You did, boss, you did, but Rosey, she…"

The house phone started ringing. It was late for a phone call, and usually nobody waits till it's late at night to break good news.

"Want me to get that?" said Rosey.

He went into the back room and picked up. Mikey's hunch was on the money, he didn't win the lottery.

ଔ

"MIKEY, THIS IS MR. Smith."

"The *famous* Mr. Smith? I been hearing a lot about you lately. You make the acquaintance of Mr. Dolly?"

"Mr. Smith doesn't have time to bullshit with all you losers."

"How come you don't call me Mr. Mikey?"

"Lorenzo has a message."

Lorenzo got on the phone. "Do what they want."

"Which is what?"

Mr. Smith took back the receiver. "We don't want nothing. I mean, we're going to take what's yours, on account it's yours, but we don't need it and we don't want it, we just don't want you to have any of it."

"You know who you're dealing with?"

"Yeah, I'm talking with the owner of the restaurant that once was called Lorenzo's. This place, which is going up in flames in five minutes, give or take. Don't call the cops, not that you would, because you might not see your friend Lorenzo alive again."

Mikey was hoping that his crew, Dolly and the rest, were in the private dining room, and he was trying to figure out how to reach them. But Mikey had it all wrong, as Mr. Smith would soon make plain.

"By the way, I like the way you do the roast chickens, al mattone, under the brick, very juicy, with crispy skin."

"It's our most popular item on the menu, in fact…"

"I'll miss eating that dish. Because in a minute, everything's gonna be cooked under a frickin' brick, and everybody's gonna be crispy."

"Mr. Smith, why don't we get together and talk, see if we can accommodate each other's various interests."

"Waste of time. Speaking of waste of time, your crew's time is done for good. Your dad, rest in peace, was a powerful man, which people respected, that's what they all say, but as far as his son Mikey—well, what can I say, you're a little bit on the pussy side. And then there's the whole problem with your ex, who's too greedy for her own good and knows a little too much, and she got a boy, and I'm going to have to take care of both of them."

"What's you and me got to do with the boy or his mother?"

"So it's true, what the word on the street is, you're getting kinda soft-headed. I'd feel sorry for you if my own boss didn't have a problem with your girl."

"She's not my girl, not really." He was flailing.

"So no big loss for you, no big loss. But I don't trust you, so I'm not taking any chances. I'm gonna say goodbye now. Got any last words for Lorenzo?"

What did Mr. Smith have to do with the senator? What sort of mess did Zayana put herself and Mikey in? "I got some last words for you, Mr. Smith. You touch him, I got a swift response for you and the senator both."

"The fuck that mean, 'swift response?'"

Too bad Mr. Smith wasn't there standing in front of him to find out what he meant by "swift response." Having no other target, he punched a hole in the wall instead. In a few seconds, there was a lot of blood dripping off the fingers of his throbbing right hand.

"You don't have the muscle anymore, Mikey. God, you are weak little pussycat, orange ya?"

"Lorenzo, he's got nothing to do with any of this."

"But he's your friend, right?"

Mikey hesitated answering the trick question.

"That's good enough for me. People gonna start dropping like flies around you, you'll see. But I'll make sure your friend is informed of your undying commitment. Cost of doing business."

Mikey was all over the map. "The senator has assolutely nothing to fear, the girl's gonna shut her trap."

"Yes, she is, I'm gonna make sure, permanently."

"You wanna go to the mattresses? I got a good crew, they're gonna track you down."

"You think Dolly and Scoop and Beppe are working for you? Think again. I can use them till I don't need them anymore. Meantime, your old world is passing you by, Mikey. Passing. You. Right. By. Hear that? There it goes. *Swoosh.*"

Mikey should have known. Those guys were going to make a move on him tonight at the restaurant after all. Funny how he didn't mention Fatso, which confused Mikey.

"Far as I can tell, all's you got left is the little mope, who I hear is the tough guy, Mo. I'll aim low when I kneecap the midget. And the fat man, he used to be fat, he got away, but since he moves slow, I can track him down by the trail of his piggy breath."

At least Mikey could count on Mo, one honorable guy left. And who knows, maybe Fatso was loyal as well.

"I'll bid you a do, or as you Eye Talians say, ciao-ciao. Say bye-bye, Lorenzo, and bye-bye, Lorenzo's. We're coming for the boy, to make a point, and then for the broad, and then for you, Mikey, to put a cherry on top of the whole thing. We know we can find you anytime we want, and your crew has cut you off, so you're not going anywhere. Can't believe those two jerk-offs got in your car, trying to steal it, which we had all wired to the ignition. It woulda been perfect, what with you forgetting your key inside the car like an idiot, and Randy telling me where to find you that day. That Randy, he's a artist with the duds, ain't he?"

So Randy ratted him out, too. Figures. Everything had fallen apart.

"You forgetting the other guy you sent to pay a social call?"

"Guess he went on his Moron Mission."

"I wouldn't leave a candle in the window waiting for him, Mr. Smith. There's a lot of bad traffic at rush hour."

"Yeah, we took a shot. No risk, no award. But I'm feeling generous. We were a little bit too late to get the boy tonight, but there'll be other opportunities. Tell me right now where the girl is, and maybe I'll let you live. That's a deal, ain't it? Where is she? She's kinda slippery. And she's a pretty girl, too bad she won't stay that way."

"Fuck you."

"Now now, no need for harsh words, Mikey. Gotta go now, I mean, Lorenzo's gotta go now."

Mikey could hear the phone dropping down on the business office desk and Lorenzo screaming, "Dolly, we shoulda killed your dumb ass when we had…" Then he stopped screaming, and the phone line and Lorenzo's voice went dead.

Chapter Twenty

When Mikey came back into the room shaking his hand, trying to get the feeling back, Rosey asked what the hell was that big thump she heard. Then she noticed the blood. "Jesus, Mikey!"

"Mo, bag of ice."

His sister asked what the hell was going on.

"Nothing I can't deal with." He wasn't certain that was true, but he knew it was the thing to say—the kind of thing his own father, rest in peace, would say. He'd get his revenge for Lorenzo as soon as he could, but he could not do that under the current circumstances, being a boss suddenly without a crew to back him.

"What did you punch the wall for?"

Reasonable question for Rosetta to ask because the hand looked mangled. He didn't think it was broken, but it was hard to tell. He must be getting old. Used to be, he could knock down a wall and not pay a price.

"Me and the wall had our differences."

"Man, boss," said Mo, and put the ice pack on the hand. "You need to go to Emergency."

"Right now," he said, "we gotta skip town."

Rosey was full of questions and just getting started: "What are you, crazy?"

"Everybody asking me the same thing."

"You made boss. You can't take off."

"Trust me, Rosey."

Zayana wanted in on the discussion. "What's going on?"

"Things have come up."

"Oh, that explains it perfectly," said Rosetta.

So he gave them a quick summary, what happened with Lorenzo's, with Mr. Smith, with the crew. Mo showed little emotion. He went into the hall closet, pulled out a shotgun, and stood sentry by the stairwell nearest the front door, in case.

"Tell you what, Z. I'll go with you, keep you company, which you might could use, given the situation, which is a little more serious than I first grasped."

Zayana was barely tracking the import of the latest information, because there was a lot to take in, so nobody could blame her. All she could say was: "You really are a crazy Italian."

"Stop with the 'crazy,' stop. No, listen, I mean it, Z. I'll look out for you, and you'll look out for me, and we'll look out for each other. Plus, it'll be easier for you traveling with your husband…"

It was like she swallowed the olive pit: she realized all over again how deep she was in to be here in the first place in Mikey's house with all this shit coming down, most of it, she had to admit, caused by her. This was not turning out as she planned.

"Play along, Z. You and me, on the road for a while, till things calm down, election's over, senator's hard-on goes limp. It's a plan." He was recalling what his dad told him, about taking a fresh look at his life. He wasn't sure he had done that for a long, long time. "It's the best I can come up with right now."

"Who the fuck's the senator?" Rosey wanted to know.

"That's not important. I mean it is important, but hold on."

"Who's going to be watching Jeremiah?" Zayana said.

"He'll be protected." Then he instructed Jeremiah: "Buddy, go upstairs for a minute, would you?" The boy obeyed.

"You and me, Mikey," said Zayana, once her son was gone, "playing husband and wife? And you with only one good hand?"

"Like those old times we were about to toast."

"God, I hope not, I really hope not."

"Gotta ask *you* a question, Z. I'd appreciate it if you'd be honest, for a change. Jeremiah. Is Jeremiah mine?"

"The fuck you talking about?"

"My little swimmers really make a successful beachhead and nine months later Mikey's Normandy invasion?"

"Your swimmers were always crashing the shore."

"We didn't do any of those tests to determine, and he always looked like me, and the timing seemed right—but maybe he had some other white father."

"I think it's past time you go screw yourself."

"The thing I can't figure is, the senator, he's too interested in the boy. Is there a chance Jeremiah's his kid?"

"Again, who the fuck's the senator?" Rosetta was ignored.

"A chance?" said Zayana to Mikey. "You're asking me is there a chance I slept with him when I was with you, using all those terms loosely?"

"That's eggs-ackly what I am needing to know."

"Define 'chance.'"

"That's helpful, thanks. Let me ask it another way. Does the senator *think* Jeremiah might be his boy?"

"I can't be responsible for what men think, because they don't know how."

"That's also helpful." The way he saw it, maybe the senator was Jeremiah's father and the motherfucking senator wanted to eliminate the boy, who was living and breathing and visual evidence of his transgression and political miscalculation—in which case Mikey felt a responsibility to protect an innocent kid who made a bad choice when it came to being born to certain parents. Or alternatively, he really was Mikey's boy, in which case the senator was trying to kill his son, and that wasn't going to happen if Mikey could help it. The other minor thing he decided was that one day he would get Rosetta to arrange for a DNA test, which would clear up the mystery once and for all. But really, all that was immaterial in the short term. Either way, Zayana and Jeremiah—and therefore Mikey— had a problem right now.

Rosey said if somebody didn't tell her right now who the fucking senator was…

"First things first, Rose. Z, lemme see your phone."

"Use your own."

"Phone, baby, I wanna take a look."

She hesitated but complied. After all, Mikey was holding if not all the cards, all the good ones.

He studied the phone number she had called and texted it to himself. "You're going to need a new phone. Where he can't call you. I'll get one for you. And this one don't work no more." Then he dropped her phone on the floor and stomped on it. The satisfying, crunching sound was like tiny facial bones, a sound familiar to him from past experience. "Road trip, Z. Ready?"

This was when Zayana quickly ran down for Rosey's benefit who the senator was, but Mikey wasn't listening as he contemplated the situation:

Lorenzo had been murdered. Mikey would mourn for him the way his dad, and Lorenzo for that matter, would have approved, the right way, by getting revenge when he could. And the restaurant was doubtless in flames now. He faced facts. These guys—Mr. Smith and Dolly and whoever else was involved, whoever these guys were—were out of his league. He had to admit this to himself. They were more capable than he and more equipped to bring on the world-class pain than he was. It hadn't always been like that, but *always* wasn't *now*. It was bracing to acknowledge this personal limitation on his part, but it had to be done. His family business was up in smoke, like his restaurant—for now. Worse than anything, he had failed his father, who had entrusted him to keep the shop going. There was no getting around that, either. But he himself didn't feel like he had the muscle or the mental and emotional stamina to stick around and fight. It was time to get out of town, one day get reorganized, then launch an offensive. Nobody was safe as long as the senator and Mr. Smith were coming on like they were.

One unexpected and strange side-benefit of losing so much: Mikey was thinking more clearly. He himself *sensed* he was thinking clearly. People determined to kill you may help in the clarity derby, not that he'd recommend the experience. What did Rosey say about limiting brain impairment by having a purpose in life? Now his purpose was big time, better than any tango class. His purpose in life was saving Jeremiah and Zayana. And look at this, suddenly he wasn't forgetting as many things as before. Maybe the Alzhammer had been blunted by these extreme conditions. On top of that, maybe he didn't need to kill himself for a while, not while there were others coming after him who were far better at it than he was. One thing he couldn't forget was this: if his concentration wavered, he and Zayana and Jeremiah and Rosetta and Mo would be history.

Zayana was reading his mind. This wasn't as hard as it sounds, and she was no mystic seer. "This is totally wack. I'm not getting in a car to go fuck knows where with you. You're crazy."

"What'd I say about 'crazy?'"

He starkly outlined her options. Did she wish to rely on the goodwill of a frightfully wealthy and powerful man who probably if not certainly would have her killed if he got the opportunity, or would she prefer to throw in with a man who used to want sometimes to kill her a little bit but had lost the interest over the years? Why didn't she trust he would take care of her? Wasn't she possibly the mother of his only son? She couldn't think that Mikey was still in love with her, but in front of each silver lining there was a cloud.

"Agreed, Z?"

"Yeah, and Fredo goes fishing in a boat."

"What the?"

"Fredo got whacked in the boat. Let's get this straight. Not going fishing with you, never gonna happen." She wasn't sure she meant what she said.

Between Tony Soprano and the Godfather, he was thinking, *all the trouble those guys started.* Watch a movie or a TV show and you think you have the skinny as how the mob works. Then again, they weren't that far off.

He might be crazy but Zayana was willing to hear the rest of his plan.

"First," he said, "right now they would go to the safe house."

"What?" said a stunned Mo standing sentry in the foyer. "You got one of them?" He believed he knew 100 percent of the crew's business, but the real percentage of his information was nowhere in that ballpark.

"Next time I tell you to stay in the car, no freelancing."

"Sorry, boss."

The safe house was a place his dad had set up and instructed Mikey to tell nobody about. There were always limits to trust, so his dad had taught him—that and you don't know who your friends really are until it turned out they weren't and if you weren't careful then it was too late. Today, being a case in point. It wouldn't be somewhere to hole up long-term, but they could certainly buy a few days before heading out by the light of the moon. In this safe house of his there was also a very special bedroom with a very generous lumpy mattress that functioned like a practically bottomless ATM machine. Mikey's father packed it with stacks and stacks and stacks of large denomination bills.

"I'll tell you the rest in the car." As soon as he figured it all out. It wasn't like there were a lot of options on the table. He instructed them: "Ten minutes. You guys got ten minutes to pack." He couldn't count on much more time before Mr. Smith and company, including the traitor Dolly, descended.

"What?" said Rosetta shaking her head as she looked at Mikey, who appeared exuberant. "You draw to an inside straight? You don't have a poker face, so what could you possibly be smiling about? People coming after you, including a nut job politician and his deadly wife, coming after the rest of us, too, your crew falling apart, you find this entertaining?"

"You got a point, Rosey, a legitimate point. I will have to get back to you."

Truth was, he felt he had been preparing all his life for whatever was coming his way. That might have indeed sounded crazy, a word he was hating more and more, but when it came to certain specialized kinds of crazy, he had the corner on the market. The senator and Mr. Smith and that rat-faced Dolly would understand soon enough, and so would everybody else, that Mikey Festagiacamo was one day going to get back in business in a way that he had not been for a long, long time.

There was one other thing that made him feel irrationally happier, too.

Now he had discovered what it meant to have one of those fuck-the-bucket lists. His newly created bucket list contained one item and one item only, which he didn't need to share out loud: take care of Zayana and Jeremiah. That wasn't a whole lot for Zayana to ask of him, not that she was asking, but for him that was better than paragliding off the Great Wall of China or swimming alongside man-rescuing dolphins, though it had a good deal in common with both.

Chapter Twenty-One

"**S**on of a bitch, look at him," said Zayana, pointing at the senator on the television screen. "Preening peacock."

"Don't make me," Rosetta pleaded.

"Nice suit," said Mikey. "Not a Brioni though, right?" The hunch soured his mood.

The safe house blackout drapes were drawn, and they were watching the debate between the glib telegenic senator and his professorial female opponent who referenced strings of mind-numbing numbers to buttress her cause. To tell by the stricken, hunted look on her face, and the tremor in her voice, however, she had no shot to defeat her incumbent opponent.

At the same time, maybe not so fast. Based on long experience, Mikey always respected, always feared the underdog. Dogs have more to fight for because they have nothing to lose—nobody expects them to win. He supposed he himself qualified as an underdog now.

"Mo, scope out the election spread, maybe we get down on the dog."

Missing the point, Mo pleaded. That wasn't a good idea, he railed, calling up the book…

"Mo, Mo, stop, okay?"

Mo caught on: Mikey was playing. "Whew, good one, boss."

Literal-minded Mo could be a challenge. Good thing he was loyal, because he was no Leonardo da Vinci or even Leo da Oakland, a freaky genius of a bookie who fixed football games until somebody without the inside information fixed him permanently. But loyal doesn't require smart and sometimes smart won't square with loyal. In loyal versus smart, Mikey signed up for the former. Smart could make mistakes, smart you could not always count on. But loyal? Loyal was gold.

My friend the congresswoman and I have positions that couldn't be more starkly different. Take, for instance, the tragic subject of abortion. She wants abortion legal on demand and subsidized by overtaxed taxpayers. I am opposed to abortion absolutely. As a practicing Catholic, I learned early on the sanctity of each and every precious life and how the unborn must be protected in a civilized Judeo-Christian society...

This view was voiced by the very same sanctity-of-life senator who would have Mr. Smith and his people fanning out to kill Mikey and Zayana and Jeremiah throughout the whole of Judeo-Christian society.

Defiantly, Zayana lit another cigarette.

"Those things'll kill you," said Mikey.

"I'll worry about that later."

When my beautiful wife and I married, thirty years ago tonight—happy anniversary, darling. We'll go out for dinner tomorrow night, I promise. In any case, she and I vowed to do all we could to protect life together. We have three children, two boys and a girl, and seven beautiful grandchildren—hey, Chrissy and Chandler, get to bed now, it's late. And we will do everything we can to promote life and protect the unborn, who have a right to life, liberty, and the pursuit of happiness under the Constitution of the United States of America. As your senator, if you reelect me, I solemnly pledge to do all I can to undo Roe v Wade, which was decided in the wrong by unelected judges and which is single-handedly responsible for the ongoing tragedy in our country, which amounts to nothing less than genocide...

"How much longer we gotta watch?" Zayana said. "Because I want to stab myself in the eyes."

"You heard about knowing your enemies?" Mikey said.

Zayana turned off the set. Nobody protested, including Mikey. If she was in the know about anything, it was enemies. It was her friends who confused her. Take Mikey. Was he her friend and how would she know for sure?

He had an announcement for the whole house: "You all nice and comfy?"

They murmured they were.

"Too bad. We're outta here in the morning."

ʘ

"Why should I trust you and throw in with you?" she asked. "Wouldn't I have to be nuts?"

"Same reason I should trust you. You and me, we're the only games in town for each other. For now, anyway."

"I do like your sister Rosetta. And she likes you, so might be you're not the asshole you used to be."

"And my sister likes you, too. Right, Rosey?"

Rosey nodded, apprehensively, because that seemed like a trick question.

"We're not gonna stay on the run forever, Z, only till the time comes for us to resurface, after the election."

Mo had picked up a car, a nondescript used Buick. Everybody's cell phones were changed out. He had also arranged for false identities—fake drivers' licenses and phony social security numbers for one Michael Jackson, born sixty-two years ago, and one Zelda Jackson, born forty-nine years ago.

Mo's handiwork upset Zayana. "Michael frigging Jackson, Mikey? Really? Michael Jackson? Why not Michael Angelo or Michael Corleone?"

"Best Mo's guy could do, short notice."

"Very eighties, like you, but don't be wearing one glove, Michael Jackson. Speaking of, you keep shaking your hand. You in pain?"

He probably did break a bone or two, but there was nothing to do or say about that.

"The other thing. I look forty-nine to you? I'm not even forty-five."

"Right, you are forty-four and your birthday is Christmas. Besides, your picture on the license is a good one."

She was touched he remembered that much personal detail.

"I got a new idea," he told Rosey and Zayana, and he was prepared to lay out the new plan he'd been conceiving in private. Big plans might be the bailiwick of chumps and dreamers—and losers—but he felt his new plan was a pretty great one. Once he finished telling them, he would wait for applause.

◌

Zayana did not see that one coming. "Old folks home, outskirts of Vegas? That your big idea?"

Mikey and Jeremiah had looked at lots of websites until they found what might be the choice rundown nowhere place, which was located on the California side of the border with Nevada, within easy striking distance of Vegas in case they needed to hop on a plane or get lost in a crowd.

The place was called Over the Rainbow Assisted Living, a veritable village, a community of old people ignored by the staff when not being abused. Not that *that* was their marketing plan or promoted by their advertising slogan, which was *To serve elderly people like persons.*

Yet that was the inescapable conclusion to be drawn from reading in between the lines of the dozens of online reports detailing complaints about a business that had had its license yanked in reaction to the latest tragedy. It seems that a resident with advanced-stage Alzheimer's had wandered off through the unlocked, unsupervised front door and got himself summarily flattened in the street. The main advantage for Mikey and Zayana and company was, nobody would think of looking for them in a place like that, somewhere over the rainbow. Somewhere over the rainbow was practically the definition of where they ought to be—as long as the senator and Mr. Smith and Dolly were circling.

"I know," he said, "genius or what? Rosey's not the only one with brains around…"

"How you going to maintain your brilliant cover nonstop in some old folks home?"

Rosetta had some information for both Zayana for Mikey. "First off, nobody says 'old folks home' anymore. Assisted living, or nursing home, some kind of elder residence," she said, trying to be helpful, and she instantly bought into the idea. "He can do it, Zayana. He's always on stage. A good liar. And I mean that as a compliment."

"Thank you, Rosey."

"Don't push your luck."

As far as Rosetta was concerned, if on the off-chance he really was early-stage Alzheimer's, as he hypochondriacally insisted, he wouldn't have to act so much. And Zayana could also keep an eye on him. Over and beyond everything, who would think to look for people like them in a place like that, located there?

It took some convincing, but it didn't take long before Zayana was starting to entertain the idea. That's what desperation will do.

Rosetta took a big chance, and gave up some crucial information to Zayana about her brother's fear of dementia—it was only fair if not quite full disclosure. Rosey said she herself harbored skepticism as to his supposed condition, and she added that her brother was very far from going there yet, that he was highly functioning. Look at how he was managing this crisis, handling this mess they were in. His moves demonstrated mental acuity and agility. If he was afflicted with dementia, he wouldn't be keeping up thus far.

All things considered, Mikey was okay with giving up that information. Zayana probably had a right to know this about her traveling companion. "Rosey," he said, "you also said it would help if I found a purpose in life. You also said pick up a new language, play chess, learn the tango—things to keep my brain firing."

Rosey nodded, that was true.

"Whaddaya say, Z?" said Mikey. "We take tango lessons some day?"

"I say your brain is firing too much," she said.

"Rosey," said Mikey, "you and Jeremiah and Mo have your tickets out of SF and your new passports. When you get to Rome, rent an apartment and lie low. You got plenty of money, and Mo'll keep an eye out. Don't go anywhere without him, anywhere. Call me if you need me, but don't if you don't."

"Mikey," said Jeremiah, "can't believe I'm going to Italy, I never been out of the country." Each time Jeremiah said *Mikey* instead of *Dad*, Mikey cringed a little. Funny, the things that bothered him that didn't use to. Then again, it couldn't have been simple for the boy—who was probably his son—to rearrange his mental and parental furniture—and it didn't promise to become simpler from here on out.

"Man, the girls, Jeremiah, beautiful girls everywhere, like you won't believe. You'll come back speaking Italian like a friggin' diplomat. It's where civilization began, that's what your nonno used to say. And always drink good wine, life's too short for the bad stuff. When everything settles down, I'll join you all in Italia, we celebrate."

"Mom, too?"

Zayana's rolling eyes intimated she would tag along on the one condition Mikey was the last man standing, and Mikey's upraised eyebrows suggested sometimes million-to-one shots come in because otherwise there wouldn't be a betting line in the first place.

"Sure, if she wants, sure."

"When you wish upon a star," said Zayana to Mikey, with that slantingly ungraphable smile of hers signifying both yes and no.

"Good," Mikey told her. "It's a date."

Chapter Twenty-Two

Big *day tomorrow, getting out of town, starting over, all of them.* Mikey couldn't sleep and in the middle of the night he found himself standing at the kitchen counter, staring at the untouched tumbler of Scotch held in his good hand. Rosetta also couldn't sleep, and she came out to have a drink, too.

"You're not the only one who had an idea," she said to him. "I got one, too, and it woke me up."

"Yeah?"

"Yeah, but don't respond right away, listen and keep an open mind, okay?"

He gave her permission to go for it, not that she needed it.

"Okay, listen. I should stay and run the crew for now, temporarily," she said. As she continued rolling out her idea, she sped up, sensing her brother was going to cut her off at the pass if she paused to catch her breath between sentences.

"You? *You* going to run what's left of the shop?"

"Let me finish. We'd be keeping the business in the family, and we could collect, and we'd send a message to Dolly and Mr. Smith that we're staying put, even when you are out of the picture for the time being. That's the gist."

"The *gist*." That gist of hers was nowhere in the zip code of what he was thinking. "Can I react?"

"Say yes."

"That's some kinda idea, Rosey. They call *me* crazy?"

"Look, Mo's worth five or six guys, so he and I put together a new crew. I can handle myself, don't worry. What they did at Lorenzo's, what they're doing to us, these guys have pissed me off..."

"Which being pissed off is already a problem. Clouds your judgment. You need to look into that, watch your blood pressure, baby."

"You become a Buddhist monk when I wasn't watching?"

"Rosey, Rose, *Rosetta*. You are making no sense. You can't deal with the shit storm that would come down on you."

"With Mo I could. He's the toughest guy you got." And look how it would play out, she reasoned. Smith and company would be too busy tracking Mikey and Zayana to bother with her, and the cops were conceivably already tracking Smith for Lorenzo's murder and the arson, so he'll have problems of his own.

"Come on, what would Dad've said?"

"That's easy. He'd be proud. Proud I was standing up for you and him and the whole family. I have Festagiacamo blood running in my veins, too."

He shut up and allowed her words to seep in. All she said was true, he acknowledged to himself but didn't admit to her. And she did have the right last name, which would provisionally buy her some instant credibility on the street—or what little was left of Festagiacamo credibility.

"How's your hand? You should get that looked at."

Farthest thing from his mind. "Keep talking."

"Lorenzo was a friend of mine, and Zayana maybe is, too, and my nephew Jeremiah means a lot to me, and that dirtbag Dolly and Mr. Smith—they did things they need to pay for."

Also on the money. He mulled and hesitated, and then confided that Fatso had been in contact with Mo. Fatso was lying low, or as low as a man called Fatso could possibly lie, and he was prepared to join up. Of course, there was a chance that Fatso was setting up Mo, but Mo himself doubted it. For one thing, Fatso was a sentimental guy who had trouble prevaricating, usually a major liability in their business, but not so much under the prevailing circumstances. Not to mention that he, of everybody in the crew, hated Dolly more than any of them did, with the exception of Mikey.

"Think about it, would you? I have nothing in my life as important as looking after you and the family."

"Rosetta, your heart's in the right place."

"Stop it."

"You have no idea what you're asking for."

"But I do, I really do."

"You don't know how to use a gun."

"When we were kids? Dad said I was a great shot. Besides, you're no Buffalo Bill. Being the boss ain't about using a gun, it's about using your brains. That's what Dad would say. Besides, Mo can handle all the fireworks we need."

To himself Mikey had to concede that Rosey—incredibly enough—was starting to make a little bit of sense—almost. It might have been the hour or the pain in his hand, but the fact was, Mo would have her back 100 percent, he was that sort of soldier.

"What would Dad, rest in peace, say if something bad happened to you?"

"We're in a safe house, Mikey, and we're all about to split up, and are we safe now? I don't think so. Best defense is a good offense."

She had made another good point.

"What about your day job, perfesser?"

"I already quit my job at the institute the day of the funeral, didn't tell you. I couldn't stand another minute. I could tell you shit that happened, but it's not important. I realized after Dad died I wanted to make things right between him and me somehow. I owe him. I want to be the kind of daughter who would come through for him."

"Thing is, I don't know about girls. Like Dad would say, are they tough enough? You gotta strike fear in people."

"Fuck off, Mikey."

Yet another unassailable point.

"We'll talk in the morning," he said.

"It's morning already."

"Sweet dreams."

"You know I'm right."

"When have I heard you say that before? Oh, yeah, my whole life."

He stayed at the kitchen counter after Rosey went to bed, downed a couple of drinks, and entertained the possibility that she had indeed conceived what amounted to a kind of plan. Mo was a beast and he would protect her with his life. She was smart. She had resolve. And she was a Festagiacomo, best of all.

◌঩

"ROSEY, WAKE UP," MIKEY said, touching her arm. She woke with a start and took a swing at him, which he ducked.

"Don't do that, you know I hate that."

"Lissename."

"Don't fucking do that again."

"Okay, okay. Thought about what you said."

"And?"

"Let's do it."

She shot up in bed, eyes wide open.

"Been discussing with Mo and been on the phone while you were beauty sleeping. Mo'll stay here at the safe house, hook up with Fatso, who is gonna be back in the saddle. You take Jeremiah to London, meet with our lawyer there, who'll connect you with people in Naples. Then you and he fly to Italy with the boy and set him up, where he'll be better protected. Zayana will love this, soon as I break it to her. I talked to guys in England and Naples and got the ball rolling. Then you slip back to America, where Mo and you will put together the crew and keep doing the family business till I return. And another thing. Along the way, you and Mo take out Mr. Smith and Dolly, instant they raise their fucking heads."

"And?"

"And until the day comes when I get back in the saddle, you are the boss."

She shook her head side to side, ecstatic. "I won't let you down."

"I know that." He really almost did. "Only downside is, Mo might start calling you boss every two seconds."

"Love you, Mikey." She threw her arms around her brother's neck.

"Bosses, they don't love nobody, Rosey."

She rubbed her eyes, wiping away a tear.

"That's not true."

"They don't cry neither."

"You're right, they make the bad guys cry."

He'd made a wise decision. "Don't forget that part, we'll all be okay."

PART TWO

Chapter Twenty-Three

Chas Blink, executive director of Over the Rainbow Assisted Living Village, sat behind his desk and his rubbed-dull doubloon eyes did not live up to the promise implied by his strange last name. He was doing all of the staring and most of the talking, while "Michael Jackson" and his wife "Zelda" were doing most of the listening. It had been a long time since ponytailed Chas had darkened the door of a barber shop.

"So nice to meet you in the flesh," he said. "I've enjoyed examining your paperwork." He was the rare sort of man whose articulation of *flesh* and *paperwork* suppurated with vague, unsavory implication. "And your material all looks to be in fine order for us at ORAL." His *material* oozed, too. He slipped on an oversized pair of black horn-rimmed glasses. His earnest demeanor suggested over-caffeinated entry-level Internal Revenue Service agent, while his red silk shirt, black bolo tie, black leather pants, and crimson cowboy boots smacked of effete religious cult, or Wild West Show orchestrated by entrepreneurial Russian immigrants.

"You'll be needing a deposit, first and last month on the furnished apartment, right?" said Zayana. "We have cash if you're down with that."

"Not to worry, ORAL can take care of all that money business in due course. 'Cash,' you said '*cash*?'"

Then he replaced the horn-rimmed with red cat-eye glasses, evidently the better-suited to address one by one Zayana's—rather, Zelda's—breasts. She had tarted herself up spectacularly, and dispensed with her bra and unbuttoned a juicy number of buttons. The less people here concentrated on her supposedly demented husband and the more they concentrated on her body, the better.

Zayana and Mikey were confused initially about how Chas Blink kept referring to *ORAL*. They would come to find out that nobody outside this man's office referred to Over the Rainbow Assisted Living that shorthand way. This seemed to provide a clue as to Blink's idiosyncratic thematic preoccupations. He also seemed to possess an effectively endless array of eyewear, including ski-goggles, on his desk, a preliminary indication that he was perennially struggling to achieve perspective.

Zayana sought some clarity of her own: "It's unclear if you are running a nursing home, or assisted living, or skilled nursing, or board-and-care, or a little bit of this and that."

"Little bit of this and that, yes, that's our mission. Actually, our stated mission is: *To serve elderly people like persons.*"

Chas Blink patiently waited for a positive reaction from these quite attractive new candidates for residency who were flesh with cash, he meant *flush*, or at least a sign of minimal brain function from Zelda's companion, Michael. He seemed destined to be disappointed on both scores.

"Nursing home, assisted living, whatever—these are terms bandied about, and there's a smorgasbord of options out there, as I'm sure you are aware, being obviously stylish and educated consumers. We like to think we are all things to all people, but without any of that stupid red tape. We're here to serve older folks as if they were human beings, as our mission stipulates, wheresoever they may fall on the spectrum of specialized need."

Mikey doubted that his and Zayana's highly specialized needs would have been located on any spectrum visible to such a man myopically presiding over the residence. As for medical needs, Mikey's hand still throbbed, and he was continually flexing his fingers, hoping to get back the feeling. He was trying but having trouble making a fist. Maybe he really had broken a couple of bones.

Noticing that, Blink inquired of Michael if he was in discomfort.

Zayana answered: "He took a tumble, landed on his hand, but he'll be okay."

"That's good. I mean, that he's on the mend, that's good. You know, your husband is going to enjoy his happy days with us, Mrs. Jackson," he mentioned to Zayana's mini-skirt. "We know how to make a man with particular health concerns feel at home and cared for—and his long-suffering wife, too. Too often caregivers suffer in silence, but they desire some TLC, too, don't they?" Blink was making all the assumptions Mikey and Zayana wanted him to make—namely that the younger wife of an Alzheimer's-afflicted man might sooner or later prove easy pickings for a person of his dubious power and sophistication. As a result, they hoped, he would be disinclined to analyze too deeply the woman's husband. "True, Michael would be the youngest male villager, and you, Mrs. Jackson, would be by far the youngest woman."

Underlying the executive director's management style was a palpable sadness that anyone in his orbit could not fail to detect. Plainly, this was a world of cognitive deficits and physical and mental disabilities, where some people, the elderly and mentally challenged, needed assistance to go on with what was left of their lives. But Blink's exaggerated sense of self-importance made it impossible for anybody to care about *him*.

The consolation he was currently imagining sweetly lay between this so-called Zelda's impressive breasts, breasts that surely, he presumed, were being ignored by her physically impaired, addle-brained husband.

Christmas had come early, the executive director had no choice but to be thinking. And when a man like Blink, who thinks the chances of this Zelda giving him a shot were excellent—that sort of man could be counted on spending hours staring glaze-eyed at pornography on his encrusted computer with pants down, which is how he spent his hours when not conducting what he liked to call "business."

Blink asked when Mr. and Mrs. Jackson would like to schedule their move in. His eagerness intimated that he was personally available for toting boxes, painting walls, laundering lingerie, whatever was called for.

"No time like the present," said Zayana. "We have our luggage in the Buick, and the sooner my husband begins to receive care at your excellent facility, the better. He's too much for me at home," she said, demurely stifling a fake sniffle.

"Ah, about your car," said Blink. "Would you like to sign over the pink slip, in lieu of rent for a month? This is a service we offer for our customers' convenience. You won't need your own car, because you can employ ORAL vehicles that we make available to our villagers."

Zayana effortlessly sniffed out that scam, and said thanks but no thanks.

"Two months?" he tried.

No dice.

"Then no time like the present, indeed," affirmed Blink, assuming that Zelda was a gold-digger and her husband's trophy wife, a deal that had gone south for her. The essence of ideal opportunity for him, in other words.

"Sounds good."

"I certainly appreciate that, Mrs. Jackson, and even more do I appreciate Mr. Jackson's beautiful wife's fantastic body." The second part of that statement of his was not voiced, but it was reliably communicated nonverbally to every sentient creature in the room, including possibly the pet Gila monster flicking his tongue in the mini-desert housed in the tank located behind Blink. The reptile brain was in universal ascendance at Over the Rainbow, or what Blink insisted upon calling "ORAL."

"We especially like that your facility is unlicensed, and can therefore serve us with flexibility and openness," Zayana said, thereby uttering a view that few if any had expressed prior to today, especially repulsed state investigators.

Mr. Blink was past master, he hoped he conveyed, of flexibility and openness, especially as it pertained to hopeful, to him, marital arrangements.

"Well, we once did have a license, but we were constrained by pestering examiners who nit-picked through our halls day and night, petty violation for this, docked demerits for that, food allegedly not refrigerated, bathrooms supposedly not clean, a string of groundless bedbug charges we refuted over and over dozens of times. Now, we are free to serve our customers—our community, our villagers, I should say, our family—in the style to which they become quickly adjusted. Because as you know, we at ORAL treat old folks..." he said, cueing her.

"Like persons?" Zayana obligingly said.

Blink chuckled. "I notice you didn't list the name of Michael's primary physician." One mystery resolved: he may have had reason to seek recourse in one set of glasses or another, but he could see *that* much.

"That's because we are being assisted by the most powerful force for human health in the whole universe: God. God and I are supervising his medical care. We are Christian Scientists."

Mikey shot her a what-the glance. She was an improviser, wasn't she? He would press her as to what Christian Scientists like they were supposed to be believed when he had the chance.

"Yes," she continued, illuminating Mikey in the process, "we're devoted Christian Scientists who believe in the ultimate healing power of God, who needs no assistance from human hands—or man-made drugs."

"Excellent, totally excellent. And so you will not be tapping the resources of private insurance or Medicare?" His eyes might well have twinkled—impossible to tell behind the donned goggles. "Reason I ask is that sometimes big, cumbersome, heartless bureaucracies have trouble dealing with ORAL."

"Don't you think we've had enough of the nanny state in the care of elders and the sickly? Did I mention we will pay in cash?"

He didn't bat an eyelid (or he could have—again, those goggles prevented ascertaining for sure), not even when she removed an envelope from her purse and counted out the hundreds on his desk, which he scooped up like a croupier at a casino and stuck in his leather pants pocket.

"One other question, strictly a formality, which the board of directors requires me to ask." In truth, there existed no board of directors except in the junky pixelations of the Over the Rainbow website. "Please understand, this is nothing but a formality: Are you private investigators or law enforcement?"

Zayana laughed out loud.

A long moment of silence passed and he reiterated the question: "Well, are you?"

"No," she said cordially, "not at all." Blink noticed that Michael Jackson himself was on the verge of piping up, and he seemed to make a mental note of this.

"I didn't think so, Zelda, if I may call you Zelda, Mrs. Jackson, but thank you so much for humoring my vigilant board of directors."

Zayana said she understood why he would inquire.

"A few more items to tick off my list, Zelda, so we're all on the same page. Any pets or firearms?"

"No cats or dogs," she said. "I love them, but I am allergic."

"And no AK 47s?" Blink said. "Doing the due diligence."

She assured him they did not have automatic weaponry in their possession. She was unaware that Mikey had secreted a few handguns in his luggage. Much as he hated guns, he would be stupid not to be prepared for any exigency, so Mo had hooked him up.

"*Michael?*" Chas Blink turned his attention to Mikey. "*Michael?* Can you understand me, Michael?" He was deploying that overtly self-conscious, sing-songy tone favored by bozos sucking up to strangers' children acting out on mass transit, who detest them heartily as a consequence. "Do you know what's happening?" He didn't follow that with the real question slithering inside: "Do you realize, Michael, it might as well be written out in your contract that once you move in, I will be hitting on your wife day and night?"

Mikey nodded, sharp as a scimitar while he stared into the middle distance.

"Good, Michael. You do understand what's going on, don't you?" He smiled at Zelda. "Very good. Most of our residents are ladies, but in fact there are a small number of nice, relatively high-functioning gentlemen here with early-stage dementia…"

"You'll find," interceded Zayana, "that my poor, dear husband, Michael, will spend all his waking and sleeping hours in the company of his loving wife, so he will be no burden to you and your cracker jack staff. He likes to be read to from the works of Charles Dickens. It's not always easy to tell how much Michael picks up on, but he communicates, nonverbally. I am a pretty capable reader, I was in the theater once." Which was technically true. Some date had taken her one night to see a clunky *Oklahoma!*

Mikey and Zayana coughed one after the other in quick succession, expressing wonderment with regard to this labored book-reading fantasy.

"Certainly that must be delightful to be read to by such a lovely reader like you. You are aware we will herd Michael into social bonding activities, like sing-alongs and bingo and old classic movies, like our most requested movie, *Wizard of Oz*, naturally." Where Michael would be distracted and when the coast would be clear for the executive director. "In no time, a new light will shine in his eyes and, if he is anything like most of our residents, he will see his whole world expand."

There existed the very high likelihood, verging on a mortal certainty, that Mikey was unlike any other resident in the sordid history of Over the Rainbow. He had no interest in expanding his world, and if anybody was unwise enough to shine a light in his eyes, it would be the last deed that unfortunate creature perpetrated in his lifetime. For when it came to his world, he was opposed to any form of expansion. He was signed up for contraction, and living in deep cover for the near future—at least through the November election.

She couldn't contain herself. "Mister Blank," she started to say.

"*Blink*," he gently corrected her, perhaps being accustomed to the predictable mangling of a name that was most unpleasant, if not vaguely embarrassing, for anybody to articulate.

"What?" she asked, unsure of what she was being advised to do.

"'What' what?" he responded.

"You want me to do *what*?"

"Name's Blink, not…" He couldn't bring himself to say it.

"I'm sorry, Mister…Blink."

"Call me Chas, let's not stand on formality, because we'll be spending lots of quality time together and be getting to know each other well."

"Mister Blink, Michael is not much for socializing."

"We don't think of it as socializing, we think of it as therapy."

"You have a psychotherapist in residence?" She might as well feign interest in a subject or two.

"Glad you asked. Yes, we do. Me! I furnish all the counseling, individual and conjugal—I mean, for the couple."

Counseling was not in the cards, either. "Good to know that that's what *conjugal* means, but in terms of group activity, Michael isn't a joiner. He likes to hear his books, likes his music, likes to be in the company of his wife…"

"I can imagine! A man named Michael Jackson *would* like his music. But our activities can be a *thriller*, too, if you catch my drift, PYT. He doesn't have to be a *man in the mirror.*" The executive director appeared perilously on the verge of bursting into song. And then, that's what he did. *"Billie Jean's not my lover… She's just a girl… But the kid is not my son."*

They waited for Mr. Blink to rise up and moonwalk. Perhaps fortunately, he did not accommodate this desire. Though not because he wasn't wearing pants today. He wore his leather trousers with new customers—that is, new villagers.

"All right then," said Zayana, forging a transition.

"Dig that song," said Blink.

"I can tell," she said.

"*Billie Jean's…*" he tried again, reasserting a point that particularly resonated for him.

"Mr. Blank," she said, endeavoring to curtail the reverie.

"Blink."

The supposedly conjugal union sighed, conveying a message of *let's not go there again, please.*

ଔ

THE UNKNOCKED OFFICE DOOR swung open and in barged an elderly lady using a walker for stability, so obviously she was an Over the Rainbow resident.

"Jason!" the villager said with blood-curdling authority.

"Yes, Ernestina." He added as an aside to the Jackson Two: "She insists on claiming I am her husband Jason. The man died last year when he wandered off ORAL grounds and met with a car recklessly speeding down the road...long sad story of an accident in which we bore no legal responsibility."

"Jason, where'd you hide my dentures?" Her toothlessness communicated the conviction that she missed them.

"Ernestina, you know you lost your dentures during the community hoedown when you..."

"You like your hoes down, don't you, Jason? Alla the time you, your jaunts to Vegas..."

"Come on, Ernestina deary, be nice."

"Too many blow jobs, that's why you got rid of my dentures, and you were scared because one time, little too energetic..."

Blink looked vaguely titillated to hear the BJ evoked here at ORAL. "Ernie, come on, Ernie."

"Too much kissing, that's how I lost my dentures, as you know. Too much kissing and sexualalatyness"—that last mangled word not easy to say denturelessly, but she somehow managed. The aged woman turned her attention to the couple and passed along her public service announcement: "The rate of venereal disease around here is through the roof, just so you know. They should pass out penicillin like mints on the pillow."

"Now's not the time, Ernestina," Blink said with a crestfallen glance, and looked fearfully at Zayana for her reaction, steeling himself to be quizzed right this minute as to any possible pandemics.

That's when Michael stunned everyone in the room including himself when he bellowed out "Wow!" He couldn't resist. It was the first thing he said during this let's-get-acquainted meeting.

He had voiced the only suitable, to him, exclamation to remark upon the shocking arrival of a buxom blonde attendant who had that instant bounced into Blink's office. She must have been in her early twenties, and the skirt she was wearing was so abbreviated that a loin cloth would have employed more fabric.

"There you are, Ernie girlfriend," bubbled the blonde, throatily, sweetly. "You gotta keep from scuttling off, sweetheart, every time I turn my backside." Scuttling off using a walker seemed like the remotest possibility, but evidence was mounting to indicate that flight seemed to the preferred activity of both Ernestina and her late, last-seen-alive-while-fleeing husband. Then again, flight might have been indicated for a man in the predicament his widow's demeanor inflicted upon him.

"Look who's here, Ernestina," said Blink. "Carololina's here to take you out to trim the rose bushes."

"Carolina..." she tried.

"*Carololina*," he corrected.

"What kinda butcher baby name is that?"

"The kind of name that is her name," he said with a we've-been-over-this-a-million-times impatience. "Carololina is from Idaho." As if that geographical detail was freighted with psycho-biographical significance. As if it is a truth universally acknowledged that a blonde bombshell hailing from Idaho is named not Carolina but instead Carololina. The identification of her birthplace somehow induced an uneasiness throughout the office, as if some compromising photo had been distributed.

"I can't say that name, 'specially without dentures. Whatever her name is. She is a sweet piece of ass. You banging that, too?"

Ernestina seemed to be onto the secret life of Mr. Blank.

Blink!

"But about trimming them bushes. She's always looking hard at my bush when she puts me in the shower every month, whether I need one or not. Ain't you jealous? Don't I make your plant grow no more?"

"I am, I really am jealous, but I think Carololina is looking out for you today, so we will see each other at dinner." He arched his eyebrows in the direction of the attendant, laying claim to her in the process, to which she readily acceded with her own elevated, severely plucked eyebrows.

"Dinner! Tuna fuck-all surprise," Ernestina said. "I saw the menu posted on the bulletin, more like bullshitting, board. Surprise is, there's as much tuna in the dish as there are brains in your foreclosed noggin, Jason. Look at me. Put on some of your glasses and looka me."

He gave up. Ernestina lumbered off reluctantly with Carololina, not before yelling back over her shoulder: "Lemme see you whip it out, Jason!"

"You forgot your walker."

"Bag the walker. You need it more'n me." And she and her ravishing handler were soon gone.

◌

"DEMENTIA TAKES MANY FORMS," observed Blink in the Ernestina aftermath, with as much professionalism as he, or any other charlatan, might manage upon the occasion of being urged to expose himself. "For Ernestina, as you can tell, it takes on a hypersexualized character, when her meds are hitting her like a nine iron. This acting out is par for the course, or at least it isn't unusual for somebody in Ernie's advanced condition."

"Interesting," said Zayana, though it might not be. "But there you are, saw it for myself, treating that elderly woman almost like a person."

"Thank you for noticing. It's my calling, to work with those who need me to be by their side, struggling with challenges that growing older..."

"So we good to go?" interrupted Zayana.

"And much better to stay!"

The Jackson Two shook their heads. Living here was going to be like shooting fish in a barrel, though this Chas Blink was one slimy eel.

"A couple of other formalities. We have our resident medical expert here, to give you both a check-up, you know, to verify you don't have TB or any other communicable diseases. But I'm not worried about you, Zelda, you'll be the youngest, firmest-body person here."

"Medical expert?" said Zayana. *Zelda!* "You mean, like, a doctor?"

"We try to keep expenses down while delivering all the key services to support our villagers in the manner to which we'd like them to grow accustomed—so, no, not, like, a doctor, but we have a medical specialist, who was once a nursing student, somebody we rely on to supervise the health and safety of the entire village. But this will be a minimally invasive evaluation of your health status."

"Good," said Zayana, "because as I mentioned, we are Christian Scientists." Last thing they needed was somebody around who possibly *knew* anything, but the chances of such an employee gainfully retained at Over the Rainbow were rapidly approaching nil.

"It will all work out, Zelda, these boring formalities. Let me show you guys your apartment now, which is tastefully and fully furnished."

As they headed down the hallway to where they would take up residence, with Chas far in the lead, Mikey whispered to Zayana, "The dog pound's gotta be more organized."

She hooked her arm into his. She pulled him down to her mouth's level and whispered into his ear: "Perfect or what?"

He was two steps ahead of her along the corridor. A hundred steps ahead of her in reality. The day would come when they would leave this place and go their separate ways and she and Jeremiah would be safe. Then he'd have the proper peace of mind to knock himself off once and for all.

TWO YEARS LATER

CAREGIVER LOG

Use this form to monitor changes and to communicate with doctors, hospice nurses and caregivers across shifts.

PATIENT: *MICHAEL FESTAGIACAMO (age 59)*

CAREGUVER: *N.B. Caregiver not "careguver"—typo on the form. Thank you. Winona Wilder is on the job.*

DATE/TIME: *Sunday Morning.*

NOTE CHANGES: *I am noticing that Michael grows calmer by the day. I wonder if seeing his sister Rosetta lately accounts for why. He does seem to brighten up visibly when she is in his room. He reaches for her very lovingly. And when she leaves, he touches my hand and my arm, with affection. I am always moved.*

FOOD: *Ate like a bear.*

MEDICATION: *As indicated and prescribed.*

ACTIVITIES: *Moving around almost fluidly.*

PAIN LEVEL: *Minimal, non-existent?*

ENERGY: *Steady.*

SLEEP PATTERN: *He sleeps! No longer sundowning. My notes: Is it possible that I am witnessing Michael's renaissance? His mood seems to be on the upswing, for which I feel so grateful if I have played any part. Diana (?), his health care manager, always illuminates me, and I am ready to learn new tricks. I feel very grateful for the opportunity to serve this kind, elderly gentleman.*
—WW

TWO YEARS LATER

To: Rosetta Festagiacamo
From: Dinah Forte
Subject: Grace (and Winona) Abounding

Dear Rosetta,

Winona is a star! They all call her Mary Poppins around the nursing home. Which I don't think has anything to do with her school-teacherly clothes or carrying around a sun umbrella or putting up her hair in a tight bun, and I think it's meant as a compliment. I mean, yes, she likes to sing to Mikey, and she says that she lullabies him to sleep at night. Sleep! He's finally sleeping! Just a spoon full of sugar helps the medicine go down! And that British accent is pure melody. Hallelujah!

Warmly yours,

DPF
Dinah Penelope Forte, PhD
Forte Care Management Professionals

Chapter Twenty-Four

All new villagers—which is how understaffed personnel cozily referred to the assorted gummers and drifters, the dandruffed, the sauce-stained, the abandoned-by-cruel-fate denizens of Over the Rainbow—all new villagers would perforce go through a period of adjustment. That was to be expected. And the experience was unique for each villager. It was not all smooth sailing for anybody. Anger could ambush them. Disappointment could put up its big top tent. Denial could bushwhack. Confusion could reign. And some would barely notice that they had been uprooted and transplanted by their families, who either could not handle them as a result of their difficult requirements, or who had had more than enough, thank you very much, of grandma or grandpa—and had the disposable income to get somebody else to babysit, even if it was at Over the Rainbow. Nobody would comment that those were the ideal customers, but that was only because it was obvious.

Thus it happened that Michael and Zelda Jackson became *villagers*. Did that mean they were also village people who were allegedly treated as village persons? They would soon be finding out.

Before Blank had left them to their own devices at the door of their new apartment home, he several times reminded Zayana: "ORAL

Orientation is Job One." Mikey picked up on Blank's telegraphed designs on Zayana, and also on himself, as how could he not? He may have been mildly impaired cognitively or, as he feared, early-stage Alzhammer. He was not a dope. Obviously, after Blink's proposed oral orientation of Zayana (good luck), Blank's Job Two was self-evident: siphon off their money.

Mikey and Zayana's second-floor digs overlooked a dry creek bed where, like gut-shot deer, supermarket shopping carts and tires wandered off to die. A few scrawny trees dotted the mostly vacant parking lot beyond, in which no self-respecting member of the avian species seemed to *tweet tweet tweet* a carefree, joyous, proprietary interest. The curtains on the window were Daughters of the American Revolution–vintage soiled white muslin, and the walls were dusky toadstool, the shadings of a fungal biker bar at end of the night. The TV was on life-support, and the microwave couldn't be discouraged from emitting a flashing blue light, and the dining area card table had lost one of its legs, and a ceiling light needed a replacement bulb, or two, to brighten the mood of any mole in residence. The kitchen cabinet was packed with cracked dishes and the counter tops were laden with fraying binders jammed with packets of obsolete or worthless information. There were indelibly stained tea cups and a drawer of tea spoons, but no knives or forks. The soap dispenser was bone dry. No ashtrays, of course. A snippy little *No Smoking* plaque had been glued to the door, but Zayana pried it off, freeing herself in theory to smoke any time she wanted.

"All the comforts of home," said Mikey.

"If you lived in an atomic bomb test site."

"Eggs-ackly."

"Shall we go to dinner?" She studied the front page of the Over the Rainbow bulletin, which featured the menu. "Salsburied steak, green peas...both of which sound appalling. If not appealing."

"I was looking forward to tuna surprise."

"Also says we get '*sop*' du jour, the idiots, and an item called '*Nealopolitan*' ice cream."

Mikey wondered if Dolly conceived the menu.

"Tetanus booster for dessert?"

"Hey, Z, had a question. Where's the boy tonight?"

Maybe she wasn't hearing him clearly.

"I mean, where'd Jeremiah go? He got a date?"

No, she *was* hearing him correctly. "You sent him off with Rosey and Mo. Remember?"

Damn, she realized that was what *not* to say. Rosey instructed her not to call attention to his memory slips. Move forward, calmly, positively, filling in the empty spaces, reducing his anxiety in the process.

"Oh, sure, I remember. Where'd I send them again?"

"It's okay, where you sent him, he's safe."

"Which is more than I can say about what kind of food's for dinner. A guy's gotta eat, I guess."

So that was a new experience for Zayana. The first time she witnessed for herself what Rosetta had given her a heads up about. This could have been a momentary glitch for him. And he did seem to scramble back to surer footing practically immediately. These transient moments of disconnection were to be expected, according to Rosetta. No need to panic.

At the same time, she was going to stay on the alert for any subtle, sudden shifts in his mental state. Rosetta had given her tips as to how to cope. Keep it simple, she advised Zayana. Don't be obvious observing him, analyzing, evaluating. And if he needs help putting on his clothes, say, or shaving, don't make a big deal. According to his sister, he was probably at the early, early stages of mild cognitive impairment, she could not say for sure—and took pains to minimize his relentless stated dread of already having been slammed by the Alzhammer. Worst case, this was a long, long process, and for days, weeks, months, conceivably years, he could well be very stable, which were considerations ultimately irrelevant for Zayana: not to be blunt, though she was, all she required was getting Mikey and herself through the upcoming election. He would appear normal for long stretches, Rosetta advised, whatever normal passed for in the life of a mobster on the run from unhinged killers. There may be challenges, of course. When he loses the thread, walk him back, gently. Make sure he gets plenty of sleep. She would be surprised how a good night's rest would help him stay on a level keel. Most important: stay close and keep your eyes and ears open. When he is under stress, when he feels pressure, that's conceivably when he will falter, so keep it simple. If one day he becomes impossible to manage, Rosetta had made her a solemn promise. She would fly to the rescue.

CR

THE TWO NEW RESIDENTS looked around the dining room, which would have been silent as a morgue if it weren't for the piped-in faux pop music of generations past bouncing off the peeling, floral wallpaper.

Mikey asked Zayana if they were expected to eat in silence. She didn't think so, but then again she wasn't positive. Her experience of old folks homes was, she mentioned needlessly, incomplete. "They might cover the subject in ORAL orientation, which I hear tell is Job One." She also wasn't certain if anybody in the whole residence had much they were inclined to, or much they were able to, say. For instance, next table over, an eight-top, all the diners were bent over their plates, their necks hanging like turkey vultures, and moving the food around as if they were panning for the gold nuggets they were not going to find. Some were using spoons, others forks, others knives. "At least," she said under her breath, "they're using utensils and not their fingers. Speaking of which, how's your hand?"

"Christian Scientists take aspirin?"

"Don't think so."

"Took six."

"We should go see a doctor, get an x-ray. Though I don't believe Christian Scientists allow them, so we won't tell."

He studied his hand in front of his face. The fingers looked mangled and bent.

"Really, Mikey, that doesn't look too good."

He instantly tired of the subject.

After he and she took a stab at the meat—he used his left hand to clumsily manipulate the fork—they were convinced of one thing and one thing only: limited calorie-consumption lay in their future.

"We can go out for Chinese or pizza," she proposed. "What kinda town doesn't have Chinese and pizza?"

"Hey, Z, look around."

"Do I have to?"

"What do you see?"

"One thing I can say for sure is, it ain't Fashion Week in Manhattan."

"Zombies. We're surrounded by zombies."

She concurred. "But let's not give ourselves up, let's act like zombies, too, so they don't catch on."

At this point, somebody arrived at their table and welcomed them to Over the Rainbow. He was wearing a once-upon-a-time white apron that was stained with multiple colors, some of them not recognizably comestible-related, all of them unappetizing. "I'm Eddie, head waiter." He wore a black net cap. "Also head cook. salsburied steak is a house spesh-e-al-ah-tee, you like?"

"Yum," said Zayana with as much counterfeit ambiguity as she could muster.

Eddie looked toward Mikey, who added nothing.

"He's kinda shy, my darling husband."

"Oh, I understand. Women are mostly the talkers around here. Mr. Blink said you would spice up the whole place. I also lead the exercise class and drive the van down to the mall, where you can shop. You need anything, van leaves everyday at ten from out front."

"We'll see you at the van, or for a workout if my husband Michael has the energy."

"You look in good enough shape to lead the class—Zelda's your name, right? And I say class, but honest, when I say 'class,' it'd probably be you and me."

"I will keep active however I can." Or she would lose her own mind.

"You missed today, but everyday four o'clock we have happy hour in the rec room, don't forget to be there, Mr. Blink pours the good stuff, especially when we have new business—I mean new villagers to welcome into the fold."

When Eddie the waiter thankfully departed, Mikey leaned over the table toward Zayana and said, "You know they're all zombies here, right?"

Okay, he was repeating himself. Did that constitute another development? "I take your point," said Zayana, "but so what?"

"Isn't that great?"

She wondered, honestly wondered, why he seemed so happy. Here they were, holed up in an old folks home that was run by a lunatic and a deviate and a possible predator, and they were being served third-world-rejected food. Did he fall on his head when she wasn't looking?

At the same time, it dawned on him that it had been a long time since that early morning when he had idled his car on the tracks and waited for his ticket to be punched on the celestial railroad. That was for all practical purposes another person behind the wheel that early morning of that strange day. But if that was so, if he had traded places with somebody else, who was he now, who? And what happened to the Mercedes? He missed that car.

"Hey, Z, I'm in the mood for some cracked crab, you?"

She didn't think there was a fish market within a hundred miles and as far as she could remember, it was the wrong season for Dungeness anyway.

"Sounds good." She played along.

"Whaddaya say I teach Jeremiah tonight how to cook your favorite pasta, cracked crab with penne in pink vodka sauce?"

"I always liked that dish."

"Yeah, and 'bout time I show the boy the fastest way to a girl's heart—her stomach."

"The second fastest way to something like a girl's heart, but good idea, let's both work on that."

ଔ

NEXT MORNING, AFTER A good night's sleep (Zayana in windowless bedroom no fire department would approve, Mikey on mossy couch no health department would sanction), they went back into the dining room for breakfast. One day in, life was starting to feel like a rut already. Now they were invited to feast upon the heaped offerings of charred bacon and runny eggs to their hearts' content. Their hearts were instantaneously discontented.

"How can you screw up bacon and eggs?" he said.

"On the bright side, at least there's a lot of food."

"Fatso would be in hog heaven," Mikey said. "Except for the egg part and the toast."

She didn't know anybody by that colorful name. He informed her he was the one member of the crew in addition to Mo who had not betrayed him.

"Long list of turncoats you got going, Mikey."

He hoped Zayana's name wasn't going to lengthen the list one day. God, he hated lists. Which brought up a vexing topic. Whatever happened to the batch of Post-its he had purchased?

☙

AFTERWARD, ZAYANA HAD A plan to deposit him in the monkey pit that passed for a recreation room. This place was easy to identify on account of the high-school-pep-club, happy-days-are-here-again banner hanging unconvincingly on the far wall: RAINBOW REC RM! The banner sagged severely at the corner, and from across the way all you could read was RAINBOW REC, which seemed telling.

The rec room seemed a popular destination, evidently the place to be seen—or in Mikey's case, not to be—as thirty or so villagers in various stages of semi-undress and non-compos-mentis were settled down for a long post-breakfast snore, self-natter, or slobber. The space was also remarkable for the overriding scent that turned his stomach, and he struggled to identify that ripe stench. Had they one and all pissed themselves? Had they all been pre-embalmed? Whatever the explanation, the whole room suffered at a minimum from a serious case of morning mouth. Did Chas Blink hire any custodians? If so, they were operating sub nosa.

The villagers appeared to be strictly on their own, left to their own insufficiency of devices, because there was no apparent supervision, and therefore no assistance was available should somebody keel over and require, say, CPR or a bandage for a boo boo. Zayana was going to use the gym, take her chances. She hadn't worked out for a while, and she would take a look at the facilities and break a sweat if the treadmill and weight machines functioned. She bent down to Mikey on the couch so nobody else could hear, as if overhearing was what the villagers were capable of, or interested in.

"Good news. Bingo begins any minute."

"Glad I got my cyanide pill."

"Can I count on you to keep your trap shut?"

Mikey vowed as much as he hunkered down on his perch on the only unoccupied and tattered couch and assessed his beleaguered surroundings. According to his preliminary assessment, only one of the residents appeared to notice Zayana, and that resident invested committed energy into such noticing by tracking her with his eyes across and out of the room. Then the man swiveled around and aimed a point blank dagger of a stare at Mikey that communicated something between "You lucky damn duck" and "What the hell are you trying to get away with?"

Mikey filed away that reconnaissance information for later degustation, as the emboldened looker kept training his gimlet sights on him. The man was another formidable-looking big guy, with tattoos on his forearms and a scratched straw fedora on top of his head and lots of glistening teeth, except for one front tooth, which was on permanent sabbatical, and he was the only one in the room who appeared observant enough to notice anything. He also conveyed a prepossessing disposition: as if to radiate his conviction that this village belonged to him, no interlopers permitted. It was a look that Mikey knew well, having continually exercised it in the past in the implementation of his own best business practices.

It was a spacious, open room with windows shut, and the ceiling was crushing down on Mikey with fluorescent illumination, and the TV was set on high volume to an insipid cable news show ideal for the memory-challenged, because the same "news" items recycled every ten minutes. Mikey never could understand why people wasted their life watching such time-filling crap. Then again, given the current circumstances, what difference would time-filling crap make here at Over the Rainbow? It wasn't like he was surrounded by budding software engineers or Tour de France racers in training.

Then the pace in the rec room slipped into frenetic, at least by Rainbow's standards. One of the residents shuffled over to the scruffy, bedented baby grand piano in her white bunny bedroom slippers and assumed a seat on the bench. The buttons of her flower-patterned housecoat were misaligned and she had applied a carnival-kewpie-doll quantity of rouge on her cheeks, which apparition made Mikey feel unaccountably sad for the poor old woman. She squinted and looked down through askew taped-up glasses at the keys as if she were fearful of the presence of contaminating E. coli, and for all anybody knew, there might have been such rec rm contagion. A bang-up rendition of "Moon River" or "New York, New York" did not seem imminent.

But then, but then…a miracle. She started to play, and play quite intricately and beautifully. He was no talent agent or music critic and this wasn't Carnegie Hall, but damn, the old gal was a marvelously gifted pianist. It was no junky pop standard or show tune she was playing, either. If he had to guess, it was—he was a good two galaxies out of his element—classical music, like from the operas his dad probably listened to while being chauffeured around by Mo.

He was eagerly steeling himself to rise to a standing ovation when she finished her number—low profile be damned. Unfortunately for the pianist, nobody in the room seemed to be impressed, or to care, or to be faintly pleased for that matter to be gently washed over by such sweet melody. In fact, it did not take long before a churlish, jowly villager stormed up to the piano and wordlessly pointed to the TV screen, indicating that the piano tinklings were irritating and distracting. The woman evidently preferred to hear news about LA freeway traffic or Pakistan bombings or thirty-minute dinner recipes, the typical manic mélange of rumors and dispatches and briefings and images that amounted to the arcane routine of the self-congratulating televised cable news entertainment racket. And of course, there was also a sixty-second clip featuring the senator, whose face he recognized and who was grinning and spinning tales before his rallying throng like he got lucky, which with any luck at all, would not be the case for the candidate. Mikey couldn't escape the guy. At the same time, he hoped that wouldn't ultimately be true.

The piano player took the critique to heart and ceased, another artist wounded by rejection. She remained seated on the bench, hands over the keys, as if the instrument needed to be kept warm and comforted.

At this cheerless juncture, the memorable Carololina emanating from the great L-shaped state of Idaho materialized. She sauntered through the room as if she were auditioning for a role in a very low-budget movie of a certain genre, like the kind where a take-out delivery guy gets stunned by somebody with physical assets like Carololina who answers the door in her white nurse's uniform, and the next thing you know they are both on a stained divan doing the grim dirty in close-up wide angle HD unforgiving of dermatological imperfections, while bad, sad rock music serves as background to the flesh-slapping rhythms. As for that white nurse's uniform—was Carololina really a nurse? Somehow Mikey doubted her life had taken that career course. He was convinced that Over the Rainbow wouldn't have budgeted for an honest-to-God professional nurse. At the same time, he did not doubt her excellent taste in uniforms, which uniform strained credulity as much as the garment's seams strained to bust free. When her promenade carried her out of the room in a minute or an hour, hard to tell which as she glided out, the space felt somehow emptier than it should have been. Her absolute indifference sizzled, the implosion of charisma.

In a flash, Carololina conducted a return sojourn into the rec room, only now she had a flannel throw over one of her impressive, bare forearms. She was heading straight toward Mikey, and when she arrived she knelt down before him in her white uniform, and as her body lowered and retracted she resembled a nuclear-meltdown of a French vanilla ice cream cone. In the process, he was afforded an unobstructed view of her majestic cleavage, which seemed from his privileged vantage point to be inhuman or possibly superhuman. He was physically closer to her than he would have ever dreamt. It was a long time since he had familiarized himself with breasts remotely like that in his close visual field—including Zayana's, renewed proximity to which he supposed would be strictly disallowed.

"Michael," she spoke to him in a smoky, raspy, husky voice reminiscent of Zayana, specifically Z in the throes—in the erotic throes of what they once knew of intimacy. That was when her voice dropped several registers, when she indulged in the alternately titillating and disquieting habit of conducting a type of monologue, which used to distract and simultaneously concentrate his attention, and which now he realized he craved and missed, and he wondered if he would hear Z's guttural gutter talk again. He had no justification to be anything but skeptical.

It had been a long time since he had been sexually pertinent to anybody, much less Zayana. He would never grow accustomed to that superannuated status, but then—what could he do about it? That party was over.

"You need this blanket," said Carololina. She gently placed the moth-eaten cover over his lap, in the process draping it over his blooming erection, which rose up like an undergirded pillar. "My goodness. I like seeing you, too," she said, imperfectly concealing a demure, vanquishing smile.

Mikey shifted his eyes from the stupendous décolletage long enough to notice a few aspects of Carololina that had thus far eluded him. Carololina had large shoulders to support those big breasts, and cruelly dominant cheekbones, and a subtly prominent Adam's apple and a faint shadow of stubble above the lip, and a nose that was a little too broad at the base.

News flash. Could it be true? Yes, it could. Carololina might be a Carl-olina, a very pretty Carl-olina, a very sexy Carl-olina indeed, but a Carl-ish-ina babe nonetheless. Then she, or he, or *they* rose up and hip-slinked away, his/her ankles thicker than Mikey had detected before, his/her calves and thighs powerfully driving her forward. *Wait till I tell Z*, he thought, as he waited for his tumescence to subside, which was taking much longer than he would have expected given the fresh data download.

ೞ

THIS EXCHANGE TRANSPIRED OUTSIDE the mental purview of all but one of the residents, most of whom sat passively, vegetatively, continuing to stare at the television screen. The rec room shelves were packed with board games like Monopoly, but nobody was playing them and rolling the dice all the way to Boardwalk and Park Avenue and collecting their Get Out of Jail Free cards, which would have been a boon around here. On one table a card game was going on, however.

One of the participants, the only man of the foursome, had tracked Zayana when she appeared and had executed his territorial stare in Mikey's direction, was clearly in command, and he seemed much more lucid than the others, not that this was saying much insofar as those competing countenances were frozen, full-body-Botox-like. They were playing poker, and each of them had a stack of plastic chips.

The man calling the shots, who was easily twice the size of any of the women, dealt out the hand, and only after that, he looked at his cards and announced the rules: "Sevens and eights wild, ladies."

Nobody argued, perhaps nobody understood. *What an evil clown,* thought Mikey, *taking advantage of these aged people and not treating them at all like persons,* which was the Over the Rainbow's mission, as the man reached under his hat and not-so-surreptitiously pulled out a card, a douchey move which went undetected by the table.

"How many cards you need, hot stuff?"

"Five?"

"You can't have five, puddin'…never mind, take five cards, won't matter anyway."

He went around the table. The betting commenced, and it was chaotic, one of the women shoving into the pot a single chip, while the others went all in with their chips, giddy and bewildered.

That's when the dealer threw down his cards and announced, "Read 'em and weep, geriatric head cases. Five Jackos, and I win, thank you very much." The players expressed little disappointment in the outcome— or comprehension.

Why should they care, Mikey wondered, *what else was there to do?* You win, you lose, what difference does it make over the rainbow? Time goes by, and that was the object, if there was one. Then the dealer noticed Mikey observing him, and once again the man took the measure of the new resident.

"Newbie," he addressed Mikey, "your pretty daughter left you here all lonely, poor mutt that you are."

Mikey stared back.

The villager was intending to have some fun at Mikey's expense. "But maybe she's your girl, your wife?"

Mikey nodded, ambiguously.

The villager addressed the captive table: "I think the newbie misses his squeeze, such a pretty wife, if they're hitched. Think he wants to play cards with us?"

Mikey rearranged the blanket.

"Hey, newbie got a woody! Carololina'll do that to a man, won't she? Proves you *are* a man, which is more than I can say about most of us around here. If you have an erection lasting three hours, see your doctor, or Ernestina. Tell you what," he said, showing the deck of cards, "want a piece of this action?"

Mikey did not reply and pretended to be amused.

"Speak up. You want to play a game of chance, which would be too bad on account when it comes to my dealing, you got no chance. *None* chance."

Mikey couldn't resist. Without saying a word, he got up, now gratefully detumescent, disposed of the blanket, and took a seat in an available chair.

"What'll we play, newbie? Five card stud, which name reminds me of me?" He didn't wait for an answer. "Five card stud it is. I deal."

Mikey had other notions. One good thing about the absence of supervision was, he could get away with anything.

"Five card stud," he said, "but newbie deals." There was no Blink and no Carololina and no Eddie around, so nobody would see him blowing his cover.

"Talkative, ain't he, people? Okay, newbie, you deal."

Mikey shuffled the deck and dealt the cards, one down and one face up. He had a three in his hand and an ace showing. "Threes are wild," he said.

His opponent was irritated, impressed against his better judgment but also irritated. Mikey won.

"You got a name, newbie?"

"I got two."

"Let me tell you mine. It's Hercules. Suck on that pill."

Mikey broke into laughter. He tried to stifle himself, but he failed.

"You think my name's funny? You think it'll be funny say I smack you around?"

"No. But it would be unusual, because it ain't gonna happen."

"You got any money on you?"

"Plenty."

"Fork it over, I need it."

"You got any money on *you*, Hercules?"

"I got what I need. But I also need yours."

"Let me break it to you. Starting right here, right now, right with me, you ain't gonna to be getting what you need. Might as well get used to it."

"I'm going to cut you some slack, on account you're a newbie, but I'm in charge around here. Not boneheaded Blink, not sex riot Carololina, not dweebish Eddie, not nobody but me. Got that straight?"

"So you are the boss of the undead?"

"You could say that, you *could* say that, but don't."

"So you really are boss zombie?"

"You're a very bold newbie." He threw in his cards, game over, it was no fun anymore. He pulled back his chair. "I wouldn't walk down the corridor at night by myself if I was you." And Hercules stood up, using his cane, which was adorned at the top with, to Mikey, a most unusual grip.

"What's that?" said Mikey, pointing.

"That's a gen-you-wine bull penis."

"For when you don't have your own dick in your hand?"

The resident's attitude underwent instant adjustment. "You're funny. I think you and me, we'll get along beautiful. I think I like you. Just so you know, they drop like flies here in the village, so no need to make friends, 'cause they don't last. Have a nice day." He theatrically tipped his hat. A king of hearts fell to the floor.

Mikey couldn't help it. He kind of liked the guy, too.

CR

MIKEY MADE HIS WAY back to the apartment, where Zayana was napping.

"You awake? You won't guess." He blurted out the shocking Carololina revelation.

She hated to be jolted awake. "You bother me to tell me that?"

She would want to hear a bombshell, wouldn't she?

"God, men are so slow. You only now figured that out about her?"

Chapter Twenty-Five

Sunday meant Visiting Day, so trumpeted Over the Rainbow's bulletin board. Mikey sat down in the lobby, where visitors were not standing in line to come in, hand out pastries, and pay their respects. He watched football on the lobby TV, already dreading dinner and the latest incarnation of Salisbury steak.

Zayana remained upstairs, too depressed by her living conditions to get out of bed. She had begun to complain a lot, and it took longer and longer for her to come around, longer and longer before remembering this remained the most viable option for her under the circumstances. When she lapsed into a mood like that, Mikey wandered away, hoping she'd feel okay by the time he came back, hopes not always rewarded. Blink was not keeping close tabs on him, or anyone besides, perhaps, Carololina or Ernestina, so Mikey could afford to take his chances walking around by himself.

It was halftime of the boring game and since noon there had been zero visitors for Visiting Day. Last thing Mikey wished for was visitors, of course. At the same time, he felt sorry for all the Over the Rainbow people who were unvisited.

Then he had some company. He was joined by the fellow who had been busting his chops during the rec rm card game.

"Mind if I join you, newbie?"

"You like football?"

"Who doesn't? Truce?"

Mikey didn't mind agreeing to the terms of a cease fire, and a little conversation might spice up his day.

"Nice hat," said Mikey, referring to the man's fedora. "Not every man can wear that type hat."

"It's mine, is why."

"You got change for a twenty?" Mikey didn't really need the change, but he wanted to see what the man would do with the question, to assess where he was mentally and to determine whether or not he was dealing with a long-term problem resident or not.

"Butthead Blink says we're not allowed to carry cash, which you might have heard, but screw him."

Then in arthritically inflected motion the man awkwardly reached into his pocket and pulled out wrinkled and what looked like much-laundered faded paper currency, the possession of which, as he explained, was strictly against those ignorable, strict house rules. No cash was the law, because cash was supposedly a bad temptation for the underpaid help. The man counted out the ten and the five and rest in dollar bills, and Mikey tested him by putting the money into his own pocket and not handing over his twenty.

The man laughed, a hollow, good-natured *ho ho ho.* "Reminds me of the trick I taught my grandson. He says he might visit me someday, though this Visiting Day don't look like it qualifies, including not for his parents, who put me here when I gave them too much trouble, which they called carousing, but which I called living and breathing. I'd go to the boy when he was a little guy, 'Buster, wanna see a magic trick?' And he'd go, 'Sure, Grampy.' 'I can make a dollar bill disappear into thin air. Gimme a buck, Buster.' And he forked it over, and I put it into my pocket.

'See? It disappeared.' Good kid, that Buster. Eventually, we changed places and anytime he'd need some cash, he'd ask if I wanted to see a magic trick. It was nice, long time ago, before I got sentenced into this shit hole."

He and Mikey had gotten off on the wrong foot the other day, so he reintroduced himself. Do-overs were important in life. Mikey hadn't experienced any of those yet, but he was hoping the day would come.

"Good to meet you, name's Hercules."

"Yeah, you told me in the rec room. That's quite a name to live up to, *Hercules*."

"Got me into scrapes when I was younger, yes sir, but which you know I looked forward to them. I don't much look like it now, but I could handle myself pretty good back in the day. I still can. Throwing punches keeps you focused. Sometimes I go to the exercise room and hit the heavy bag a few times—on the bad days. I may be an old man but I can handle myself, a little bit. Call me Herc."

Mikey was not the type to doubt such self-promotion or his name.

"You keep flexing your hand, Mikey. I see you can't make a fist, you hurt yourself?"

"Long story."

"My hands hurt sometimes, too, arthritis, from the old days in the ring. You know what I do that helps?" Hercules pulled out of his jacket pocket a tennis ball and tossed it to Mikey. "Squeeze on that, you might feel better."

Mikey experimented, nothing to lose. Did feel pretty good.

"Keep the ball, I got a lot of them."

Hercules explained how he arrived in the village ten years ago. "Not like I got anywhere else to go, with my bad ticker and my brain going maple-oatmealier by the day. Next week, birthday number seventy-nine, my boy might could visit, but I'm not putting a candle in the window. Seems like he lost the map here since the day he dropped me off, threw me in the dumpster. But my grandkid, Buster, one day he'll come through. The whole bunch, he's the one that phones time to time, that Buster."

"Family," said Mikey, philosophically.

"Another word for people who let you down when you're old and got nowhere else to go," said Hercules.

"You never know, sometimes people change." Mikey was thinking about Rosey, how she came around—and did that count as a do-over? "Bet the grandson, someday he'll come visit you."

"I think he will, and it'll be a first. Here's the crazy thing. The kid I used to walk around in the stroller, that kid I used to change his diapers, the kid I taught how to shoot a .22, that kid? That kid's a grown-ass gangbanger. His tattoos have their own tattoos. Now he has weapons I wouldn't know from how to use. He runs a whole crew in Long Beach, which is a very tough town. But he's always been sweet to me. I hope he stays outta prison, don't kill nobody. And you know what? I like that kid better than my son. My son made so much money. He's a real estate developer, which I think means he steals other people's property."

"There you go, Herc. The kid'll walk in the door when you least expect it, you never know." Mikey surprised himself. He didn't know where his sunshiny optimism—if it was sunshiny or optimism—was coming from.

Hercules turned his eyes toward the front door and changed the subject. Family was always a gloomy subject.

"Eddie, he's a talker, you met that wart-face mongrel. He told me about you and your wife, who's very pretty, if you don't mind my say so. Don't trust him, is what I say. Word spreads, I was going to say fast, but nothing spreads fast around here 'cepting death and venereal disease and more than a couple times food poisoning, which since everybody's here's mostly all already in the land of permanent *what was that again?* they already forgot. One interesting thing. Since there's about one goose for fifteen ganders, well, you do the math. Most of these gals are lonely, and that means they're more than willing. Which is good and bad news for a guy like me, with a sticky ticker. Watch out for that Ernestina, she's friggin' insanetiable. Girl like that with a cauliflower head, I wish I knew her forty years ago when she had teeth of her own she brushed. You wouldn't happen to have any Viagra on you, would you? Not saying I need the NASA rocket launcher."

"Nah, but wouldn't expect Hercules would."

"Got that right. Got that right."

All of a sudden, meeting Hercules was the next best thing to being down here in the lobby in the first place, out of the line of fire. "Here I thought I was surrounded by nothing but zombies."

"Sometimes feels like that to me, too."

"How many guys like you, able to hold conversation?"

"Let's see, there's me and now there's you and we should keep an eye out for the third guy so we can start a friggin' book club."

Mikey wanted Hercules to give him the inside scoop on Over the Rainbow, and he was pleased to comply.

"Well, you got your *Goners*, they live on the third floor, in the ville called Goner Town, which they call the Memory Wing, which is not the right term, because none of them can remember their own name much less your name or the time of day. Then you got your *Limpers*, because they are supposably transitioning to *Goners*, and they got canes and walkers and are one banana-peel slip away from the wheelchair, which getting in the wheelchair is punching your ticket to the crematory, you ask me. Me, I'm not really a Limper, I just like the bull penis cane."

"Like who wouldn't?"

"Then there's the *Indies*, independents, like you and me, and nobody pays attention to us, long as we pay our bills, which I can because of my military disability and Longshoreman pension. You probably got one of them type pensions."

Mikey didn't disagree with him.

"People look pretty beat down around here. How come not you?"

"Oh, man, some nights are long ones. Some days are longer. Which is when I go hit the heavy bag. I'm glad you moved in."

Mikey had a delicate question that cut close to the bone for him, but he felt compelled to ask, as he reflected on all the misery visible in the eyes of the residents. "How come these people, so miserable and all, how come they don't up and take themselves out?"

"You mean like hari-kari? For one thing, they couldn't pull the trigger if they had a weapon. I mean physically. They also couldn't muster the strength to throw themselves off the roof, or get to the roof. Ask me, it's already too late to do something constructive like offing themselves. I myself never considered it, but I guess I'd say it's irrelephant now, that's why. When we were dumped here, we were already family suicided. Now buying the farm is, like, who cares? Tell you what. I ain't going nowhere, I got a bucket list to check off. My list don't include seeing the Taj frickin' May-Hall. Hey, my own bucket list is short, which is one last piece of fabulous fresh tail and I don't refer to the patriotic Ladies Auxiliary here in the village."

This bucket list concept was making progressively more sense for Mikey, his distaste for all lists notwithstanding.

"And right alongside tail on the bucket list, I put pizza, it's been so long since I had the right taste of either one. Because can't you smell what's in the air here? That's death coming on, through the vents, through the floorboards. It's so weird, 'cause finely, finely, *finely* death is a sweet gift."

Mikey was in complete sympathy with those jumbled sentiments, or had been until recently.

One of the teams on TV scored a touchdown, and Mikey's attention was riveted.

Hercules asked an innocent question: "Who's favored in the game?"

That query really got Mikey's attention: Hercules might be a man after his own heart after all, so he picked up the Sunday paper on the table in front of him and found the betting line in the sports pages. He always preferred betting a game if he was watching, which made the experience more interesting.

"Tell you what, I'll take the dog, plus seven, for twenty."

"Milk from a baby," said Hercules. "I'm gonna like having you around. Don't die for a while, okay? Only now you gotta give me that twenty I made change for a few minutes ago."

"Can't fool you, Herc."

"I'm smarter than I look. Probably a good thing, no?"

When the game was over, Hercules won the bet, but Mikey, for a change, didn't mind paying off, and that partly explains how come he had an inspiration. It wasn't much of an inspiration, but then again any inspiration went a long way these days.

"Take me to Goner Town," Mikey said. He could not have quite articulated this next point, but for some reason he needed to see what was inevitably waiting for him upstairs, if not here, then somewhere else.

Hercules was reluctantly willing, but he wanted to be clear: "No man gets out alive from Goner Town. You sure you want to?"

"No, let's go."

CR

No Sunday afternoon, already by definition the saddest and longest part of the week, is as bad as a Sunday afternoon when everything a man thinks about Alzhammered life turns out to be worse than he could have expected, which is what happened for Mikey being introduced to Over the Rainbow's Goner Town.

Hercules spelled out instructions: "Move like you shit yourself but don't know what to do about it, or you don't care. Like you been staring at an eclipse of the sun without sunglasses. Like you got a drum going on in your gut," he said. "Mostly, act like you belong."

That was easier for Mikey than he might have assumed.

Some of the Goners were in formation around yet another booming TV, to which nobody seemed to be paying the slightest attention. Some were gathered around the card tables, not playing cards, others around the juice bar, studying the offerings as if they had not seen an orange before.

The banks of fluorescent lights cast a yellowish blue radioactive glow. It was like being inside a bunker in the atomic desert. Didn't they use to, long ago, test bombs nearby? And the smell. Curdled milk. Mixed with the sulfuric undercurrent of spent wooden matches. The toilet door was wide-open, which might have explained something. Mikey had zero desire to investigate. His olfactory sensibility was growing more and more acute these days, a development which had taken him by surprise. Then he remembered the smell: it was how the zoo reeked near the elephants.

Meanwhile, he watched one Goner who was unzipping his jeans. Then rezipping and then unzipping again. Generations of tomato sauce splotched his shirt front.

A female Goner was applying blood red lipstick in the vicinity of her face but missing her mouth.

A male Goner was weeping and complaining into a pillow. "Pete," he cried out, expecting a response. "Pete!"

A cackling woman was handling a book that seemed to have enraptured her. The book was held upside down.

Another woman was looking intensely at the green apple in her grasp as if it was from another planet. Her jaundiced skin looked like vintage lampshade.

Someone else was energetically picking at her face, as if there were worms squiggling.

And then there was the wheelchair brigade, which was lined up against the wall. Bodies barnacled to their seats, the riders' arms tied down by means of restraints, people who, to judge by their look of resignation, had long ago given up resisting.

Carololina ambled up: "Looking for the pool room, boys? Or did you take a wrong turn at Disneyland?" A he who was a she, or a she who was a he, Carololina was not easy for Mikey to understand. He grasped this much: Carololina was nonplussed, this side of contemplating whether or not to invest in a smile for Mikey and Herc, or to grant them a free peek into the generous cleavage of her enhanced chest. Mikey wondered if she were ever liable to lose her cool, and he doubted it. Living the life she was living, and doing it without breaking a sweat, she was formidable.

"Seeing if you need any help, darling," said Hercules.

"That's considerate, Herc. We're getting ready to serve the people dinner, but we're set, thanks. Seen what you need to see? You don't want to linger in Goner Town."

Carololina knew everything. She was in charge.

As they walked toward the elevator, Hercules expressed his admiring view of Carololina. "She has some balls."

"Tell me about it."

"No, really, Mikey, Carololina has *balls*."

Always the last to know, was Mikey.

∽

IT WAS NOW APPROACHING five o'clock, and Mikey and Hercules were ensconced again downstairs staring at the TV where the game had finished, and dinner was around the corner. Goner Town had been an eye-opener. Mikey resolved: no way would he take up residence there. He'd do whatever it took to make that not happen. Right now, he cultivated another, more fundamental worry.

"I'm dreading what the so-called cook thinks is dinner," said Mikey.

"Dog meat most every frigging night. Salisbury steak, which ain't that hamburger? And then the other days there's Beef Jackenoff, but which they call Stroganoff. Man, I wish I had some real food. I'd settle for a can of Spam and a bottle of Cheese Whiz."

Mikey had a brainstorm. "Wait here."

He went to his apartment, where he found Zayana on her laptop.

"I hope you're not sending out emails, Z."

She wasn't that stupid. She was merely trying to stay connected, however tenuously, to the world.

"The senator is leading in all the polls," she said, disconsolately.

"Like I am interested."

"Well, you should be. Wait, what's wrong?"

"I'm hungry. And the idea of dinner doesn't eggs-ackly thrill me. Do me a favor." He asked her to conduct a search online.

ℜ

Downstairs Hercules was waiting for him when he returned. The de-cartilaged and de-ligamented and multiply concussed retired stars were rehashing the game on TV and it was pleasant, virtually normal for Mikey on a Sunday afternoon during football season.

About twenty minutes later, at the front door appeared a middle-aged delivery man in a triangular paper hat anybody could sense he felt humiliated to wear. He reeked of beer suds and had an announcement you could tell he was embarrassed his bosses from the national pizza chain office required him to make:

"Family Business Pizzeria," he said in a flat, uninflected, anything-but-enthusiastic voice. "Today we settle all family business."

He deposited ten pizzas on the table, and Mikey paid him with bills he snapped in front of his reindeer-red nose and told him to keep the change.

"You guys are Johnny on the spot," said Mikey, impressed.

"It took me longer, accident on the freeway. Actually, if you want real quick delivery next time, go half-bake, which we always got laying around. 'Course, you'd have to finish it off in a oven about eight minutes at..."

Mikey said he'd keep that in mind for the future.

"Beautiful," said Hercules, "you're beautiful, Mikey."

"Hope you like pepperoni."

Like it? It was his favorite.

In no time, the aroma of pizza spread throughout the village, and soon the TV room was packed with ravenous Indies and some Limpers, who dug into the boxes as if they had not seen a live pizza before.

Eddie materialized at the reception desk, which was supposed to be manned twenty-four-seven, but was never destined to be. He was fuming at the sight of the flagrant and fragrant pizza, so he got on the phone, and a minute later, Blink showed.

"Eddie, what is going on here?"

Eddie spluttered he had no idea.

"Who ordered the pizzas?"

No answer, but lots of appreciative mumbling from the gumming residents with slices in their hands.

"Ordering outside food is against ORAL rules," said Blink to the assemblage, which ignored him despite the rage in his voice. "Your diet is strictly managed to maintain health and longevity"—and rent-paying, which he did not add. "And your appetite will be ruined for dinner that Eddie has slaved over all afternoon, a new dish he's experimenting with called chicken a la king, with real chicken parts. So I want to know. Who ordered these pizzas? Hercules, was it you? You know better."

"No, Mr. Blink, I most certainly did not. But this is pretty good stuff, Mr. Blink, you should dig in."

"I know it wasn't you, Michael." Blink knew that much because he was operating under certain erroneous assumptions with regard to his newest resident, which Mikey saw no need to disabuse him of. He remained mute. For one thing, Blink might as well think what he needed to think for as long as it was convenient. For another reason, it was hard for Mikey to talk with that mozzarella and pepperoni in his mouth. The pizza in question wasn't bad, to tell the truth.

The zombies were devouring pizza as if they had found fresh flesh and there was nothing the director could do to stop them, so he wheeled around and left.

Hercules had sauce on his face from wolfing his slice.

"Best dinner, ten years," he said. "I'm glad you're around, Mikey."

That was going a bit too far for him to say so himself, but Mikey was pleased enough.

"Now," said Hercules, "I got one more thing to tick off my bucket list."

"Thanks for the tennis ball, Herc."

Chapter Twenty-Six

Thus it came to pass that that day might enter Over the Rainbow local lore and be fondly remembered forevermore as Pepperoni Sunday, assuming villagers were capable of remembering anything. Not to be counted among the absolutely cognitively-challenged, tabula-rasa throng were Hercules and Mikey, who coined the appellation. And Chas Blink himself would never fail to recall the flouting of his instructions. He was gunning to nurse a grudge based upon the anarchy unleashed by the illicit pizza apocalypse.

Consequently, Blink took counter-measures intended to assure there would be no subversive tradition established. Next morning, he posted an oversize, preposterous, nonsensical, threatening sign in red marking pen on the glass door entrance:

FOOD DELIVERY ESP. _PIZZA_
IS FORBIDDEN BY LAW
—BY ORDER OF ORAL Mgmnt. AND
CALIFORNIA STATE HEALTH DEPARTMENT—
Pizza subject to _fine & imprisonment_

"Nice while it lasted," said Hercules, standing before the door. "What are you doing, Mikey?"

Couldn't he see? He was ripping down the notice.

CR

MIKEY WAS SURPRISED TO find he had acquired a friend in Hercules on the first and probably last PS, Pepperoni Sunday. Of course, being boss of a crew is not the most failsafe road to friendship. So he didn't have many friends. If he were honest with himself, he might say that he didn't have any. Maybe he *never* had any. Unless he counted Zayana, but he would not be so rash as to put her in that column. Hercules, on the other hand, was somebody who might possibly, conceivably, perhaps qualify.

"Where'd you get such an ugly ass hat?" said Zayana to Mikey, who was wearing one.

Hercules had bestowed upon him an extra he had unearthed in his closet. In fairness to Zayana, it was battered and beaten, a black stingy brim, which Hercules didn't wear anymore, but Mikey felt jaunty underneath it. He had forgotten how wearing a hat could change a guy's mood. And seemingly Zayana's, too. At some point he regretted that he had left his Borsalino hat collection at home. A lot was left behind in the wake of his former life.

"Mikey got a new friend?" she teased him, not altogether gently.

"He's a good guy."

"What do you two talk about?"

"You wouldn't understand, white guy stuff."

"What do you do, arm-wrestle, dodgy shit like that?"

"We get pedicures mostly, watch soap operas. Does it bother you, Z, that I like hanging with the old guy?" Implying in the process that he was having trouble hanging with her continually belly-aching self sleeping far away from him in the next room.

To tell the truth, it sort of did bother her, not that she would admit to feeling any jealousy—which was Mikey's accurate read on her temperament.

At the same time, she was awakening certain uncertain feelings within him. The other night he wished he could slip into bed next to Zayana, so near and yet so far-fetched away, and his designs were not really sexual, he would have wished to qualify, though he was only fooling himself, because that describes what they were. He wasn't dead yet, was he? She was insanely desirable, right? He may have been memory-impaired, but one thing he never would forget was located in that complicated juncture between her beautiful legs. Still, he couldn't work up the courage to risk rejection, and he fell asleep, by himself, night after night after stupid night. By morning light, he was relieved he had not made any kind of move. Better to keep things—what was the word? Professional? Impersonal? Neither term seemed appropriate.

In any case, they had only a week till the election, and when the senator crossed the finishing line and strutted into the winner's circle, he would have minimal incentive to track Zayana down, because there was no further damage she could visit upon his political aspirations. Sure, she could hypothetically inflict damage upon his squeaky clean rep if news came out post-election, but politicians and their hired guns know how to survive hits like that. Her greatest leverage, and his greatest exposure, existed with voters on the way to the polls.

One short week, that was as long as they needed to hang on. Seven more nights of his sleeping alone. When this was over, Mikey was going to miss Zayana. He came close to telling her so. But why upset the woman? She had been through so much already.

And yet, one week, it would turn out, is a long time for people who are hiding out, biding their time, and for people tracking them down, like Mr. Smith, the wild card. His connection to the senator was threatening enough for Zayana, of course, but his animus toward Mikey was personal and irrational.

One week. A lot could happen in one week.

"How's your hand feel?"

"This tennis ball helps. I'm getting the feeling back, everywhere."

She hoped that wasn't true.

og

When Hercules's birthday arrived, and given that PS prospects for future celebration looked bleak, Mikey came up with a new plan to show his appreciation for the company of his friend. He was appreciative that there was somebody who had current brain function and liked to talk sports and share Over the Rainbow Village inside information and gossip.

Every other day the two men, along with Zayana, would get into the van for the scheduled excursion to the mall. It was a way to pass the time, to get out into the world a little bit. They didn't need to buy much, but they contributed to the local economy. The morning of Hercules's big day, Mikey asked Zayana if she would mind staying at the residence and not heading into town today. She didn't mind in the least. She had been waiting for such an opportunity. And she would be safe for a few hours by herself, he felt confident.

"You two young bucks in your high hats, you and Hercules—what a ridiculous name—you two going to rob a bank?"

"Hadn't occurred to me, Z, but don't take off your thinking cap."

That morning eight residents loaded themselves agonizingly into the van: Mikey and Hercules along with six from the Ladies Auxiliary.

Embarkation seemed to require more effort and coordination than loading containers onto a cargo ship. Those who got into the van for their excursion were by definition and by virtue of self-selection, and grading on the curve, the sharpest of the lot. There was Ernestina (party girl who never missed an opportunity), and five others in their upper seventies, all of them relatively mobile, extremely relatively.

Each excursion morning the same pattern obtained. Eddie, the driver, always scurried back into the office because he said he forgot something, but he usually went to the bathroom for a long time and would cavalierly leave the vehicle running, warming up the cranky engine. If he wasn't doing lines of coke, he was sticking his nose into chalk dust. Mikey had anticipated this opportunity. He casually slipped behind the wheel and drove off as fast as he could.

Destination? Forget the mall.

Most of the duffers barely noticed they were in motion, but the exhilarated Hercules did.

"What's the plan, Chief? Race track?" He was joking.

"I don't know any track close by, but you're warm."

Hercules was stunned. This Mikey was a piece of work.

Ernestina caught on to the new development.

"Michael, you cowboy, we leaving behind Eddie, the dickless weasel?"

"Life's too short, Ernie sweetheart. Keep waiting around, the world passes you by—as you may have not noticed."

"I got to pick up condoms at the drug store."

"Thought you hated the old umbrella, Ernie," said Hercules.

"Not to worry, girl," said Mikey. "Meantime, field trip!" He shouted as the old van rumbled down the road: "Let's hear it from all of you! Field trip!"

"Field trip," they mumbled, practically in unison, obviously unclear on the concept.

"Hey, wish Hercules a happy fucking birthday. We gotta celebrate. One two three…"

"HAPPY FUCKING BIRTHDAY," they answered, this time as one.

As is commonly remarked, the secret to real estate is location location location. One of the best things about Over the Rainbow was also its location location location: on the border of the wild and wooly state of Nevada. What the Nevada location meant most promisingly today consisted of this: casinos, some of which located in smaller towns sufficiently far outside Vegas to drum up nickel and dimer business. Mikey had done the research on Zayana's laptop when she was asleep. There was a small gaming establishment not twenty minutes from the facility. That wasn't the only research he conducted on Zayana's laptop. Knowing Blink's casual attitude about residential security systems and Eddie's nasal Northwest passage history and the lack of any other Over the Rainbow vehicle, he figured he had about four or five hours before he headed back. Plenty of time to get in and, if necessary, out of trouble, plenty of time. They did need to make one other stop before they were able to gamble.

ʘ

THERE IT WAS, AS expected, what Mikey was looking for. At the end of a dusty road loomed a series of interconnected double-wides, painted a color that once upon a time was fire-engine red. They had arrived at the Minx Ranch, which name burned in neon on the desert floor, a compound situated against the side of a scruffy hill and dedicated to an age-old business proposition. The parking lot designated for customers was empty, a good or terrible omen, depending. Right now, based on Mikey's plans, that was an excellent thing.

"Do my eyes deceive?" Hercules asked with a hush in his voice.

"Can't pull the wool over you, Herc, what *do* you see?"

"I see a dream, a dream coming true."

"Soon you can cross the other item off your bucket list, buddy."

Mikey and Hercules helped the ladies out of the van and they passed through the chain link gate and entered past the sign that said MUST BE 21 TO ENTER PREMISES. The establishment was devoid of patrons—which was part of Mikey's plan, correctly intuiting at this hour: what sort of loser goes to a loser brothel in the early light of day? And he had the answer to the ready: *losers like us, from Over the Rainbow.*

The bartender was a beanpole topped with a blue Dodgers baseball cap and he wore patriotic red, white, and blue suspenders and bow tie. Upon seeing these new clients, the man did a double take and dropped the glass, which he had been wiping with a bar towel, onto the rubber-matted floor. The man had no idea what to venture by way of greeting, which was understandable. When had he seen a posse such as this inside the Minx? That was easy. Never.

"Nothing to fear," Mikey said with authority, and took out a roll of bills and put a hundred down on the bar. The investment instantly eradicated the bartender's apprehension.

"We won't be taking up a lot of your time, but in the meantime would you make some tea for your lady visitors? What's your name, sir?"

"Hopper."

"You in charge at the Minx, Hopper?"

"Since I graduated from high school I been working here back when…"

"Hopper, this is Ernie and Colette and another Colette—who may be twins born to parents who ran out of names to name them but I don't know for sure—and Wanda and Blanche and Merilee, I think, all ladies of a certain age and distinction who I bet will have no recollection later today of where they spent their morning, or at least nobody'd believe them if they did tell them. Hopper, please keep them amused and entertained, would you?" He put down another hundred to sweeten the pot, and Hopper was heartened by the prospect of serving premature high tea and earning with no trouble in the process his big bucks.

"But Hopper, my friend here, name's Hercules, he would like to see the menu."

"We got sandwiches and like that, if the kitchen opens."

"Hopper, follow the bouncing ball." Mikey tossed his tennis ball in the air and snatched it, for emphasis. "Talking about—come on, what *is* the Minx Ranch?"

Hopper was slow but nobody was that slow.

"Oh," he said. "No shit?"

"Eggs-ackly."

Then Hooper got into the spirit. "Give us a minute. The girls are all in their rooms, it's kinda early, but I'll get them out here for your pal."

"That's the business, right, my man?" Mikey caught himself feeling nostalgic for his old crew back home, for practically the first time. This was the kind of place somebody like him in his line of work would have asked for a piece of the action, and it wouldn't be an ask. Take his dad. His dad hated mugs who specialized in running girls. But here Mikey was, doing business at this place. It was too hard to think through the implications, and fortunately he was about to be distracted.

Because in a few minutes three yawning Minx Ranch employees teetered on their high heels onto the scene, having slathered on make-up and hitched up their scanty bikinis, their skin goose-bumpy on account of the ratcheted-up AC. For their part, they were visibly amazed and disappointed to be called in for this senior citizen car wreck of a party, and they muttered about grandmas and grandpas and wondered under their breath what the hell was the big idea, getting dragged out of bed for no good reason. Hopper, to his credit, and with two hundred of the easiest bucks he was going to make today in his pocket, was chatting up the lady villagers, who seemed, for a change, to be enjoying themselves, especially Ernie, who would have been batting her eyelashes in Hopper's direction, had she had any.

As advised by Hopper, the girls begrudgingly introduced themselves to Hercules and Mikey. The Thai girl said her name was Me-ow. The Big Mormon Hair Extensions girl introduced herself as Come Come, a name which had to strike patrons of the Ranch as being clever. The French Girl in a beret and pigtails went by the Parisianly pedestrian name of Chantale. Come Come was the mouthiest of the bunch and more than a little cynical with regard to Hercules.

"Grandpa, you sure? I don't want anybody getting CPR in my boo drawer."

"Well, I hope you don't have a heart attack either, sweetheart, when I am on the job."

"Herc, this is on me," said Mikey. "Take your pick."

"You're beautiful. You know, I never paid for it, not once."

"Your record will be intact, because I am picking up the tab. I don't want to hurry you up, but let's not camp out here too long because Ernie's going to apply for a job if we're not careful."

Hopper spoke up. "There's one more for you gents to meet, who's taking a little bit longer to get ready, and who's a house rarity."

No need to delay. Hercules chose Me-ow, and that was simple for Mikey to understand. She was petite with silky long black hair, and a shockingly angelic face. She was practiced in showing feigned pleasure to be selected, so she went up to Hercules and put her Thai palms together in prayer and bowed slightly before putting her arm through his and guiding him out to her double-wide.

"No hurry, Herc, but—well, you know what I mean."

Big Mormon Hair and French maid looked nothing less than relieved not to have made the cut, and they sent glances Mikey's way, inquiring wordlessly *What about you, sailor?* As long as they roused themselves out of bed and put on makeup, why not?

This was the moment when the last prospect showed up, heading in from the opposite direction, and it was somebody Mikey knew.

Carololina.

For a second his mind tipped sideways. Had he been teleported back to Over the Rainbow? Did Minx Ranch double as an assisted living satellite residence? Then he blinked hard and, clearing his eyes, he concluded he was indeed where he thought he was, and Carololina worked alongside Me-ow and Come Come and Chantale. She was not wearing a bikini. Instead she was dressed in her nurse's uniform, demonstrating that certain fantasies were time-tested winners in both bordellos and assisted living residences. Not to mention that her uniform was capable of split-duty if she took the night shift at the village. Mikey had to whisk Carololina away before the Ladies Auxiliary caught a glimpse. He grabbed Carololina's massive hand and winced and walked himself and her back to where Carololina had come from.

"I knew he was that kinda guy," said Mormon Hair girl.

Hopper noticed this development and he realized he'd better advise Mikey. "Sir, so you realize what you're getting into…"

The two of them were gone before the man could inconsequentially elucidate.

⟡

CAROLOLINA'S ROOM PRODUCED IN Mikey a woozy effect, as if it was pumped with a dentist's office nitrous oxide, and the scene was shadowy and gauzily fascinating. On one wall hung posters of sports figures in action—slam-dunkers and swinging-for-the-fencers and touchdown-reception snaggers, all in the act of scoring, which was the essence of his hostess's joke, he supposed. On another wall, framed photos of Marilyn Monroe, kittenish and come-hithering, as well as the famous skirt-billowing one over those subway grates. The bedding on the King-size was pink and the dozen billowy pillows blue. The lampshades were red and black, which made for plenty of illumination for an industrious vole to find a food object on the floor. It may have been too early for any man to be legitimately drunk, but Mikey was reeling.

"Darling, you're not going to tell Blink, are you?"

"Not if you don't."

"Think Ernie saw me? She is sharp, too sharp."

"She was probably busy propositioning Hopper."

"Pervert's probably considering, too. How about Herc?"

"He's occupied with Me-ow."

"That's sweet. She's a good girl, prettiest at the Minx. You know, her parents sold her in Bangkok when she was a teenager and worked the blow job bars. I don't know how she got to California, but she says life's a lot better here. Speaking of which. What are *you* doing here, Michael Jackson?" As if it weren't obvious, as if he had taken the wrong road, and might have confused the Minx Ranch for a real assisted living residence.

Michael Jackson. He was sick of the name. He explained it was fake—an abbreviated account, as there was no need to go into detail. He also told her that the Minx Ranch was Hercules's birthday present. But he could ask the same question of Carololina—what was *she* doing here?—but that wasn't necessary because she read his mind.

"Well, we all enjoyed a good chuckle over the Michael Jackson sighting. Thing is, I don't make enough at the village, I have my own parents to support at a real nursing home, which is expensive, so I work here, few days a week. And hormone injections are not covered by insurance and they're not cheap. They do work, don't they? Along with a little state of the art cosmetic surgery, you see?" She cupped her breasts, leaned over and bent at her waist to show them off.

"Your equipment's fabulous, really fabulous, no question, and your secret's safe with me at the Rainbow."

"So we have a deal. But long as you are here, and Hopper's got you on the clock, what are you in the mood for?" Carololina rotely ticked off the options and the non-standard variations upon the options.

Mikey was not one to blush, but he might have a little then. "Carololina, I don't think my tastes run in your direction, no disrespect."

None was taken, he was assured.

"I mean, you are a fine-looking…specimen."

"What I have to offer"—Carololina ran her hands down her sides for visual emphasis—"is for a lot of guys irresistible. But not for everybody, I get that."

"I bet you don't lack for loyal repeat business, again, no disrespect."

"Your head would spin if I told you who's walked into my room—and came back next time for more. You sure you don't want to take a walk on the wild side? One time? No disrespect, but you won't forget it."

He could not remember everything he once forgot, but he hoped the no-disrespect derby had crossed the finish line.

"One thing I did realize about you from the jump is, you don't belong at the village. You're not the type. So I do wonder what brought you to the place. It's not like it's a destination vacation spot, so you have aroused my curiosity."

"Same here, same here."

"Blink, of course, doesn't give a rat's, long as he gets your money."

"Yeah, but you and Blink, man, that must be complicated."

"I gotta throw him one now and then, a freebie. He's not so bad, really, when you get to know him."

"Bet he's probably worse."

"It helps a lot he's clueless, I admit, and he's also half-blind, which is why he keeps rotating his twenty pair of glasses. And he doesn't mind me working at the Minx Ranch. He hired me after he, uh, *met* me—here, in the uniform. He's got needs, like any man. A guy like that, once I get going working my magic, he has no idea whose lips are wrapped around him. Why should I burst his bubble?"

"Blink and I, different planets."

"Your wife ain't your wife, is she?"

So they were in truth-telling mode now. "She and I have history."

"None of my business, Michael, she's been cool with me."

"*Mikey*. Zayana's important to me."

"*Zelda?*"

He had no choice. He explained her name.

"I can see Zayana's important to you. But wives or girlfriends don't really mind what I do with their men, if they find out, which they don't have to, pinky swear."

He was doubtful about everything pertaining to Carololina. *She* was complicated herself. *He* was complicated, too. Maybe everybody is, when you get down to it. His life had taken unpredictable turns. The crew's betrayal. Mr. Smith. Zayana and Jeremiah, reemerging. And look, here he was talking with somebody like Carololina in a Nevada brothel. Way better than wasting his time with the likes of Dolly. A few months ago, he could not have imagined such eventualities.

"It all began in Idaho," she said.

"Blink did mention Idaho."

"Yeah, my potato-state origins turned him on, God knows why. Started when I won the lumberjack competition, junior division. I was in high school, star of all the teams, strongest boy in town, and I could work the ax like a chopstick, vertical chop being my best event, and I was good at the ax throw, too. I knew it was different when the winner of the senior division lumberjack competition, he was my mom's ex-boyfriend, he took a liking to me, and it was no liking. But I liked him a lot myself, more than I would have guessed. He asked me to wear his other girlfriend's silk underwear, which felt cool and sweet on my skin. Went from there. Just so you know, I didn't do anything I didn't want to do—still don't. Next thing I knew I was in California where nobody knew me. But *I* knew me, which is what matters, and I was pretty close to what you might call happy."

Hearing *happy* made him turn his head, quizzically.

"Happy *enough*. Never told anybody here at the Ranch my story. One day, if there's any money left of my inheritance, which I doubt, considering how the money keeps flying out the door for my folks, one day I go under the Big Knife, get the Big Cut, can't afford it now."

"You were a lumberjack?" That image was hacking away at him, along with the Big Cut, which made him feel fleetingly queasy and defensive about his own equipment.

"But like they say, once a lumberjack… You know, one way or the other, I gotta collect from you, sorry. Hopper'd be all over me with the bosses. Once you walked into my room—hey, you like my room?" He nodded. "*Good*, I'm glad, did it myself. Once that happened, meter started ticking, that's how it works at Minx Ranch."

"No problem." When she told him the number, he couldn't stop himself from saying with awe, "That's real money."

"Gave you the half-off friend discount, sweety. Last chance for you to reconsider, long as you're paying."

He was not used to how business was conducted in a place like this, and he was thankful he never would be. He counted out money for her. He was not prepared for how he was all over again visualizing her with a swinging ax, wearing flannel over her silk panties, felling trees and the men who felled them, an image that was strangely somehow not incompatible with her current profession.

Now is when Carololina appeared confused, and also a little bit concerned.

"What's wrong?" he said.

"You gave me way too much."

He went blank. He was pissed at himself, another breakdown when he wasn't expecting it, not that he ever expected a breakdown, because he wouldn't have had one if he were expecting one. But then he rallied, best he could.

"A tip, that's a little tip," he lied.

The day would come when he wouldn't realize he had been exposed like that. And then he couldn't cover, because he wouldn't notice that the day had come. Then it would be too late for cover. Some days he feared it was already too late.

He should find the closest train tracks and finish the job he started.

"Here, really, please take it back. I'm not going to take advantage of a friend from the Rainbow. A girl's got her integrity or she's got nothing."

"Spend it on your folks. The day'll come you can help me out."

Carololina winked.

"Not," he assured her, "not like that."

Chapter Twenty-Seven

Mikey made sure all the riders in the van had buckled their seatbelts, though he himself neglected to, before he drove off. Hercules was sitting in the back of the van, but by his tone of voice Mikey could tell he was beaming.

"You know why that pretty girl calls herself Me-ow?"

"I can take a wild guess."

"Yes, you can. Now where to, *boss*?"

⚔

It had been a while since anybody had called him *that*. He missed being boss. He may have missed being *called* boss more—especially by Mo, which surprised him. As for the acting boss, back home Rosetta was in occasional communication with him. Fatso was back in the game along with Mo, and they were doing what they were accustomed to doing, and if her information was accurate, doing it better than when he was on the job. On this front, Mikey was reeling from yesterday's telephone exchange.

She had filled him in on Jeremiah's status, and how the boy was safe and secure, enjoying himself in the cowboy town of Naples, going around with his two bodyguards from club to club, he teaching them English along the way, they teaching him Napolitan dialect. He also had taken to wearing fancy silk neck ties, frequenting that famous tie store called Marinella's, renowned throughout the world, where people stand in line outside to gain access, where they counted on enjoying the privilege of spending lots of Euros. Jeremiah never waited in line, not with his entourage. That tie tidbit moved Mikey. At least he taught the boy how to tie one.

"We expanded," Rosey had told him, news flash. "I figured we needed more soldiers. So I recruited Mo's two boys…"

"Wait, wait. Mo has *kids*?"

"Omar and Beatle, in their early twenties. I think Beatle's a nickname for Benny."

"*Mo* has kids?"

"I told you that. They're adopted and adorable. Funny thing, they are both huge guys, they tower over the old man. They are black belts in karate, and they are like gigantic versions of Mo, down to the same mannerisms, they like to say 'all due' and not 'all due respect.' They worship their dad. Actually, they worship both their dads."

"What's that mean, both dads?"

That was considerably more information than Mikey was counting on hearing.

"Mo lives in a house?" he asked. That was a relatively innocuous landing spot from which he could launch a few interrogatories.

"You think he lives in a cave?"

"I guess I assumed Mo had some kinda family." He had not previously experienced any difficulty restraining his curiosity as to Mo's domestic arrangements.

"Beautiful little Cape Cod, picket fence, planter boxes, the whole thing. Mo's a great cook, and his partner Joey's a peach. He's an ER nurse, head taller than Mo with a buzz cut and a beard, and the house, it's spotless, you can eat off the floor. We all watched the sunset sitting on the veranda, and we drank to your health."

"Mo has a veranda and he *cooks*?"

"Middle Eastern is his go-to cuisine."

"Mo has a cuisine that's go-to?"

"Mikey, you going deaf?"

"Go back. What you say a second ago? *Two* dads?"

She explained. When her lucid explanation was greeted with her brother's incredulous-bordering-on-gobsmacking silence, she re-explained. All the pie charts, graphs, and op-eds in the world would not have aided her cause. This sort of household set-up was happening all the time these days and not only in California, so she told Mikey, who had somehow missed this development, having usually never gotten past the sports page of the paper or the betting spreads online. "How long you been living in a vacuum cleaner?"

He must have been in a vacuum cleaner because he was having nothing but trouble processing her explanation, and he determined this was one subject he was not going to comprehend for the time being.

"Fatso come over for dinner? Man, I would've paid to see that. What kinda bacon dish Mo make him?"

"Matter of fact, Fatso enjoyed his vegetarian dinner. Perfect table manners, by the way. Even took off his suit coat."

With each additional data point, Mikey was feeling ever-increasing anxiety.

"I put the boys, Omar and Beatle, outside the construction lease company, figuring Mr. Smith would show up again someday to collect, but so far no dice. If he does, the boys will put him down. What we hear is, he's full-time out of town, coming for you, him and Dolly."

"And the money?"

"It's rolling in, hand over fist, like the old days, Mo says, with dad. Other day, I went over preliminary plans with the architect to rebuild Lorenzo's, because the pier amazingly retained structural integrity. Insurance settlement was good, but it's going to take a while."

Hearing what Rosey had shared with him today, he would not have been more astounded had she also advised him she had dyed her hair orange and gotten a nose ring.

"Mo and I want to call it Mikey's Place."

Mikey was touched, though he wasn't sure it should be named anything other than Lorenzo's, rest in peace. It took him a while to formulate what else he was burning to know. He asked her a question.

She heard the question: "What do you mean?"

"It's not a trick question, Rosetta. What do Mo and everybody on the street call you?"

From his serious tone of voice, she sensed it was a crucial consideration for him, so she wanted to frame carefully the response. "Sometimes Mo calls me Rosey, most of the time they all call me Boss Lady. You okay with that?"

"Sure, why not?" he said, though he was not quite sure. "Dad thought you were *born* boss lady of the house."

"Dad was always the boss and you're the boss from now on. Nobody'll forget that."

So Mo had a male partner named Joey and they had two adopted kids who had two dads and they ate Middle Eastern food on a veranda in a pretty little house where Mikey'd never been invited, not that he could fault anybody, not at all. What else had he missed?

CR

"Mikey," Hercules resumed his tale of Minx Ranch conquest as Mikey drove on through the desert, "she calls herself Me-ow on account…"

"Herc, I got it already, man."

That curt response dampened the celebratory mood, if only temporarily. For a while, the only voice audible in the van was Ernestina's, as she narrated her imaginary quickie dalliance with the Minx Ranch floor manager, Hopper, which had to be both biologically and logistically improbable. In a minute her voice trailed off: she had run out of steam. It had been a long morning already for her, and for all of them.

Hercules asked where they were going.

"You'll see."

"Day started out bad for me, till the Ranch, I mean. My grandson, Buster, called this morning before we left, said he wasn't gonna visit for my birthday, guess something came up. Something always gets in the way, but you made it all better, Mikey."

There was one more stop on their journey, and before long Mikey guided the van into the Desert Gold Casino parking lot.

Hercules's mood instantly zoomed into the stratosphere. "This whole morning," said a joyously teary Hercules at the sight of the gambling establishment, "is way fucking better than a birthday cake."

"Here we go, people," said Mikey. "Don't wander off into the desert, okay, or play with any coyote pups. We'll stay for a couple of hours, and be back for a late lunch at Over the Rainbow, which I am pretty sure is tuna casserole topped with potato chips. Let's keep an eye on each other."

Ernestina had a different idea: "Michael, whaddaya say you and me we grab a room, some sloppy soap bait and tackle?"

"Flattered, but I'm spoken for."

"How about you, Herc? You used to like it when we played Sneak the Flag."

Hercules considered the prospect, but he had to demur. "I'll take a rain-check, Ernie, let's grease up the flag pole in another lifetime, all right?"

"Why'd I bother? You old coots can't keep up with me. 'Sides, bet in the casino I can find a rodeo rider to play bucking bronco."

"No broncos," stipulated Mikey, "and stay out of anybody's corral, would you? In fact, let's all keep in pairs. Ernie, you stay with Colette Number One. Colette Number Two, you and Blanche. Wanda and Merilee, you two are a tag team."

"Teams of two," said Ernestina. "That's a great friggin' idea. We might get lucky and put together a regular manage a tuna. You game, Colette, you phony little blushing whore?"

One other thing Mikey had in mind. "Here we can all play games of chance. Fat chance mostly, given the dicey casino opportunities we got here. Speaking of which, you can find me at the blackjack tables, where I plan to make a killing of these pigeons. So let me help you all out."

As each woman stumbled out of the van onto the asphalt parking lot, he gave her a hundred dollar bill. They looked like they had not handled paper currency before, so Mikey didn't harbor much hope for them, or anybody else for that matter, at the slot machines. "Go have some fun, you girls. Remember, we meet at the van at one o'clock. Tell me. What time we back?"

Ernestina played cheerleader: "ONE, OH, COCK!"

&

MIKEY AND HERCULES SHOULDERED into the seedy casino side by side, feeling for all the world like behatted gunslingers strolling down Main

Street in Dodge at High Noon, but looking more like tin horns who run the feed store.

Once inside the refrigerated confines, Hercules announced, "I'm getting that very special feeling again."

"Me, too. I see the blackjack pit that's got my name all over it."

"Yeah, I can see that. And cards are tempting, true. But I can also see that redhead in the mini, standing at the bar at this early hour which means she's open for bidness. My name's all over that sweet thing and if she ain't a pro I ain't a randy'n ready old man."

"Man, you ready to saddle up again so soon?" Mikey was impressed. "Hey, wait a second, you said you never paid for it."

Hercules shrugged, caught out. That was okay with Mikey, who had plenty of his own secrets he wasn't about to divulge to anybody, even a pal like Hercules.

"You need some cash, Herc?"

He didn't, because he said he had plenty of his walking-around money in his pocket, so the two split up, each to his own diversionary vice.

Mikey assumed his seat at the highest-limit table in the house, in this instance a modest $25 minimum, $500 max, which were the low stakes to be expected in a tiny dive casino like this. He placed five hundred dollar bills down on the green felt, which was worn out by lonely generations of gamblers who lost it all chasing a dream. The gopher-mug, bearded, and toothy dealer scooped up the cash and counted out his chips. Mikey was the only player ponying up and he put four quarter chips in the betting square, a hundred bucks. First hand he was dealt: blackjack. This might end up being a better day than he imagined.

"Beginner's luck," said Mikey cheerfully to the dealer, but he could tell he had already attracted the dismayed attention of the anti-Brioni suit pit bosses who were huddling up to monitor. Mikey couldn't really count cards anymore, but he grasped the principles, so he played what he recalled of Basic Strategy, though he wasn't as competent as he used to be. As it happened, however, he could not lose, and at the end of the second or third two-deck game, about forty minutes into his session, he was up several thousand, in all likelihood not an insignificant number for the Desert Gold drop.

A pit boss strode up to the table and whispered into the dealer's furry cavity that passed for his ear. The dealer ostentatiously fanned the cards across the table, clapped his hands for the benefit of the sky watchers overhead to signal he wasn't palming any chips, and walked off.

"You guys closing down the game?"

"No, sir, not at all. But the dealer's going on a break, you know, unions? And his replacement is coming on."

"Okay, where is he?"

"Ah, here *she* is, right now." And a new dealer showed up with big shadowy wrap-around glasses that enveloped her in mystery, or more like chicanery. She also wore glittery costume rings on most of her fingers, both of which sartorial accessories communicated a couple of obvious, urgent takeaway messages to Mikey. One, he couldn't watch her eyes. And two, bling was not allowed on dealers in the bigger casinos, but here they were intended to function as a distraction for the rube they supposed him to be. She was a cheat casinos call a mechanic. You want a good mechanic for your car, but it's the last person you want dealing you blackjack.

"I will try my luck at another table," Mikey said as he headed over to another dealer at an empty table.

Funny thing, the new dealer followed him to his new destination, and relieved that other dealer of her duties.

Mikey addressed the pit boss: "Again with the union? They must be Teamster Longshoremen, all these breaks."

"You have no idea, sir."

"Sweetheart," he said to the mechanic, "you stalking me? I'm getting a funny feeling inside."

"Well, old man with funny feelings," she said, "if you need, you can piss in your Depends or you can go to the Little Boys Room, down the hall."

"You're a comedian? I don't like comedians. Okay, deal the fucking cards." Mikey himself knew this was a dumb move, and he should have picked up stakes and declared himself winner. But he was taking their disrespect personally.

She shuffled the cards, and judging by how dexterously she manipulated them, she was talented, an expert brought in to fleece the unsuspecting sheep. There is one very curious aspect about dirty dealing. Sometimes, admittedly rarely, dumb luck can trump professional trickery, and that's what transpired. She dealt Mikey a pair of tens and he split them, managing a nineteen and an eighteen, whereupon he stood. After all, she was showing a five face-up, a terrible card for the house. But she flipped over the down-card to reveal a six, which caused her to beam, because that totaled eleven, a great situation for the house, at which point she hit that with—another six. Of course, she had dealt herself a second, not the card on the top of the deck. There may be no justice in the world, but sometimes it turns out cheating doesn't pay off. She paid Mikey's winners and muttered curses as she did.

"If you were a little bit sweeter, I'd slip you a nice tip."

"If you were a little bit smarter, you'd be a moron."

"Awe. We were off to such a pleasant start."

She dealt and she stayed ice cold, despite her best mechanic's designs. And he kept winning. Before long, he was up over eight thousand. It wasn't big money, not for him, but when is winning not better than losing? He knew he should pull up and get out of here, but he was outraged, so he wouldn't.

"Hey, doll face, why don't you take off those shades? I like to see the eyes of who's trying to fuck me."

The dealer audibly sighed and stared at the pit boss, who was watching closely and conveying his simmering ire.

"What do you want me to do, Sonny?" she asked the pit boss, which was brazen on her part. "This old prick can't buy a losing hand and I can't steal a winning one." Not adding the unneeded-to-be-stated: *and this was when I am doing all I can.*

"Take a break."

Mikey addressed the pit boss. "Man, Sonny, I want to join that union. Who you bringing in to cheat me now?"

"Nobody, table's closed. In fact, I think *you* have been cheating and I am going to have to confiscate your chips. You are a counter, another word for cheat."

"I can barely remember the day of the week, hell if I can remember the cards flashing by."

"Nice try, grandpa," he said, and signaled to two members of the security team who descended on the table.

"Where we going, fellas?"

"*We're* going nowhere," one of them said. "But *you're* going bye-bye."

"I ain't going no place without my money."

Out of nowhere Hercules materialized and hustled up to the table. He was not wearing his pants and his skinny ghostly white legs looked veiny as an old tree. He did have his hat on his head, however.

"You're walking without a cane, Herc?"

Hercules looked down, saw that was the case, and said: "Guess that's true. Must be feeling pretty damn good, thanks to you."

"You happen to notice you ain't got pants on?"

"When I went to take a piss, which pissing takes a long, long while these days, the honey pot stole my cash and left me in my drawers—before I got to spring my surprise on her." Hercules was simultaneously laughing and lamenting, admiring that he'd been taken and at the same time deploring that she absconded with both pants and cash.

"Get out of here, the two of you, you're both barred," said the pit boss. "Security, throw out these decrepit sacks of shit."

They physically pulled up Mikey from his seat and, as the two friends stood side by side, Hercules looked into Mikey's eyes to verify they were in accord. They were a team. If only Mikey could have had Hercules in his crew in the past, he was thinking, that would have been fun.

"We got nothing to lose. You thinking what I'm thinking?" said Hercules.

"Yes, I am." Mikey nodded toward the security guard on *his* left and Hercules to the security guard on *his* left. "We were having such a great start to the day, too. We can't let these toy cops get away with this, can we?"

"No, we can't let these high school dropouts jump in our shit."

"Not saying anything's wrong," said Mikey, for whom formal education perennially remained a point of sensitivity, "dropping out of high school, but becoming a fake cop, that's plain wrong. This situation, I say it calls for a *swift response.*"

"As my grandson Buster'd say, word up, Mikey, word up. Least I think he'd say that."

"What's that supposed to mean," said the twitchy security cop, "*swift response?*"

The guards couldn't be faulted for not anticipating what was coming from the two old men, who were perfectly attuned to each other. Practically in unison and without benefit of practice, as if they were plunged into some old black and white movie, they threw right crosses into the jaws of the guards, which knocked them back, stumbling along the carpet.

Mikey yowled, he couldn't believe the pain. In all the adrenalized excitement, he had forgotten about his damaged hand, but now he had little doubt he had re-broken a few bones and knuckles.

Then things got serious. More security rushed up in force and the two friends were boxed in against the blackjack table while the guards formed a semicircle to contain them. One of the guards pulled a taser, and he pointed it at Hercules. Last thing Hercules would need, an old man with a challenged ticker, was to be tasered. And a guy who had been ripped off by a hooker and left depantsed needed to be protected—especially on this day, his birthday.

"You pussies are outta control," said Mikey. "Put that thing down."

Then Mikey stepped in front of his friend and absorbed the full impact of the shot. Mikey dropped noisily like the transmission of a street-car-racing Chevy Trans-Am and trembled. It felt like somebody turned on the coldest shower in the world. And also like somebody had electrocuted his balls.

At this point the ladies of Over the Rainbow descended and, seeing their fellow villagers in extremis, attacked the guards, swinging their little spindly arms to no effect. Soon all eight of them were cuffed, including Mikey flat on the floor, placed under house arrest, and then dragged bodily into the back room, along with their hats.

That was where the police showed up and couldn't stop from laughing, mocking everybody in sight. They obviously despised the casino bosses and did not bother to disguise their contempt for the security detail that couldn't control a kindergarten recess uprising.

"You little girls couldn't manage eight old geezers and wheezers, including these nice old grannies, without a taser, and had to call us in? You are pathetic, mixing it up with the old folks. Pathetic."

They did have to determine whether or not to take Mikey to the hospital, but the man was coming around with a vengeance, and he told them he wasn't going to any hospital in this cow town. They might taser him again.

"You really okay, sir?"

"They'd need a real gun to put me down."

"You got a pair, old man."

Mikey nodded, not altogether convinced his pair was intact and he was reluctant to administer a self-check. A taser blast will inculcate some doubts on that score in a man.

"You should sue these clowns," said the cop loud enough for them to hear.

How could the police officer know that was precisely what Mikey would not do?

"I want my money, which I won."

The cop turned toward the pit boss and said, "Man's got a point, and if I were you, I would give him his money and hope he doesn't come after your ass in a court of law."

But the humiliated pit boss was adamant. He wanted them all placed under arrest for disturbing the peace. The cops had no choice but to take them in, because casinos call the shots in Nevada, so that is what they did.

Hercules was shouting as they hauled him off: "Give me my fucking hat, right there on the floor, that's my lucky hat."

The pit boss was intoxicated by his moment of triumph. "You mean this piece of Goodwill shit?" And he stomped on it, crushing the crown, and then for good measure stomped on Mikey's hat as well.

ଓ

AFTER FINGERPRINTING THEM, THE cops put them in a holding cell, all eight together.

Hercules looked somehow more naked without his hat than he did without his pants.

Ernestina took the opportunity to flirt with one of the desk-jockey officers.

"Never serviced a man with a service weapon," she cooed quasi-toothlessly, then turned to her arrested associates and added, not caring if the cop heard her, "that's not really true, what I said about not servicing a man in uniform bearing arms, because men get turned on when you play with their big guns."

Hercules, meanwhile, was strangely elated for a hatless man in yellowy boxer shorts who had been ripped off and had not enjoyed the female attention he swore he had legitimately paid good money for.

"You okay, Herc?"

"Like a million bucks. You?"

"Remind me never get tasered again."

"Mikey," he said, "let me tell you. Thanks for taking a bullet for me. First Minx Ranch and then the casino? Best fucking birthday I ever fucking had."

Chapter Twenty-Eight

Casino brass stepped in, fearing a PR backlash, and elected not to press charges, though they did keep the money, so they were released from custody and driven in a police van back to where they came from. Returned from his abbreviated sojourn in the slammer, Mikey took brain- and ball-bungled refuge in the place Over the Rainbow preposterously designated the library. He was moving slowly. He was somehow sitting slowly. Despite Zayana's fantastic attestation to Chas Blink of Mikey's so-called love of Charles Dickens, he had never before in his lifetime broken into a library, or a bookstore for that matter. Mastering the Dewey Decimal System did not threaten to make an appearance on his nonexistent bucket list.

Nonetheless, he was in something like a library because he couldn't stay in his apartment. Zayana professed no sympathy, she shouted, for his "tasered white ass," and she was furious with him for getting in trouble, making such a public scene. What was he thinking? He disgusted her and she wished she had taken from the jump her own chances without relying upon somebody as unreliable as him. Again he had let her down, yet again.

It had been a long time since she had yelled at him like that.

The dim dungeony nook that was the so-called library shared a wall with a very popular destination toilet. Every bio-hazardous human ministration and every single flush and throat-clearing expectoration was queasily audible. The room had six teetering, unbraced bookcases jammed with *Readers Digest* and *TV Guide* back issues and a biblical number of Bibles. There were also multiple copies of *The Good Earth* by Pearl Buck. Mikey presumed this to be a farming manual. There was also a legion of *Ben Hurs*, which he himself knew was a movie starring Charlton Heston he saw as a kid, and which also didn't threaten to elongate his aggravated attention span.

In addition to enjoying safe haven from Zayana's indignation, Mikey approved of the isolation afforded by the library, which meant it was a good private place to make a call.

"Mikey," said Rosetta. "You okay?"

He wanted to know what she was implying.

"I don't know. Making small talk?"

No need telling her what happened today.

"How's tricks, Rosey?"

"Let's see. Brownie paid up, he's square first time in years, said Mo."

"Where'd the hell he get the money?"

"Fact is, he does better than we thought for an old school book."

Rosey was doing great, Mikey had to admit to himself.

She thought he might be interested to know Randy's store suffered an unfortunate accident the other day that Mo arranged. "He won't be doing any tailoring anytime soon on account of the casts on both his arms."

"Goddamn rat."

"Mo and I went to the shooting range today, target practice."

"Don't tell me."

"It's true, I outpointed him with the Browning."

"Dad's pistol?"

"Sweet piece, a classic. And that construction equipment leasing company you always liked—they opened a second location and you know what that means."

Double the income, of course.

"Eggs-ackly," she said.

"But no Mr. Smith?"

"He's keeping lower profile than an ostrich."

"And Dolly?"

"Mo called him."

"That's not right, Rosey, reaching out…"

"Hold your horses. Mo invited him to a sit-down, but Dolly wouldn't take the bait. Mo was going to…"

"Don't trust that son-of-a-bitch."

"Of course not. And then I was sent a dozen red roses, typical Dolly, which arrived anonymously, without a card."

"What a dick."

"But it wasn't Dolly, it was Judge Keily who sent me the flowers. A little token of professional courtesy. Nice of him, no?"

If Mikey could whistle, he would have done so now.

"Mikey, what about these unruly teenagers in the neighborhood? You have a beef with them?"

He denied provoking the tattooed mullet-haired suburban punks.

"I sat down with them and convinced them they had better things to do with their time than TPing the house and leaving dog shit at the front door. And besides, if they did it again, Mo let them know they wouldn't like what happened to what was left of their houses. They seemed to listen to reason."

Teenagers listening to reason? What was she going to do next? Persuade the senator to back off, convince him of the error of his ways?

"Actually, I think we got an idea how to deal with the senator."

He wanted to know what that idea was.

"Don't you worry your pretty little head. Less you know, the better. Besides, we got a lot of new action going on. You're going to like it when you get back to town—after we take care of Smith and Dolly and the senator."

Spoken like a real boss, which he was beginning to suppose was what Rosetta was fast becoming. He should have expected that.

He didn't expect that.

ʘ

THE CALL UNSETTLED HIM. His sister was stepping up, taking care of the family business, doing precisely what she should have been doing all along, so why was he rattled? Maybe it was the taser's after-effects. Sitting gingerly on the pillow placed on the seat of the big red Naugahyde easy chair in the library produced some nostalgia for him, bringing back memories of his combat-zone social club, and he was drifting off to sleep, exhausted after the hard day, when in stepped Mr. Blink, who took a chair from across the room and placed himself directly in front of Mikey, who was now wide awake.

"Looks like you hurt your hand again."

Mikey didn't respond. Why start now? It was a reasonable enough question about his hand, considering that he had a bag of ice on it and he couldn't imagine squeezing a tennis ball anytime soon.

"You and Hercules had a very big day. Hope it was worth it. Was it, was it really worth it?"

Mikey stayed silent. For one thing, Blink was wearing yet another pair of glasses, wire-rims that hooked behind his stupendous ears, and when he smiled sarcastically, as he did now, his face resembled the beady, carnivorous grill of an American automobile manufactured in the fifties.

"Let's be clear. I really don't care what you think about anything, as this is a pretend polite conversation."

Mikey decided to expand the dramatic range of his dementia performance. He decided he would violently pick at his ear lobe for a while. Then he decided he would hum and hum and hum, tunelessly. Then he stood up and took off his shirt. What else, he was thinking, what else would an Alzhammered guy do? He drew a line at playing with or pissing himself.

Blink did not convey any curiosity with regard to these behaviors, nor did he try to manage Mikey before he did a crazier-seeming thing.

"Where is your lovely and fresh-as-springtime wife? Oh, that's right, she is probably taking lessons from the fitness trainer, in the gym, far from here, getting in some steamy aerobics. Tell me. How is your sex life these days? I am asking purely in the interests of your treatment protocol. We wouldn't want you to jeopardize your heart by imposing too much stress upon the old muscle. Zelda must really be frustrated, sexually speaking, a woman of her age, energy, and passion. Whereas you, well, *you*? Boom boom was oh so long ago for you, wasn't it, Michael"

Mikey wasn't going to stroll into Blink's version of the honey trap.

"I know you understand what I am saying. I know you have been fooling us all along, pretending to have Alzheimer's, both of you pretending to be Christian Scientists, which was a good one, I have to grant. But you are not clever enough to fool Chas Blink, not by half, Michael, if indeed Michael is your name. Is it your name? And Zelda—or whatever her name is—is in on this, and you are both cons, or grifters, or carneys. On top of that, you and Hercules have been having your fun, deceiving us, you and your Pepperoni Sunday fiasco, showing us up, but your circus tent is coming down and the show's going to be heading out of town soon enough. Yes, there will be some new controls put in place, starting tonight at dinner. You'll be plated your reliably delicious two ounces of

Salisbury steak, only this time you'll be served that protein-packed meal in the discomforts of your own apartment. We're going to close down the dining room till further notice, till order is restored in ORAL. People who are demented—people unlike you, Michael—demented people thrive in an atmosphere of order and regularity. You are an anarchist, somebody whose role in life is to destroy routine and organized expectation. I could justify tossing you out on your ass, I could easily, easily justify that, not that I answer to anybody but my board of directors, which doesn't really exist in the first place, as I may have neglected mentioning to you priorly."

Mikey was operating on the assumption that the man may not like him much, but he liked plenty the income flowing from people like him, and his paying his bills in cash, so how could Blink risk burning a bridge?

"But I am also a man who likes a challenge. I am going to help you grow and adjust to your circumstances. I plan to spend a lot more time with Zelda, for starters. You okay with that? I really don't care if you aren't, because you wouldn't be here in the first place if you could be anywhere else, had any other option."

Which was the baseline story, Mikey believed, of each zombie lurching through the halls, shuffling down the steps, face-planting onto the uncarpeted floor from time to time. Every Goner, Limper, and Indie. If they could be anywhere else, they wouldn't be here. But clearly, Blink believed he had Mikey by his nuts, his taser-aching nuts.

"You heard the sad news? I know you are listening to me. You and Hercules had such a wonderful old time, and evidently so did the girls. Too much fun, as it turns out. Ernestina in particular. Yes, poor little sexpot Ernie, who pleasured so many of us at the village. Well, you didn't hear, I guess. In case you didn't catch the latest, she died. Yes, about two hours ago. She stroked out, we've preliminary determined. And for that, I blame you, you and your irresponsible adventurings. Have a nice life, Michael, or whoever you are. And another thing. The board voted a rent increase, not that we really have such a board, like I said. Expenses are going through the roof, let's say for the sake of discussion, not that that is true. And because you and Zelda have the nicest apartment, your rent doubled, effective today. Meanwhile, put your shirt on and let me show you something."

They departed the library and passed into the hall and rounded the corner. The villagers were standing sentry outside Ernestina's open door, forming, very loosely, a receiving line. They didn't strike Mikey as anything like zombies now. They looked like people who had lost something very precious, something like a friend. Hercules was there, too, hat-short, a condition which rendered him more forlorn than ever. He was shaking his bare head, this side of weeping. They were all shaken by what happened to her, and shaken as well by the prospect of what lay in each of their futures.

The gurney was slowly guided out the door, pushed by sorrowful Carololina, on which wheeled metal stretcher evidently lay the body of Ernestina, decorously covered in a white sheet. It rattled somberly down the hallway, and each of the villagers touched her sheet as it passed, maybe somehow hoping to raise the undead. After Ernestina passed into the elevator, the door retracted shut, clanging loud as an ironworks factory, and she disappeared from view. The villagers from Over the Rainbow held their position as if they had no idea where they were supposed to go and as if standing in place was the most they were capable of.

Chapter Twenty-Nine

Zayana was watching, horrified, the local TV station when Mikey returned to their newly rent-doubled residence. He'd share that ultimately trivial financial development later—after all, they weren't going to stay anyway. She appeared ashen-faced as the breezy, folksy newscaster in an ill-fitting travesty of a sport coat flashed white capped teeth and a tinselly smile.

"Z, how about I buy a new TV?" A make-up present, he was thinking.

"Shut the, listen for a change, here comes the end of the world as we know it."

Now, here's one I didn't see coming. Grandma and grandpa causing a wild ruckus? In a casino? Biker gangs going at each other in a Nevada casino, sure, but old folks from a nursing home? As it turns out, local senior citizens were at the center of commotion at the Desert Gold Casino. Seems that a van full of residents of Over the Rainbow Assisted Living made an unsanctioned visit to the gaming establishment. Some of them are afflicted with dementia and various other disabilities, and they caused an uproar in the blackjack pit. According to the casino, there was a dispute about a bet, and about some alleged cheating on the part of the old folks, and fists were soon flying. I'm not making this up, people. Casino security broke up the melee and police detained the six women and the two men, both of them in dashing fedoras. One of the men, one Michael Jackson, his real name, apparently, had to be controlled with a taser when he threatened security. He recovered at the jail and did not require hospitalization. Purportedly, he is suffering from dementia, but he is strong as a bull, said a casino spokesman.

Footage of the Rainbow Eight's weak-kneed, sheepish perp walk into the police station rolled.

Mikey had an observation to make: "It's true what they say, TV puts extra pounds on people."

"Yes," said Zayana, "but unfortunately, TV puts no extra brains in their heads."

Mr. Jackson and his gang were released on their own recognizance, and a Desert Gold spokeswoman indicated no charges will be pressed. Word from the nursing home executive director, a Mr. Chas Blank, is that the trip was not authorized, and he thanked God no one was injured. But he was also lighthearted. He said that the eight of them will be denied dessert and TV privileges tonight. Just when you'd heard everything, right? Now, here's our weather guy Farley Garnet. Looks like unseasonal weather on tap. Scorcher tomorrow, right, Farley?

She clicked off the TV. "If you don't think this information and that video goes viral, you are from Outer Mongolia," Zayana said in a hushed voice. "I bet there are a thousand hits of you guys on YouTube already." She checked her laptop. "I was wrong. It's up to a twenty thousand now."

Mikey was annoyed. First, he had to be educated as to what going viral and U-Too meant and where Outer Mongolia was. Once up to speed, he concurred it was bad.

"Straight up, fool. Here's another thing I don't get. Why'd you take them all in the van? Why didn't you go in the Buick with Hercules and keep Over the Rainbow out of it, what is freakin' *wrong* with you?"

"Buick?"

"Our car, talking about our car. The one Mo got for you?"

"Don't drive a Buick. More like a Benz. Couple of other cars, too, which I left at home, but I'd never drive a Buick."

"Mikey," she started, "please don't..." But she was too dismayed when she completed the connection he seemed incapable of making.

Another thing else was eating away at Mikey. "That fucking taser hurt. And they're not going to press charges because they're crooks, is why. The arresting officer said the casino was full of scum bags, and he gave me his card, and told me to call him, I need anything, which I might."

"You don't get it, do you? The Keystone Cops might have screwed up and not identified you—not yet anyway. But those other guys coming after us? They may be idiots, but idiots like them watch television, they read papers, they turn on computers, they Google. What do you think they're going to do?"

Mikey didn't know what to say—he felt very stupid. That wasn't part of the plan. All he wanted was to celebrate Hercules's birthday.

"What possessed you to go there in the first place?"

"Desire to live? Little bit of fun?" He didn't go into details about the Minx Ranch and Carololina. What Zayana didn't need to know she didn't need to know.

"Are you happy, Captain Fun?"

Well, bring it on, Zayana. Best defense, always a good offense. When you don't have a leg to stand on, run the ball into the line. He had had his fill of being on the lam, hiding out. Whatever was to happen now, he would be prepared. As he reflected upon that, he realized he was not thinking clearly, which didn't stop him from doubling down.

"You know what, Z? I *am* sort of happy. I did make a bad judgment call. But I wouldn't change a thing. You're right, though. Sometimes I'm thinking clearly, other times..."

"How soon before you think the senator puts this all together? Now your face has been on television. The Old Folks Home Gang, whatever they're calling you. Who knows how soon before he and Mr. Smith and Dolly the Dick swing into action? If you don't care about yourself, that's one thing. But you could at least pretend to care about me, the mom of your son. We need to blow it all up and get outta here."

"You *say* I have a son?"

"Fuck all, don't start up again."

"If the senator's coming, I'm ready. I'm done running. Anything to relieve the boredom."

"There you go. You're crazy, Mikey. But you're feeling good about yourself, aren't you?"

"I was. I *was*. This is a bad development. I give you that. Don't know if you heard what else happened. Ernestina went to the great swinger's party in the sky."

Zayana felt downcast over the news, but she and Mikey had more immediate issues, and they were looming large. She was also baffled, and pointed down at Mikey's shoes, his gorgeous shoes.

"What? These are my favorite shoes."

Everything about him enraged her. It was open season now. "You trying to look cool now, tough guy, not wearing socks? Least you lost the hat in the brawl, which made you look the way guys look in hats, like a dope hiding male pattern baldness."

"What are you talking about?"

"I just said what I am talking about, you going out in your hat, not wearing socks."

"What hat?" He ignored the remark about socks because it made even less sense.

Zayana studied Mikey, wondering what was going on inside his head. That was a subject for later. She didn't have time to talk that through. "We gotta leave. We're sitting ducks."

Mikey rallied. She was right: they were totally vulnerable. "I got a idea. You pack. I'm staying. I started this problem, I'll finish it." And a phrase popped into his head: his fuck-it-the-bucket list. He looked over at the luggage where, unbeknownst to her, he had stashed his guns.

"You want to split up?"

"Till I can take care of these guys coming after us. Cause you're right, we got hours, day or two tops. Let's get this over. They want you, but I won't let them have you. And they want me, but they won't get their way either. Trust me."

Mikey wanted Zayana to trust him? After his screwball stunt today, why should she?

"Here's why. I'm thinking clearly now. I don't know how long I will be, but I am thinking clearly right this instant."

"Does it involve you going back to a casino?"

No, he was electing to stay here, in plain sight. "I got a idea, I told you."

"What about me?"

"Don't worry your pretty little head." Where had he heard that lately, where?

He realized he needed to tell her about the brothel. But not too much. "You, you're going to hide out at the Minx Ranch." He was improvising. It felt good.

"Sounds like some whorehouse."

Zayana always was sharp.

"There's gotta be a better way, Mikey. I can't keep hiding alongside you. I gotta look after myself now." What she had also figured out was what Rosey had warned her about: Mikey was at the point where he was not to be trusted.

"I'll explain my plan later. Pack your bag, Z," he said, heading out the door. He had work to do. And he was glad he had hidden those guns. They were going to come in handy.

"Okay, honey," she said sympathetically, no need to give him another problem. "Whatever you say, honey."

He staggered out of the apartment, he was reeling. All he was thinking was this: Zayana called him *honey*. He remembered when she did that all the time. He actually remembered.

ଔ

CASH IS GOOD, CASH is king, and thanks to his dad's mattresses, Mikey was glad to have access to lots of it. First, he tracked down Carololina folding towels in the laundry room. She appeared glad to see him. He was about to capitalize on his generous investment that started out as overpayment in the cash transaction at the Minx Ranch. He had a proposition for her, he said, and she lifted her eyebrows.

"Keep telling you. Not that kind of."

He asked her to watch over Zayana at the Minx, and he was prepared to make it worth her while. Carololina was amenable. One thing she needed was more money, she had let on to him, for her own folks, for the hormone injections, and one day if she was fortunate and flush enough, for the radical surgery.

"Mikey, you want me to call you *Mikey*? Fine. But you and Zayana, are you in trouble with the law?"

"Other side. Nothing I can't handle." He believed that this time. Then again, he had no alternative.

"There's a little camping trailer I keep at the Ranch, Zayana can stay there. It ain't the Hilton, it used to be my folks' only now it's my personal hideaway and I keep it tidy."

That sounded promising. He gave her some more money. If he didn't pull off his plan, he wasn't going to be in need of spending money. But now he needed her help. "Come with me." He'd tell her on the way. He could use her powers of persuasion. But Carololina was troubled about the money again.

"Don't think I can take all this money, it's too much—you're too sweet to me."

He wished she would get over her scruples. People needed help, that was adequate reason for him, and that was all the compensation she needed. Still, Mikey was touched. He made a vow to himself: he would somehow get the money to her later, when the dust cleared, if ever it did.

CB

"Door's open," Blink called out breathlessly from behind his desk. When Mikey and Carololina walked in, he quickly slammed shut his laptop, which was likely related to his breathlessness. He was spectacles-free. His eyes gleamed prehistorically and the swath of pale skin resembled a mask and made it appear as if somebody had ripped away a huge bandage around his head.

"No need to be shy about your porn," said Mikey, whose attention was sucked into the sight of the stock-still pet Gila monster, patiently sizing up a small white rat cornered in the glass aquarium.

"Hallelujah, now the man speaks in complete sentences," Blink said, impressing himself with his own righteous disdain. "We heal them all, we work miracles at ORAL, don't we, Carololina?"

"I don't have a lot of time, Blink, so lissename. I want you give me a room upstairs, in Goner Town, and one for Hercules, too. Nothing permanent, few days is all." He'd follow up with Hercules. His friend would go along for the ride, Mikey had no doubt.

"You're no Goner, neither is Hercules, so no can do. Besides, what do you want a room up there for? You have your rent-gouged, overpriced apartment you are paying for, and I'm not giving any discounts tonight."

"How much it take?"

"I don't like you, so no amount of money…"

Mikey blurted out a big number. There usually *is* an amount of money that works for somebody like Blink, the owner of a failed assisted living residence, or whatever the place was, a man whose dick was permanently connected to his computer's port. Then again, Over the Rainbow had now lost Ernie's rent money, so chances were the man was negotiating.

Blink's head lolled back against his desk chair. "Double it."

Carololina had a better idea, which she was about to roll out. "Chas baby, you should make this little accommodation for Michael out of the goodness of your heart."

"Sweetheart, baby cakes, you know I don't have any goodness in my burned out heart. We warehouse these pathetic old buzzards at exorbitant rates, because they don't have families or because nobody in their families gives a rat's ass, and nobody in the great state of California seems the least bit concerned for them, now that we don't expect to get licensed again, thanks to that stunt at the casino. Speaking of rat's ass." He pointed toward the aquarium where the white rat's tail was sticking out of the lizard's mouth and twitching. "They say human beings possess what they call the reptile brain. You can relate, can't you, Michael?"

Carololina could have anticipated what he said—maybe not the part about the Gila monster. She was doing the due diligence and the negotiation. She explicitly offered some additional personal services in the way of compensation, as if she were a car salesman talking about undercoating and trunk tie-downs, which were not completely unrelated.

"Enticing. That would be a new thing or two for us, true, but right now you already do other things for me, which you enjoy and are expert at, Friday afternoons right here in my office, our love nest, right before I sign your pay check, which you earn like a good girl."

Bad move for Blink. "Not anymore, Chas. I have reconsidered. My lips are now sealed and I won't be servicing you anymore, unless, that is, you want to help this man, but you know what? You want to stay in business?" She took out her phone from her hip pocket and held it up for him to see.

"Gotta get one of those."

"Amazing what this little computer can do. Like recording somebody incriminating himself. It's very easy to do. And I can post it online by hitting this button—see it here?"

"You recorded me? It's illegal to record somebody without their express…"

"That could be so, but somebody somewhere will be interested in hearing the words coming out of your own mouth. And I can hire a lawyer, and bring on my own sex harassment case. Who knows who else will be interested in how you sexually exploited a poor, helpless, adorable tranny like me."

"What are you trying to say?"

Carololina showed Chas Blink in all its sizeable glory precisely what she was trying to say.

TWO YEARS LATER

CAREGIVER LOG

Use this form to monitor changes and to communicate with doctors, hospice nurses and caregivers across shifts.

PATIENT: *MICHAEL FESTAGIACAMO (age 59)*

CAREGUVER: *CAREGIVER CAREGIVER CAREGIVER!!!*

I GUVE UP.

MRS. WINONA WILDER, BA, SARAH LAWRENCE COLLEGE

DATE/TIME: *A gorgeous Monday Morning*

NOTE CHANGES: *I think we are witnessing nothing short of a miracle.*

FOOD: *Devoured seconds of everything, all three meals. Three-egg omelet for breakfast. Tuna melt for lunch. Roast chicken for dinner.*

MEDICATION: *Per normal.*

ACTIVITIES: *Is he going to drop to the floor and do pushups in a minute? Is he going to run a four-minute mile or do the pole vault?*

PAIN LEVEL: *I have all the pain keeping up with him!*

ENERGY: *Energizer Bunny.*

SLEEP PATTERN: *Ten blessed, tranquil hours.*

When I saw him jump out of bed with a spring in his step, I practically spilled my cup of tea. Then he turned on the television set—with the remote!—and watched a Seinfeld rerun and laughed at the right times. Then he practically hopped into the shower and afterwards shaved himself and brushed his teeth and picked out his clothes as if he were going to a fancy Dan party.

One concern, tiny as it may be in the grand scheme of things: he asked me who I was and what I was doing in his room and was I his girl. I was not sure how to answer him, and I await instructions. In the meantime, I have packed my bags and, if my work here is done, I am ready to do what is required under these fascinating circumstances. I am so happy for Michael and his family.

—WW

TWO YEARS LATER

To: Rosetta Festagiacamo
From: Dinah Forte
Subject: totally astonished

My dear Rosey,

In all my experience I have never witnessed a metamorphosis like this. The other day, as you said, you saw it with your own eyes, but I have to tell you I have never seen such improvement before.

His primary called in the neurologist and the psychiatrist for a consult, and they are all making similar pronouncements. Such a radical shift—such dramatic evident progress—is not completely unprecedented, but you have to dig pretty deep into the annals of treatment when an advanced-dementia patient evidenced such a sweeping turn-around. I wouldn't be surprised if the doctors are already drafting a piece for the journal of the AMA. In the meantime, they are sending him in this week for MRIs and other tests.

I know we want to keep a proper perspective about this development. These sudden shifts are anomalous, to say the least, perhaps inexplicable, and finally perhaps unsustainable. His base condition remains the same, but let us relish the new springtime of Mikey as long as we can and count on enjoying this phenomenon while it lasts—and let us all hope it is not a one-off transient development.

By the way, when I visited him today we played poker. You should have warned me! That man, your brother, is a card shark! And he looked so handsome in his pristine robin's egg blue French cuff shirt, with links of gold, too!

One last thing: hospice is conducting its own evaluation. I would not be surprised if they pulled out at this point—at least for the time being. But if I have learned anything in my thirty-year career, when it comes to the mysterious course of Alzheimer's, that's all we have to go on: the present. And yet, the present in Mikey's case is so very sweet. Enjoy it, Rosey. I have confidence Mikey is enjoying it. I know I stand in wonderment.

Thank you once again for retaining me—this has been the case of a lifetime, because as we learn from dementia over and over again: a human being is not a case, a diagnosis, the sum of his symptoms, not at all. Mikey is a man on his own unique, startling journey. And let's not forget the obvious: Alzheimer's is a story-teller with a complicated tale to tell—struggling and failing to find the words.

We shall see what meets us down the road.

Affectionately,

Dee
Dinah Penelope Forte, PhD
Forte Care Management Professionals

Chapter Thirty

That loneliest, most dismal of calendar markers, Visiting Day, came around once again. Of course, it was otherwise known, at least for the Over the Rainbow Underground consisting of two, Mikey and Hercules, as Pepperoni Sunday. Before the sun set this occasion would ultimately live up to the promise, or threat, implied by the name. Two men in baggy suits arrived and passed unimpeded through the unlocked front door. They were not bearing pizza, delivery of which, in case they were interested, they could clearly see, thanks to the re-posted sign, was forbidden by what Blink believed was Management. Beyond that, they were not qualifying as visitors anybody in their right mind would want to receive—at this residence, or anywhere else on earth.

As for Blink, he had been keeping a very low profile since that discouraging, deflating audio-recorded conversation in his office with his all-time favorite employee, and heartbroken as he was, he had begun contemplating making changes in his life, soon as he figured out what that self-help book he read called "driving passions." He was sure he had one or two of them.

The two men approached Carololina, who was manning the desk and energetically painting her nails, and identified themselves as old friends of Michael Jackson, here in town, they said, to pay him a little surprise visit. "Which he ain't expecting," redundantly added the smaller, talkative guy.

She said that was nice of them, and Mikey would be so pleased. "We'll see about that," he said. She asked them to sign in on the Visitor's Log, which she pushed across the counter, careful not to smudge her fresh Damask Rose Pink nails. The Log page was utterly blank, because no visitors had yet signed in because they did not exist. The two men brazenly, inanely inscribed their fake names: Mr. Smith registered as Mr. Jones and Dolly Leone as Mister Lion.

The smaller, talkative of the two said, "You can call me Dolly."

Carololina pleasantly said, "Hello, Dolly."

She would not have predicted that he would greet her words with dismay.

"Or do you mean Dalí, like after the famous and arguably overrated surrealist painter?"

Dolly tugged on his lapels, his easily bruised ego abraded yet again. "I look like I climb up on a ladder of steps, drop washcloths, am I?"

She saw no point antagonizing the man with a mangle mouth like that, so she smiled.

"When I was bred, they Christianized me Delancey, get it? So Dolly, which is got from Delancey?"

She said she did get it, and his hopes were visibly buoyed. He appeared undiscourageable, which often struck Carololina as being the case with many a deluded patron who skulked into the Minx Ranch.

"To be discontinued, gorgeous. We go clubbing and have dinner and dine in Vegas? Right now, we have certain labors and work and we gotta skoodaddle, goodbye farewell for now. Whereabouts can we come across and find old Mikey, and won't he be supersized?"

CR

ONCE THOSE TWO WERE out of earshot, Carololina called Mikey on his cell phone in Goner Town.

"Game on," she said. They got on the elevator—the creakiest, slowest, most unmaintained grinder of an Otis lift in all the great state of California—so it would take a while before showtime commenced. One man the size of an offensive lineman—or more like big as half an offensive line—along with some creepy guy tagging along who wouldn't shut up and who repellently hit on her, she said.

It had taken the senator's henchmen close to three days to track Mikey down after the news report on the television news that had presumably gone, as Z predicted, viral. This led Mikey to speculate as to whether or not he had overestimated his adversary. Mr. Smith may not have been as sharp or as efficient as he gave him credit for. Then again, the man might have a sick sense of humor: after all, he did show up on Visiting Day.

"Mikey," she said, "the big guy's scary."

"What he say?"

"Nothing much," which to her was the most ominous aspect, and which told her she should call that cop whose card Mikey gave her, to use in case of an emergency.

"Mr. Jones gotta be the famous Mr. Smith and the other rat is my old crew member Dolly," Mikey said. "What I figured. Only two of them, good. Follow the plan, Carololina. These guys don't want any part of you. Well, Dolly does."

"Which part, you think?"

Mikey asked about Zayana. He hadn't been able to reach her all day.

"Remember, I told you cell phone reception sucks out there in the desert?" He remembered no such thing. "But don't you worry about her.

I got her covered. Gave her my best silk sheets and two bottles of Scotch to tide her over."

It was three nights ago when he last saw her. It seemed like a lifetime ago. Strangely, in her absence, he had somehow inched closer to her, which was always the case in the past when they continually practiced breaking up. Their best moments had always been making up. She had him figured out. All she had to do to win him over again was to vanish. There could have been a moral to that story, but he wasn't inclined to be drawing one, if there were one worth drawing. He missed her badly right now and now was all he had, or all she or they ever had together, but she was out of reach.

"You sure she's okay?"

"Trust me."

"Where's Blink?"

"No idea. Man won't look me in the eye anymore. He pretends I don't exist, and we don't anymore, *you know*, thank God. He comes and goes like a ghost, so you don't know when he's going to appear."

"Whatever happens to me, one thing: don't go out with Dolly, promise?"

"Jeez, what makes you think I don't have standards?"

He apologized. "Everything on schedule?"

Details had been taken care of. She calculated that all she needed was a ten-minute window to stick in the final piece of the puzzle, and the clock was ticking.

&

MIKEY AND HERCULES HAD organized Goner Town with Carololina's aid, on Blink's blackmailed hear-no-evil, see-no-evil say-so. The residents had all been freshly sleeping-pilled and shuttered in their individual rooms.

Then the two friends created a kind of stage, with theatrical props. They were positioned in side-by-side wheel chairs, tattered plaid blankets over their laps, portable oxygen tanks rhythmically hiccoughing tiny ooooshes, decorative tubes in their noses, while the television set mumbled at low volume in the semi-darkened room. Cable news on TV, of course, which was relentlessly covering the upcoming election.

"Herc, you can take off, you want to. You didn't ask for this shit, it's all about me and Z, and this could get screwed up fast."

"Come on, what are friends for?"

So Mikey really did, as it turned out, have a friend.

"Nice touch, oxygen," said Hercules. "Kind of makes me high. If I'd've known that before I'd…"

"Try to look like a zombie," said Mikey.

"Easy sleazy," said Hercules. "You, too."

"If we get out of here…"

"*When* we get out of here."

"*When* we get out of here, you come live with me. You'd like my house, all the fancy wine you want. Hope you like Italian. I want you to meet my sister and my boy. I'll take care of you, you won't worry about nothing again."

"Man, Mikey, you are like family. You're better than family, which never comes see me."

"First chance, I take you to a great little restaurant my dad owns, place called Lorenzo's, down by the water. My old man'll like you, too. Lights on the boats and everything, sea gulls, flags flapping. Pizza, pasta, chicken under a brick, Herc, like you can't believe. My girl, she works there. She's a beauty. My son works there, too."

Hercules was having trouble tracking Mikey. Something wrong about him was not right.

CR

THE SUN WAS FILTERING in through the windows and they were inside, but a howling wind picked up far away in Mikey's head. He heard what sounded like a hard rain on a corrugated iron roof. Then a cycle song of the coyote pack on the hillside broke in, celebrating a deer kill.

CR

"YOU HEAR ME? GOT a full bar at the restaurant?"

Mikey became confused all over again.

"I'm asking, being curious and preferring my vodka gimlets, you got a liquor license? At your dad's place, Lorenzo's?"

Mikey couldn't be sure what was wrong. Why was this guy asking him about Lorenzo's? What did the man know that he didn't? And who was he?

"Dad, I'm the boss, right?" he muttered.

"You okay?"

"What the? I'm in a wheelchair."

CR

MINUTES PASSED AND HERCULES was willing to write off Mikey's oddness. Considering what was about to come down, oddness was predictable.

"You ever killed anybody, Mikey?"

How would Mikey, having now returned from his mental wandering, begin to answer? He was glad his friend had changed the subject, even if he changed it to a topic like that. Nevertheless, that was a tricky question to answer one way or the other. Things happened to people that he determined and actions were authorized, of course. Did he himself pull the trigger? Technically, technically…no.

"You, Herc? How about you?"

"One time, the great bloody Battle of Anzio, the Big One, WWII. I was a kid, and I was a Marine. It's you or the enemy on the battlefield. As you can plainly tell, that time, it was them. Man's gotta do what a man's gotta do."

"You ready for the shit coming down?"

"My two Purple Hearts say I am all the way up on over it."

Which, Mikey believed, was what it was going to take if they had half a chance.

He wasn't sure they did.

"Follow my lead." Mikey had put together a complete plan, at least one impractical part of which involved oxygen tanks and a lighter, which he had seen work in a movie but not in real life, but his head was now a howlingly empty plain where the plan used to be lodged. He wasn't worried. He'd either get out of this alive, or he and Mr. Smith and Dolly would be goners in Goner Town, only sooner rather than later. And you know what? So be it. Forget the oxygen and the lighter. The other part of the plan was better.

With his good—left—hand, Mikey pulled out from under his blanket his three handguns and presented the offer to his friend: "Walther, Beretta, or you want the Glock?"

Hercules whistled and made his selection.

"Good choice," said Mikey. He showed him how it worked. It was a simple enough mechanism. He didn't have to like guns to know how to use them. "You got time to scram, Herc."

"We talked about this, I'm all in."

CR

THEY FELL SILENT AND listened as the elevator door yawned open and they heard the slow, heavy tread of the men approaching to commit a few quick and doubtless well-compensated murders.

"I'm looking foe word to the reunification of my old friend, which we all called Mikey boy," said Dolly in his unmistakably grating voice: cement mixer with undercurrent of growl. "I shoulda brung flowers, them forget-me-lots."

"Y'ever shut up?" said Mr. Smith, reasonably as could be.

"Not really," said Dolly, after a small pause, as if there were an authentic mystery on the table.

"Here we go," Hercules and Mikey said to each other under their breath.

The men rounded the corner and then stopped dead in their tracks at the shocking sight of disheveled, immobile Mikey alongside another comparably withered old man, both gathered before a TV.

Hercules couldn't help himself. He gasped. Anybody similarly positioned would have done the same. This was not the Battle of Anzio in the offing, after all. This was shaping up as more like the Visiting Day Massacre.

Of course, this was the first time Mikey had seen Mr. Smith. He would have preferred putting off the experience till the next life, because the appearance lived up to the legend.

The would-be killers proceeded toward them. The linoleum floor winced with each advancing step the big man took. The joists in the walls flinched. The fluorescent bulbs flickered off-yellow. The window curtains sucked in their breath.

Mr. Smith's hands were large enough to wrap around the neck of a race horse, his shoulders broad enough to support a Greek column. But his face, that was the most startling, frightening aspect. He had the impish, joyful countenance of a little girl on a playground swing, a girl who had spent the afternoon pulling off butterfly wings. The face of a man who could kill anybody he wanted any time he chose.

Mikey had witnessed close up the fear his father or he himself had instilled in others back when they had the power. He'd seen grown men whimper and piss themselves when they couldn't pay what they rightfully owed. And Mikey felt sorry for them—which his dad was incapable of feeling because a debt was a debt—and Mikey sometimes sentimentally cut them a break when he was calling the shots. He himself was an outsized man, and his bulk proved sufficient to intimidate when the occasion called for that. But Mr. Smith wasn't another sort of man, he was a volcano in a failed suit liar Randy himself couldn't convince you made you look like a million bucks. And what do you do when you see Mount Etna about to blow? You run for your life. But that prudent course of action was not an option for a man relegated to his wheelchair. Maybe, Mikey considered rationally, this time it was indeed all over for him. He had finally crossed paths with the absolutely wrong guy. It happens to everybody, he reflected, sooner or later. And for him it looked to be much sooner than later. He regretted roping Hercules into this mess he had made of his life. They were outnumbered, two to two. And he was outgunned, even with the pretty Beretta. The gun was by his useless right hand under the blanket, but if he could lift the gun, which he doubted, his fingers wouldn't permit him to squeeze a trigger. He hoped that Hercules had absorbed enough knowledge about the Glock to use it.

"Dark in this joint," said Dolly.

"Why don't you take off your dumb sunglasses?" said Mr. Smith.

Dolly acted upon that sound suggestion. "Better, thanks," he said.

Mr. Smith called him an idiot once again. Dolly was tired of hearing that point of view.

Mr. Smith and Dolly pulled up chairs and positioned themselves in front of Mikey. When Mr. Smith sat down the chair looked like it was a cast-off from a kid's playhouse. It creaked in abject misery.

"Mikey boy," said Dolly, cheerily. "How's it shakin, man?"

Mikey stared into the middle distance.

"Not too good, looks like. That's okay, it's gonna get worst."

Dolly turned to Hercules. "And who would you be by accident and chance?"

"Hercules, I'm with Mikey."

Mikey's eyes shot to the TV screen, to which they were instantly riveted.

Dolly was amused. "This your new crew, Mikey? You and—did that guy really say the name was friggin' Hercules?"

Mr. Smith was not amused.

"Is Mikey sennil?" said Dolly to Mr. Smith.

"You mean *senile*?"

"Yeah, said that."

"You said…never mind, you idiot. Where the hell are we?"

As if on cue, Carololina appeared to illuminate them. She was not following her script and her arrival was not a tactical feature of any plan Mikey had concocted, which would have absolutely precluded risking her.

"This is where we at Over the Rainbow treat elderly people like persons," she said, sharing the mission that fell dumbly on the tone-deaf ears of thugs like these. "And this is the memory wing of the residence, where advanced Alzheimer's patients reside when their impairment renders them incapable of taking care of themselves."

Dolly couldn't stop himself: "That's where we come in, sweet cheeks, we going to take care of this guy for good, once and for real."

"Once and for *all*?"

"Everybody's fucking correcting me. What, I can't talk English?" Dolly gave evidence of a disappointment surging within: "I am getting a bad feeling, I gotta say. This ain't gonna be the fun I was anticipating counting on. It'd be like whacking a zucchini. 'Cause Mikey, he's a vegetable," he said to Mr. Smith. "A squashed what's dead already." Then he spoke with venomous frustration to Mikey: "My chance to take you out, like you deserved and earned, and you forsake away all my fun."

"We got a job to do," noted Mr. Smith, "which we got paid for already."

"Was wondering thinking about that. Where is my money?"

But Mr. Smith addressed Carololina. "So Mikey's kind of like dead already, along with the rest of the vegetables here in the memory wing?"

"I wouldn't say that," Carololina said, protectively. "These are human beings struggling with an illness."

"Which will kill them eventually?"

"We don't talk like that here in the memory wing."

Even under the prevailing conditions, Dolly was helplessly excited all over again by the succulent spectacle of her. "How *do* you talk? Like, do you like to talk dirty?"

"Depends on who I am talking to."

"Like to your boyfriend?"

"Don't have one of those."

"So I got a chance?"

"What's a man without a dream?"

"Yeah," said Dolly, "what *is* a man without a wet dream?"

"You're kind of disgusting, aren't you?"

"Thanks. I knew we'd get along if you gave me the clime of day."

"Speaking of which, we're about to serve lunch. Would you visitors care to join Mikey and Hercules?" She fully expected they would spurn the offer.

"You'd be there to accompany us together, too? If so, we'd be dee-lighted."

Mr. Smith had long ago lost patience with Dolly and he had no interest in food. He normally never chowed down when working, including at Lorenzo's that time, when he could have eaten everything in the walk-in if he so wished. "I think I should kill you, too, Dolly. Then I'll kill Mikey, then all the witnesses. Sorry, pretty girl, but that's where this is all going in a few minutes, so we'll take a pass on the grub, but thanks, hate to work on a full stomach. But you might have some information I can use. Where's Zayana? That's what I really want to know. If you told me, it might be your lucky day and you won't get killed too much, after all."

"I don't know anybody named Zayana."

"I need to show you how quickly I can lose my temper?"

"I'll take your word for it, Mr. Smith."

Mr. Smith beamed. Ah, that was beautiful, what she said. "How'd you know my name?"

Carololina's bad mistake. "You introduced yourself downstairs?"

"Don't think so."

"Lucky guess?"

"Yeah, that's some kinda lucky guess, but I don't think so. *Mikey*? He told you?"

Carololina went in another direction: "Mikey's had a long day already. I think he needs to rest now, gentlemen."

Mr. Smith didn't like that direction: "Mikey can rest when he's dead."

Dolly said that was a good one.

"Shut the. But lissemame, hot stuff. If you know who I am, you must know where Zayana is. You got a very pretty face. Want to keep your face intact for the funeral parlor, so you can at least have an open casket?"

Dolly was beginning to enjoy his assignment all over again. "Plot dickens."

Mr. Smith and Dolly were getting ready to take some lives. Mikey could not stop them—even if he was skilled with the gun resting by his hand, which he was not. If he once had had a plan, it was now wandering, lost in the brain blizzard.

¨

AND THEN HIS BRAIN was jolted as if by a bolt of electricity.

"You losers," said Mikey in a clear, assertive voice, "you are going to be met by a *swift response*."

Mr. Smith and Dolly cracked up, couldn't help it.

"Mikey speaks," said Dolly, "with words."

"Whatever response you got up your sleeve," said Mr. Smith, "I got a feeling it ain't gonna be swift."

"You're wrong," Mikey said. "Here's my *swift response*. I'll tell you where Zayana is."

"Where?" said Mr. Smith, expecting a trick.

"Mikey," said Carololina, "what are you doing?"

"Yeah, Mikey," said Hercules, "'cause you don't know where she is."

"But I do. First I had a question for Dolly. Dolly, you monkey-face dick-licker, where's Beppe and Scoop?"

"We gave them all a very early retirement package, permanently, 'cepting Fatso, who roly-polyed off into the bacony sunset. But it cheers me up, you're feeding your goats."

"Okay, Mikey, enough with the shit chat. Where's the girl?" said Mr. Smith. "Tell me or I will show you *my* swift response."

"She's right under your flat nose."

"She's in the building?"

"No."

"You got three seconds."

Mikey counted off: one, two, three. "*Swift response*: she's right *there*."

Mikey pulled his left hand from under the throw and balled it into a fist and raised it before his eyes, as if preparing for the sort of *swift response* he reliably provided in the past.

"Mikey boy," said Dolly. "You're making me urinate into my pissed pants, you're so funny."

Then Mikey opened his hand, unfurling his fingers, and pointed his index finger up to the TV set. Dolly and Mr. Smith tracked in the direction of Mikey's finger—to the TV.

For that's indeed where Zayana was, on the screen. She was present for a live televised press conference, which was packed with reporters, and she sat shyly alongside a confident woman wearing a blue Chanel suit with big black eyeglasses. A menacing stack of papers loomed before her.

Mr. Smith told Carololina to turn up the volume.

"*...but the senator has vehemently denied the woman's blockbuster allegations. Two days from the general election, the senator has released a statement denying that he had an affair with this woman or fathered a child by her. Let's listen as her attorney is about to address the crowd of journalists here in Los Angeles... Here she goes now...*"

"*My client has sought my representation because she needs protection from the senator, who has stalked and threatened her if she came forward with the truth. She and the senator conducted an affair over the course of several years, while the senator was married, and before he was elected to the Senate. My client had no choice but to go public because she feared for her life and the life of her son and her son's real father, who has also been threatened by the senator. A man like the senator with his immense wealth and his effectively infinite resources has terrorized this brave woman, who never sought the limelight, who would never be before you today if she could have protected herself from him in any other fashion. But she sits here because out in the open is her best chance to withstand his assault on her. We are not currently seeking civil damages, though we reserve the right to do so, as is our prerogative. We do understand the US Attorney has begun an investigation of the senator at our behest, and she has asked for our cooperation, which will be furnished. I want to be perfectly clear. My client has no political agenda, and has no interest in derailing the senator's reelection hopes, but if that happens, so be it..."*

"Is your client going to make a statement?"

"Go on, Zayana."

"*I always wished,*" Zayana read from her prepared script, shaking in the blinding camera lights, "*always hoped to live my life out of the glare of the public eye, but I see now that is not possible. I made the mistake many years ago of becoming involved with a powerful man who was married, which I did not know when our relationship commenced—and he told me for a fact he was not. At the same time, I was unfaithful to my common-law husband, for which I will always be sorry and I will work to earn back his trust and forgiveness. All I can say in my defense is that this was a long time ago, when I was a young and foolish woman. I hoped I had put my past behind me. But the senator would not let me live my life. He told me that if I told anybody that I would regret it. And so would my son and so would my common-law husband, who is the true father of my child. I couldn't let the senator destroy our lives. Now, maybe now, he will let me have some peace and I can live freely and without fear again. That's all I have to say. Thank you.*"

"Is it true that you were blackmailing the senator and he has stopped paying you?"

"Is it true that you are a political supporter of his opponent and the reason that you are coming forward at this late hour is to wreck his chances at reelection?"

"Are you currently in rehab for drug and alcohol addiction?"

"Are you an employee of a Nevada brothel?"

"Is your son's father a mob boss?"

"Who is paying your lawyer?"

"That's all for now," said her lawyer, *"we have nothing more to add at this point. Good afternoon and thank you."*

Mr. Smith spoke to the television set: "She wants to live in peace, does she? Everybody's gonna be at peace, starting right here right now."

Mr. Smith's cell phone went off. It was ringing with the rhythms of the marimba.

"Yeah…Yeah…I'm right here…I don't…But…You sure?…I got him right here, where I want him…okay…You're calling the shots…I knew all along you didn't have the balls…You and your husband, both chicken-shit, you know that, right?…You're welcome…Tell your husband, the senator, have a nice life…I'll just kill Mikey, long as I am here, nothing else on my calendar the rest of the day…" And he put the phone back in his suit pocket.

"Foot's on the other shoe," said Dolly.

"Time to take care of business," said Mr. Smith.

"Cops are coming," said Carololina. "I called them." This was the cop sympathetic to Mikey after the casino.

"I could kiss you," said Hercules. "No really, I mean it."

ꙮ

"DAD," SAID MIKEY OUT loud, "what are you doing? Where's Mom? I'm losing more than I'm winning. The boat's here, the gate is open."

ꙮ

THERE YOU HAVE IT. What a shocking development for the senator's campaign. His spokeswoman will be holding a press conference in a few minutes, but the word we are hearing is that the senator will admit to having an affair with this woman. He is alleging that he begged his wife for forgiveness many years ago, which she granted him. This woman later became pregnant and intended to get an abortion, but the senator and his wife, who are both adamantly pro-life, purportedly urged the woman to keep the child. And to that end, they paid her, according to them. It was not blackmail, he will say, but it was a way to save the life of the unborn and to provide for the child's support. There may be more news coming out soon, but that's what we know now. Who can predict how the race will be affected by this blockbuster? And who knows if the senator will be able to withstand those inevitable calls, already pouring in, for him to step down? Now back to you in the studio.

Mr. Smith pulled down the flat screen from the wall and threw it on the floor, where it clanged and cracked.

$$\infty$$

SIX YOUNG MEN WEARING black bandanas, jeans hanging down their asses, flannel shirts untucked and buttoned to the neck, big wrap-around shades lodged on top of their heads, strutted into Goner Town like conquistadors claiming territory.

"Look who's here," said Hercules, whose teary smile would warm the hearts of anybody not named Dolly or Mr. Smith.

"Hey, Grampy."

"Thought you couldn't make it, Buster."

"Me and the fellas been wanting to visit you for your birthday. Told you I'd be here, didn't I? Better late than never. What you doin' up here, Grampy? Smells funny in this place. You okay?"

"Buster, want you to meet some people. This is my friend Mikey. He's been a real good friend to me. And so is Carololina here, ain't she pretty? Only she wants a sex-change operation so don't get your hopes or anything else up for now. And then, you see these two other guys here?"

Buster turned to face them and nobody like Buster, who had his street radar switched on when he was awake and sometimes when asleep, was going to require excessive explanation.

"Yeah, Buster, these two guys, they showed up to kill us."

Buster and his running mates whipped out their own Glocks and trained them sideways on Mr. Smith and Dolly, emulating the way they saw them do that on *The Wire*, which always looked cool. As for Mr. Smith and Dolly, they had looked down a barrel of a gun once or twice in their lives, but not six guns trained on them by LA gangbangers.

"No shit, Grampy?" Buster said, keeping his eyes on Mr. Smith.

"No shit whatsoever, and here it is Visiting Day." Then Hercules pulled out his own Glock to show off and get in the spirit.

"Grampy, that's a pretty piece you got, where'd you get it?"

"Mikey, he gave it to me in case."

Buster turned his attention to the two would-be hitters. "That's not a nice thing to do on Visiting Day, is it, threatening my grampy, 'specially around his birthday?"

"They came here to kill Mikey," said Hercules, "but they were going to take out me and Carololina, because we're witnesses."

"Why you want to hurt my grampy? That you guys' idea of what goes on Visiting Day?"

"I can explainidate," Dolly began but gave up, because he couldn't.

"You really wanna hurt my grandpa and his buddies? That true, big man, and you, you big nose mother?"

"No need for sticks and stonesy name-calling," tried a sorry-sounding Dolly.

"Oh, man, I think we are only getting started with you guys. I'm gonna teach you guys a magic trick. My grampy taught me how to be a magician. I can make shit go poof. Suck on that the rest of your lives, long as that might be. You listenin'? Don't *nobody* fuck with my grandpa."

Mr. Smith had a point he wanted to get on the table. "Son, your grandfather, I want to put this respectively, is not firing on all cylinders. He's misread the situation."

"You called me 'son'? I wouldn't do that if I was you, you ain't my dad. And you're saying my grampy's bat-shit?"

"Senile's a tough word, but yes, there it is. I wouldn't trust him."

"Grampy, you heard Big Man. Says you're nuts. What you have to say?"

"What I got to say is, you wanna see a dollar disappear, Buster?"

Buster smiled, and doing so he looked like a little boy. "Gotcha covered, Grampy."

"We don't really want to harm your grandpa," said Dolly. "Just the other guy, which is called Mikey, boy, and we'll leave with him right now. It's purely a business matter concerning very important VIP peoples. No need for you to get involvplicated."

"Mikey's my friend, Buster," said Hercules.

"Well, which that means is, I'm already involved. If he's in my grampy's posse, he's in mine. That's my move. What's yours, douche mouth?"

Suddenly blinkered Chas Blink ambled in from the back, and trailing behind him were Rosetta, Mo, and Fatso. Blink was saying in a chirpy voice to her, "He should be right here, Ms. Festagiacomo, your beloved brother, and one of our all-time favorite resident villagers." He was also holding a tray of little plastic cups for some inscrutable reason. When he noticed the array of trained weaponry, he dropped the whole thing.

Rosey needed to know fast: "Mikey, you okay?"

Hercules answered her: "These guys came here to kill Mikey and me."

CR

MIKEY DID NOT SAY a word and he was looking off into the distance. It was unclear what, if anything, he was focused on. Hercules could see his friend was not tracking and somebody else was going to have to speak for him. From the looks of things, it was going to be him.

ଔ

THE GANGBANGERS' ATTENTION HAD been distracted by the dropped tray, and in that opening, Mo and Fatso pulled out their Smith & Wessons.

"This party ain't getting started," said Mo, "don't nobody move."

"Which guys want to kill you, Mikey?" Rosetta said. "The gangbangers, or our old friend Dolly who's keeping company, I'm guessing, with the famous Mr. Smith, or both?"

"The kids are with Mikey and me," said Hercules, "but not these other two motherfuckers."

"Mikey," said Rosey, "Zayana told me you'd be here, we drove down as fast as we could. She said she was going to be on TV today, put an end to all this foolishness."

"Which she was," said Hercules. "She did great."

"Hey, lady," said Buster, who was a little bit annoyed because he had been planning on arranging his own big finish, "we got the situation under control."

"That's my brother and nothing bad is going to happen to him."

"So we got a common enemy, lady."

Rosey addressed Dolly. "The young man might be right, Dolly. You guys are the common enemy, how's it feel? Mikey, you feeling okay?" He didn't look it.

"Come on, Rosey," said Dolly, "you know what's going on. We was looking for to find Zayana, and she ain't here, so we can safely leave and exit right now."

"All due, you're going to exit and leave, all right," said Mo. "Dolly, you and Mr. Smith, take out your pieces, very slowly, put them on the ground. Listen carefully to what the boss says."

Dolly looked toward Mo with puzzlement. "Mikey didn't open his trap, Mo."

Mo didn't need to, but he clarified: "Rosey, *she's* the boss lady, Rosey is. Slow, Dolly, go very slow with your piece, I said, or I'm gonna enjoy putting a slug in you."

She may have been the boss lady, but Dolly and Mr. Smith were nothing if not reluctant to comply with Mo's orders.

"Rosey can't be no boss," said Dolly, "she's a broad. If she's the boss, the pie is falling, the pie is falling."

In the meantime, a savory distraction loomed, and Dolly was by happenstance correct.

Three seriously stoned high school boys in red pizza parlor shirts and red paper cone hats had breezed in laughing under a cloud of pot. They were carrying pizza boxes and entered with a rehearsed, management-trained flourish that might have been an indication to Hercules and Mikey that Pepperoni Sunday was in the offing.

"*Family Business Pizzeria. Today we take care of all family business.* And we got twenty half-baked family-style pepperoni specials for somebody name of…says here *Carolina*?"

"North or South Carolina?" said his far too easily self-amused sidekick.

Blink shouted: "It's *Carololina!*" But the man was feeling desperate, it was now or never for him to declare his intentions. "Carololina baby, can we make up, please? Give me another chance, please. I miss you so much."

Carololina almost felt sorry for her onetime employer: "Miss you, too, Chas, but that pizza has left the oven."

"Whatever and that's nice," said the delivery boy in charge. "But who's paying? You, with the pony tail and goggles?"

But Blink and his pony tail and goggles were not done, and much as he missed his girl and possibly boy, he didn't want anybody to forget that he was supposedly in charge: "How come you didn't see the goddamn sign I put up on the goddamn door, about no pizza being…"

Hercules told Blink to shut up. The pizzas smelled too good to be argued over. Name one situation that wasn't seriously improved by the appearance of pizza, just one. Then again, the situation before them was unprecedented in his experience. More to the point, Hercules was silently cheering that Mikey and Carololina had masterfully orchestrated such beautiful mass chaos. Fog of war was one thing. Fog of pizza, another. When matters were out of control—like people wanting to kill you—additional confusion can only help. Hercules hadn't been told in advance that that was what those two cooked up, and he was impressed. Pizza smelled irresistible, too.

"Okay," said the delivery boy in charge, remembering the script he had been trained to articulate, "you gotta heat these bad boys up for eight to ten minutes at four hundred degrees and then… What the?"

He reached that conclusion because that was the precise moment he noticed through his weedy haze the guns drawn throughout the room.

"Whoa now, we don't want no trouble. You guys can keep the pizzas, on the house, we'll mosey on outta here…"

But the pizza boys couldn't make a move anywhere because there was yet another complication. That was when two police officers hustled out of the elevator and, seeing what they saw, but not able to wait to sort out what it was that they were seeing, they drew their weapons, too, which was quickly appearing to be the thing for everybody to do up here at Over the Rainbow.

"Everybody, put your guns down! Now!"

Dolly asked an anything but rhetorical question: "Ain't this what they call a semicircular firing squab?"

Buster and company, along with Rosey's crew and Hercules, grudgingly obeyed the cops.

Buster addressed his grandfather: "Grampy, when this bullshit's over, you're leaving this fucked-up place, everybody's packing heat, you're coming home with me, where I can take care of you."

Mikey stunned them all when he shouted: "Hello, Dolly!"

The room fell silent, and everybody marveled, eyes drawn to Mikey.

Buster said, "Grampy, your buddy can talk?"

"Mikey's having a bad day, which'll happen, people trying to kill him and all."

Dolly informed Mikey that was the last time he would say "*Hello, Dolly*" to him. Famous close-to-last words, and the first and the last time in his life that Dolly would be right.

"Never liked you," said Mr. Smith to Dolly.

"Feeling's mutual off Omaha."

"You don't make sense but it don't stop you from talking."

Fatso weighed in, given a golden opportunity: "That's what I been telling you, Dolly, your whole miserable life."

"Can't argue, Fatso. You been coninsistent in that disregard. You never say nice things to me, never offer your condiments."

"*Compliments*, you idiot." Fatso wasn't done: "You're a dinosaur, Dolly, you know that?"

"I don't think so. There ain't no more dinosaurs, they're distinct. And you, Fatso, you always been one of them pessimists. I am a optometrist. Always been a bra half-full kinda guy."

Mr. Smith, disgusted, addressed Dolly: "Had my filla you."

Dolly grabbed his balls and said to Mr. Smith: "Fill *this*."

For once in his life, Mr. Smith was hungry in the middle of a job. He slowly lifted up the top of the pizza box and picked up a big slice of pepperoni, which he fairly consumed with one crocodilian snap.

Dolly was amused and disdainful. "Stupid mope. You hear the delivery guy? It's half-baked."

"Like you."

"And needs to be cooked."

"You need to be cooked, too."

"Here's your chance."

"You're an idiot."

"So they all say."

Mr. Smith and Dolly hurriedly reached inside their jackets, pulled out their pieces, and everybody else not wheelchair-bound or in a police uniform scrambled and hit the deck as they simultaneously shot each other point blank in the chest. They dropped and splattered like sacks of groceries in a rainy parking lot.

Afterward, Mr. Smith lay flat and motionless on the floor, alongside Dolly Leone, pizza crust on his bloody shirt.

Then there was the loudest echoing silence anybody had ever heard.

Mikey was present for those fireworks. He couldn't have told you a thing about it.

⁊

THE DOORS FLUNG OPEN throughout the wing and zombies rushed into the room. The pizzas had attracted them—and that was certainly part of Mikey and Carololina's planned chaos. But when did zombies start moving so fast? They gathered around the pizza boxes as if there were salvation contained inside, and in a way there was, for a minute.

❧

MENTALLY, MIKEY WAS IN his Bobcat. The machine was digging. How it worked, or who was operating it, he had no idea.

❧

MR. SMITH HELD MIKEY'S head in his enormous hands. So Mikey imagined. His thumbs gently shaded his eyes, and all went black for Mikey, deeply blue black. And Mikey welcomed this moment, which he had been awaiting for so long, and he let go. Mr. Smith was, like Mikey's Alzhammer, too big to stop, too big to see clearly.

❧

NO, MIKEY HEARD THE *caw caw caw*s of crows on their perches around the room. Crows conduct rituals for their dead. Many people are unaware of their practice of mourning. But it is true. Here in Goner Town crows are known for flapping their wings. They are always about to take flight. And then they don't.

❧

NIGHT HIT HIM BETWEEN the eyes and the darkness fell and Mikey did not know it.

❧

MANY TYPES OF HAMMERS exist, to name a few: ball peen, claw, chipping, soft mallet, upholsterer, framing, finisher, sledge. There's an art to their selection. You have to use the right hammer for the job at hand. This is crucial. But take the Alzhammer. It's quite an extraordinary tool. There is a very important job reserved for the very specialized Alzhammer. It has a particular, blunt application. It is the one hammer that self-selects.

A hammer is a blunt-force multiplier, and nothing multiplies force like the Alzhammer. It is a hammer that hammers a man's world and leaves it in so many fragments that he spends the rest of his remaining time trying to connect them all back together. Hard as he may try, desperate as he feels, he will fail, he will fail, he will fail forever and forever.

PART THREE

TWO YEARS AND TWO MONTHS LATER

CAREGIVER LOG

Use this form to monitor changes and to communicate with doctors, hospice nurses and caregivers across shifts.

PATIENT: *MICHAEL FESTAGIACAMO (age 59)*

CAREGIVER: *Now the typo is corrected at this late hour, why now? I can't explain, but this correction breaks my heart.*

DATE/TIME: *Wednesday*

NOTE CHANGES: *I can't believe how abruptly his condition has deteriorated.*

FOOD: *Nothing.*

MEDICATION: *Morphine, as necessary.*

ACTIVITIES: *Nothing.*

PAIN LEVEL: *I don't know. I could say high, but the morphine seems to work.*

ENERGY: *Zero.*

SLEEP PATTERN: *He is sleeping all the time. I say all the time, but actually he wakes up and tries to talk to me, but it is so painful to observe because I know he can't find the words. Then he gives up. And I give up trying to understand.*

Hospice is back on the scene, and they have been counseling me as to how to proceed on the next step of Michael's journey. "Comfort care," that is the watchword. He is so brave, so strong. I hate hate

hate this cruel disease. What kind of life is this for a man to live? I will take this subject up with God when I get the chance. In the meantime, I pray Michael finds a lasting, loving peace soon.

The end approaches, any day, any hour. And now we wait. —WW

Chapter Thirty-One

"Ice chip?" asked Mikey's sister, standing over the hospital bed as she patted his soft, disfigured, motionless hand.

Mikey's eyes fluttered and then opened and he stared at her, as if he had no idea who she was and what she was doing. Shook his head. Closed his eyes again.

"Have an ice chip." No extraordinary measures, that was the hospice mantra at this point. The protocol was pain management, comfort care. Morphine was working its magic. Ice chips only, it was too late for water. He might aspirate.

"Carololina, sit with me for a minute?" said Rosey.

"Sure, darling. How you feeling?"

Rosetta wasn't sure, but she also had a private matter to conduct, which she wanted to address right now.

"Mo, I'm going to speak privately to Carololina."

"All due, boss. Want I should leave?"

"Before you go, fix Mikey's blankets, would you, dear?" Mikey's toes stuck out from the edges. The curling toe nails had taken on the blue and red blush of bruises.

Mo snapped to it, glad to be of some small use, and departed.

Rosetta told her what she wanted to tell her. "I appreciate all you did for my brother." She announced she had a gift for her, a gift from the family, meaning from her, in gratitude.

When she heard how much money she was being given, Carololina was rocked, and tears cascaded down her cheeks. If she wanted sex reassignment surgery, money wouldn't stand in her way. And if she wanted to quit working at the Ranch, that was possible, too. "I can't believe this is happening. You and your brother are kinder to me than I deserve."

"Nonsense. You are the brave, the kind one. By the way, when was the last time you saw Zayana?"

"She was here this morning, early. She is working at the Ranch, doing the books, managing the office. She's good at the job. And she is a wreck about Mikey."

"Hope she'll be okay."

"One thing I've learned, it's easier to die," said Carololina, "than to watch somebody you love die."

Rosey couldn't argue.

"Too bad you didn't know him before the Alzhammer bashed him. This crazy, crazy, crazy brother of mine."

But you know what, perhaps it was better she didn't know him before. Because what she couldn't explain to anybody who didn't already know was how Mikey had changed, in strange and incredible ways that she herself would never comprehend.

TWO YEARS AND THREE MONTHS LATER

To: Rosetta Festagiacamo
From: Dinah Forte
Subject: My condolences

Dearest Rosey,

That was a beautiful service you conducted for your beloved brother, Mikey. You eulogized him beautifully, courageously. I was honored to be present, and privileged to have been associated with him at the end of his life. I hope I was of some small benefit to you and to Mikey's son, Jeremiah.

The next part is harder to write about. As news about who he had been has filtered out, the kind of life he had led, the struggles and the battles and the violence and the danger, my mind reels. I had no idea. No idea whatsoever. I feel like my whole professional world has been upended. Human beings are impossible to understand. And so is this disease.

Truth is, some of my clients get to me deeply, and Mikey was one of them. In fact, I don't think I have met anybody quite like him. He was a very complicated man, not that I need tell you. Despite his afflictions, and despite his, shall we say, colorful past, he was never less than a gentleman around me. And despite his terrible, constant struggles with his disease, he conveyed an overriding sense of humanity. I can see why you loved him. He was lucky to have you by his side throughout.

No ending is easy, and Mikey's ending is particularly hard to take for me—and I know for you.

Finally, I received your extra bonus check in the mail, which I did not expect, along with your kind note. You didn't need to do that, but you did. Your generosity touches me deeply and, in this rough economy, I appreciate it very much. Thank you. If there is anything I can do in the future for you, please let me know.

Words don't always do the job. But words are sometimes all we have. Here come mine. I am truly sorry for your loss, Rosey.

xo,

Dee
Dinah Penelope Forte, PhD
Forte Care Management Professionals

TWO YEARS AND THREE MONTHS LATER

To: Jeremiah177
From: Rosetta Festagiacamo
Subject:

Dear dear Jeremiah,

I have been meaning to answer your last email, but I kept putting it off, don't know why, sweetheart. It's been hard for me, to tell the truth.

I am so very sorry you lost your dad. And as the DNA tests showed, he was your dad, no question. I checked the calendar, because I could not believe it. It's been an entire month since my big brother passed.

Writing that last sentence takes my breath away, because he was such a force, and it seems impossible for me to believe he is gone. Given his debilitated condition, his disease, somebody might say it's better for him now. I can never go there, because I loved Mikey and I will always miss him.

When I visualize him, I don't see a man mumbling in bed, lost in his brain. I see a big, tough guy with a heart, a fractured heart. Sure, he was a difficult man, and we had our differences, but now, so what? It's all irrelevant. He'll always be my big brother.

One month, unbelievable. Did you see that the senator resigned "to spend more time with his family"? I think he should have said, "to spend more time with his money." I can't believe he got reelected, or was elected in the first place. But now he's got to deal with the Justice Department, who will never let him out of their sights. What a wretched, poor excuse for a man.

More important, you were so good to visit your dad every single day during the last part of his life, to hold his hand and tell him it was going to be okay. When he went that night, he went painlessly, and I believe peacefully. He knew you had been reliably there by his side, and I have no doubt he took great comfort in your presence. He loved you without qualification, Jeremiah, you know that, don't you? He may have had his issues with your mother, but he was always on your side. He always wanted the best for you.

I spoke to your mom a few times around the funeral. I am sorry she chose not to attend, but I understand. She said she couldn't take it, seeing him like that. She wanted to keep in her head an image of Mikey alive. I do hope you and she will always be close. Your dad and she made their peace toward the end, and that made him glad, I believe. I always liked Zayana, and a powerhouse and a beauty like her will always find a way to make it.

As I told you after the funeral, you will be sent a check from our attorney the first of each month. If you need anything else, let me know. The money will be there for your education and, when your life changes, your children's education. You will want to put down roots and buy a house someday. You will, I know, be wise when it comes to spending. If you want to help your mom, I would understand. That's a complicated proposition, with her drug history, as you yourself know better than anybody. But I promise to keep an open mind, so let us discuss as time goes on.

In case you are curious, one reason Mikey never told you about the money is that he wanted you to make it on your own—and not get involved in the family business. That was a good idea. And now that you are about to begin college next year, which would have made him proud, you should not lack for anything essential. Again, let me know. One thing I would advise is, splurge a little bit—and I mean a little bit! Don't buy a Maserati! Though that is a pretty car, I know. Buy something nice for yourself, whatever you have always wanted, and enjoy yourself, and then come up with a plan. Or maybe you'd like to go back to Italy, where you picked up lots of beautiful ties and where you had such a great time, despite everything. I think you found a girlfriend there, but here I'm relying on what I heard from our guy in London. You handsome boy, how could an Italian girl not fall in love with you? Only now you won't have those Italian bodyguards around to step on your action.

I'll tell Mo you asked for him. He will be pleased. I don't know what we would have done without his protection. He and Fatso were the only guys in Mikey's crew who stayed loyal to him— unless you want to say that in the end we put together a whole new crew, with Mo's boys and you and your mom and Carololina and Mikey's new pal from the home—the amazing Hercules, who's living now with his grandson, Buster, who along with his crew saved the day at Over the Rainbow.

Jeremiah, this is the bottom line: you won't have to worry about money the rest of your life, if you are sensible. Most of all, take this gift for what it is: your dad's wish that you take care of yourself and enjoy your life. Mikey had his faults, plenty of them, like every man, but he was a generous dad in the end, and you were, and are, a wonderful son. Your aunt loves you, too. Never forget that— and never forget you will always be a Festagiacamo.

Much love always,

Aunt Rosey

TWO YEARS AND FIVE MONTHS LATER

To: Rosetta Festagiacamo
From: Dinah Forte
Subject: Checking in

Dearest Rosey,

I am sorry to trouble you, but I should touch base.

I received this morning snail mail a second letter from you, which was very similar to the first one, practically identical, along with a second extra thank-you check.

Perhaps you forgot you had sent the earlier letter. I don't want to take advantage of you in your grieving. I think I should send this check back to you.

Please advise.

I hope you are okay. Let me know how I can help.

I'm going to take a big risk here, Rosey. Hope you won't be offended.

If you'd like referral for a work-up please let me know. I'm here for you, Rosey. I know an excellent doc who is on the cutting edge of the latest brain research.

xoxo,

D.
Dinah Penelope Forte, PhD
Forte Care Management Professionals

TWO YEARS AND SIX MONTHS LATER

To: dpforte
From: Rosetta Festagiacamo
Subject:

Dr. Forte

Thank for services

Rosetta Festagiacamo

Chapter The Last

Once upon a time, Mikey had this dream.

This dream occurred toward the end, as his days dwindled down, and he may not have been sleeping, and it may have not strictly qualified as a dream, but he would have remembered it, if, that is, he were capable of remembering anything. Then again, morphine makes meaningless all such distinctions. It can also generate a dream like this one, the dream he may have dreamed.

☙

LIGHTING IN THE DANCE studio was moody as soft evening rain on cobblestone streets, and the music was encompassing and intense, *dah dum dah dumdum dadadadumdum, dah dum dah dumdum dadadadumdum.* Zayana and Mikey could have been in a romantic night club, in a city like Buenos Aires, say, not that they'd ever been. The silly, incongruous disco ball swirled overhead, shedding fragmented stars all over them as they smartly stepped and spun and twirled. The floor was filled with students, coupled and taking lessons in the tango.

The hazel-eyed dance instructor had a flaming red rose behind her ear and her long hair was tied back fiercely and she was explaining: "*Slow slow quick quick slow…*"

Her voice illuminated the room like South American moonlight.

"*Like this. See? Watch me. One two one two three. One two one two three. One two one two three. Slow slow quick quick slow.*"

"You're good, Z."

"*Don't be shy. The tango is a dance of seduction. Come on now, act like you know each other, people! One two one two three. One two one two three. Slow slow quick quick slow. Bend your knees, bend your knees, you must bend your knees to tango. There, now you are getting it, yes, that is marvelous!*"

"You're not bad yourself, Mikey."

"*Ladies, resist but resist only partially, resist unconvincingly.*"

"She knows you well, Z."

"*Give your man the feeling anything might happen, that something wonderful could be in store for tonight.*"

"Anything might happen, Z, you hear that?"

"You're a good dancer, for a…"

"Don't."

"*Gentlemen, hold your woman close but do not hold her tight. Make her feel she is yours whenever she desires to give herself to you. One two one two three. Slow slow quick quick slow.*"

"Close but not tight, Mikey."

"I'm trying, I'm trying."

"*Dance as if your very life hangs in the balance.*"

"I know you are, baby," she said.

"*When you tango, you dance not on your feet, but on the wings of your soul, you dance according to your heart's enflamed longings, with your whole being. Dance as if your life depends on it, because what is life without the possibility of love?"*

She didn't ask what life would be like with the impossibility of love. That's one thing everybody knows.

"One two one two three. Slow slow quick quick slow. Your whole life is nothing but a tango."

Mikey had his arm around Zayana, holding her close but not tight, and he had no reason in the world to believe the tango and the night would ever come to an end.

Acknowledgments

The author is deeply grateful to:
Tyson Cornell, publisher of Rare Bird Books.
Elizabeth Trupin-Pulli, JET Literary Associates, his agent.
Kristin McCloy.
Anne Rosenthal.
Regan McMahon.
Alice Marsh-Elmer, Julia Callahan, and Winona Leon
of Rare Bird Books.

ᘒ

Patricia James, especially, as ever and always.

About the Author

JOSEPH DI PRISCO IS the author of the memoir *Subway to California* and three previous novels, including the notable *All for Now*. His third book of poems is *Sightlines from the Cheap Seats*, and his poetry has won several prizes. His poems, essays, and book reviews have appeared in many journals, newspapers, magazines, and anthologies. He is also the coauthor of two highly regarded works on family and child development. Born in Brooklyn, he lives in Northern California with his wife, photographer Patricia James. For more information, visit diprisco.com

CPSIA information can be obtained at www.ICGtesting.com
Printed in the USA
LVOW11s1036100216

474335LV00001B/1/P